C000255356

# THE GLASS BOX

KARL HILL

First published in 2022 by Bloodhound Books.

www.bloodhoundbooks.com

Print ISBN: 978-1-5040-8186-3

# ALSO BY KARL HILL

# 1

## THE INITIAL OUTRAGE

Two brothers. John and Billy. One fifteen, the other seventeen. John was the younger, but two inches taller. John was lean and lithe. Billy was heavier and stronger. He had fists like clubs and liked to use them. Billy had a quick temper and could be wild with it. Worse than wild. Manic.

Their parents were solid middle class. Father was an accountant with a mid-sized firm in town, mother taught geography in the local secondary school. They lived in a nice house in a nice area of Glasgow. All normal. Except it wasn't. Billy was trouble. Billy didn't seem to understand the difference between right and wrong. This had become apparent from an early age, escalating as the years progressed, until Billy hit seventeen, when matters reached a grim crescendo.

A new family had moved in next door. Mr and Mrs Purkis and their fifteen-year-old son Chadwick. Chadwick Purkis was a quiet, solemn boy. Some might have described him as reserved. Others, shy. He went to a different school from John and Billy. Chadwick went to a private, fee-paying school.

For some reason, this irked Billy. John, however, was unconcerned. It never occurred to him to dislike someone because they went to a different school, private or otherwise. He and Chadwick became fast friends.

At seventeen, Billy had left school and was at college. He had enrolled in Coaching and Sports Development, for no other reason than it sounded good and to please his parents. Plus, it looked piss easy. He took little interest in the course. More profitable was his extracurricular activity: selling drugs. Working for a dealer he'd met by sheer chance at a club, the dealer had seen Billy's potential – that he lacked scruples. Billy saw money, and Billy loved money.

Billy sold class A drugs. Cocaine, MDMA, crystal meth. He got his batches from his dealer friend, sold them anywhere and everywhere. College campus, car parks, clubs, lock-ups, houses. There was no shortage of users. Their age was an irrelevance to Billy, so long as they handed over the cash. Billy got a ten per cent cut of the gross. He was the one taking the risks, but he didn't care. The money was too good to pass. If he didn't do it, someone else would. He was supplying a need. And the need was real.

One summer afternoon. July. The air was warm and still, the sky cloudless and pale blue. School had finished for the holidays. John and Chadwick were running. Training for a half marathon. John was fit, Chadwick still had work to do, but John kept his pace slow. It was 3pm. Queen's Park was the best place to train – a mile from their houses, lots of inclines. Grass surface, so easier on the knees and ankles. No traffic. Plus, drinking fountains, which was helpful.

After maybe twenty minutes of running, the conversation between the boys tended to dry up. Certainly on the part of Chadwick. Talking used up too much energy. They jogged, silent and sweating in the heat. They reached a section of the park where the path snaked through dense shrubbery. They turned a corner. Suddenly, before them, a guy wearing a hoodie, and two young kids. They jerked round, startled. The kids ran off. The guy had a wad of money in his hand. The guy was John's brother.

John and Chadwick stopped. Chadwick was puffing hard.

John spoke. He knew what he'd seen, but he asked the question anyway. "What you doing, Billy?"

Billy's face, shadowed in the hood, contorted with anger. "What's it fucking look like? You got a problem with that, Johnny boy? Tell me if you have a problem."

John raised his hands, trying to soothe the situation. "No problem, Billy."

"You breathe a word," Billy said. He stared at Chadwick, slit-eyed. "You, Chadwick. What type of name is that? It's only turds with arsehole names that can get into that fancy school. Am I right?" He switched his gaze to Johnny. "Am I right, Johnny?"

John didn't respond.

Billy stepped closer. "What you looking at, Chadwick?"

"Easy," John said. "No one's going to say anything."

"You trust him?" Billy said. He took another step closer. "Chadwick, you going to talk?"

Chadwick, blinking, confused, darted a glance at John. "I don't know…"

Billy's arm darted forward. A quick, savage movement. A flash of silver. Billy stepped back. In his hand a knife, its silver gleam a vibrant new colour.

Billy backed off, pointed at John. "Not a fucking word." He sprinted away.

Chadwick stood for five seconds before his mind acknowledged what had just happened. He looked down at the hole in his running vest, an inch below his ribcage. He put his hand over the wound, and his fingers turned red. He tried to speak but was unable to articulate. He sank to his knees, toppled into the soil and leaves.

John remained still, caught in the moment, breathless,

transfixed. Disbelief, horror. He experienced a range of emotions. One second, running in a park. Next, his friend lying in a puddle of blood. John knelt, tried to staunch the wound. Chadwick was unconscious and bone white. John screamed and sobbed. The blood kept coming, pumping with every beat of Chadwick's heart.

John wept. But that didn't stop the blood.

---

Chadwick Purkis lived. The blade had punctured a kidney, nicked an artery. But the boy survived. He stayed in hospital for three weeks. A month later, Mr and Mrs Purkis sold their house.

Chadwick never told a soul who had stabbed him. Neither did John.

The day after the incident, Billy disappeared. He never came home. His parents, distraught, did what they could, but he was never found.

## 2

---

### THIRTY YEARS LATER

One of the men carried a turquoise zip-up Lonsdale sports bag, which, for effect, he dropped on the floor of the hotel bar. The contents clanked. It was 2.30am. The bar was empty, save the man with the bag, his associate and a third man, who was the owner of the hotel.

The man who dropped the bag was large, muscular to the point of ungainly. Hair shaved to the bone, a face flat and moonish, a splayed boxer's nose, heavy lips, button-black eyes. His associate was the opposite – lean, face all hard angles, a thin-lipped mouth twisted in a sardonic smile. Thick black hair slicked over to one side. The third man – the owner of the hotel – was middle-aged, overweight, balding, and watched the two men with moist blinking eyes. He was terrified and showed it.

The smiling man did all the talking.

"I miss the smell of cigarettes in a bar. Don't you?"

The owner swallowed, licked his lips, opened his mouth but said nothing. His forehead shone under the soft glow of the downlighters.

"But then I'm a smoker. I've been smoking since I was

fifteen. I suppose I'm what you would call an addict." His voice was soft, educated, each word clear and lacking any trace of an accent. He raised an eyebrow, prompting the owner to respond.

"I've never smoked," the owner mumbled. "My mother did."

"Filthy habit," responded the smiling man. "My colleague here doesn't smoke either. He's an addict of a different sort. A keep-fit addict. Power lifts and bench presses. Isn't that right, Mr Halliday?"

The man referred to as Mr Halliday reacted with the slightest shrug of his heavy shoulders, keeping an impassive gaze on the owner.

"We can work this out, Jacob," the owner said. "I can get the money. I just need a little more time. Things are slow. Tell your boss there's no problem here."

When he spoke, his eyes blinked, darting from one man to the next, like dancing fireflies.

"My mother didn't smoke either," said Jacob – the smiling man. "Hated the things. You want to hear something funny, Raymond?"

Raymond – the owner – seemed bewildered. "What?"

"I said *you want to hear something funny, Raymond*?"

"Sure."

"To be perfectly candid, it's not very funny. It's tragic. My mother died of lung cancer. Imagine that? You know how?"

Raymond shook his head, jowls reverberating like a slobbery dog.

"Passive smoking. My dear old dad. Smoked twenty cigars a day. You know what that is?"

"No."

"Sheer bad luck."

Raymond nodded, more blinking, sweat dribbling into his eyes. "Bad luck," he said.

6

"Which brings us back nicely to the situation in hand. Doesn't it, Mr Halliday?"

Halliday remained motionless, features lacking any clear expression.

"This matter of the money you owe," continued Jacob. "Your failure to pay the allotted instalments is your bad luck. You've reneged on the wrong man. If a debt is owed, my employer doesn't waste his time with the usual paraphernalia – letters and lawyers and suchlike. What does he do? He cuts out the wastage, deals directly with those individuals who owe. When I say 'directly', he uses us as his representatives. This method is simple and effective. So, to keep this matter completely by the book, we are here to collect £20,000 on his behalf. And I believe you're telling us you can't pay. Is this correct? For the record."

"Jesus Christ," croaked Raymond. "What the fuck is this? Give me a chance here. Business is shit–"

"Will you please just answer the question," interrupted Jacob.

"That's correct," said Raymond, voice a whisper.

"Now we have clarity. And above all else, my employer welcomes clarity. Your response allows us to move to the next phase."

"Next phase?"

Jacob gave a delicate shrug, nodded at Halliday, from which he appeared to derive exact information. He bent down to the sports bag at his feet, unzipped it, placed both hands inside, rummaged about, all to the sound of rattling metal.

He pulled out a carbon steel claw hammer.

"Phase two," said Jacob, voice soft as silk.

Raymond took a step back, tried to speak, emitted only an inarticulate moan.

Halliday's face registered no emotion. He turned, swung

the hammer, let it fall on one of the wooden tables, causing it to splinter, the sound like the sharp crack of a gunshot.

Raymond jumped, started to sob.

"That noise," said Jacob, "is very similar to the sound of a knee bone cracking. Or a skull splitting. Isn't that right, Mr Halliday? My friend is experienced in this sort of thing. When it comes to administering pain, he is... how can I put it... an *artist*. He knows all the sensitive spots. I would go as far as to say he has a gift. Show Raymond what else is in your bag of tricks."

For the first time, Halliday's face displayed emotion. His jaw widened into a grin. He bent down once again, dipped his hands into the sports bag, pulled out a pair of pliers, which he placed on the table beside him. Then again, pulling out a Stanley knife. Then a coil of wire.

Raymond's legs buckled; he sank to his knees.

"Please," he whispered. "Just a little more time."

Jacob regarded Raymond, his lips pursed, as if he were coming to some inward conclusion.

"We'll give you more time," he said.

Raymond looked at him, face flickering with a glimmer of hope.

"Two minutes," said Jacob.

"Two minutes?"

"As long as it takes to come to an arrangement."

"I don't understand," said Raymond.

"Why would you? But maybe speaking to the man himself might help."

Jacob, wearing a close-fitting leather jacket, produced a mobile phone from a pocket, pressed the keypad with his index finger, and spoke softly to the individual who answered.

"He's on his knees," he said, looking at Raymond. "He doesn't have the money, and Mr Halliday has opened up his sports bag."

Jacob nodded as he listened to the response, then stepped towards Raymond, and handed him the phone.

"He would like to chat."

Raymond raised the phone to his ear.

"Yes?"

The voice spoke. Raymond listened, nodded.

"Okay. Thank you."

He handed the phone back to Jacob, who wiped it on his sleeve, then once again raised it to his ear. He smiled, disconnected.

"Easy, yes?"

Raymond heaved himself up, ran a fretful hand through the few remaining hairs on his head.

"What now," he said, unable to keep his eyes from the objects Halliday had placed on the table.

"You have two daughters?" said Jacob.

Raymond's lips twitched. "Yes. Ten and twelve."

"That's right. Let me think. Abigail and... Katie. One has little blonde curls. The other red as copper."

"I don't understand..."

"And Katie's the one with braces. Abigail wears cute silver-framed spectacles."

Raymond remained silent.

"As I said earlier," continued Jacob. "My employer likes to cut out the middle man. Especially lawyers, who he believes are worse than sewer rats. However, despite his disgust for them, he understands their importance. In the next two days, his lawyers will contact you. The relevant papers will be prepared, you'll sign what you have to sign, and that will be the end of it. Mr Halliday will not need to open up his sports bag again, and you can be secure in the knowledge that your lovely daughters won't find themselves in a ditch with their throats slit. Everyone's happy."

"Yes," mumbled Raymond. "Everyone's happy."

Jacob glanced at Halliday, who placed the tools back in the sports bag.

He took a deep, satisfied breath, and made a show of looking about.

"A new venture," he said, to no one in particular. "Who knows what tomorrow brings."

He reached into his jacket pocket, took out a packet of Marlboro Reds and a silver Zippo lighter, lit up, took a deep inhale, and turned to Mr Halliday.

"Looks like Chadwick Purkis is the proud owner of the Royal Hotel."

## 3

For John Smith, the memories would never leave. As if someone had dropped a boulder into the well of his mind. There it would remain. Solid. Immovable.

The army doctors were good, but they weren't that good. He'd been referred to those who specialised in mental disorders, and ultimately, after months of treatment, the consultant psychiatrist had rendered the whole sorry episode down to this – *Acknowledge the problem. Confront it. Don't be fearful. If you can master it, then you can beat it. But the worst thing is to deny it. Do not run away. If you do, it will catch you, and devour you.*

*Devour you.* Savage words, and ones he would not forget. But he chose to ignore the advice. He *had* run away – both physically and mentally. Turned his back on society, and now lived like a hermit in a log cabin deep in the Cairngorm forest, at the foot of the mountains. He was, he reflected, the perfect cliché. Broken soldier immersed in his dark thoughts, existing in isolation.

Fucked up and self-loathing.

And mentally? He hadn't run away. He'd *sprinted*. During

the day he shut them out, those events which had taken place far away in a distant land. But at night, when he slept, they crawled into his dreams, and the terrors returned in full blazing glory. The same thing, night after night. The fear, the pain.

The guilt.

The psychiatrists said confront. He had fled. Like a coward.

Daytime was all about the routine of movement. Movement kept him sane. Movement kept him alive. Get up, fix strong coffee from a one-ring stove, get his running shoes on, get out. Running the mountain trails. Running kept him straight, focusing on each step, the rocks, the sounds of the mountains. Mindfulness in motion. He could run all day, should he choose. One thing the army had given him – a bedrock of deep fitness.

He bathed in the freezing cold waters of a lochan a hundred yards from his front door. The cold was good. Sharpened the senses. Forced him to forget. He ate sparingly and was unconcerned about quality, a cupboard in the cabin – the only cupboard – stocked with tinned food, some fruit. He shaved every day without fail. The process involved routine. And routine was good. He chopped at his hair every month with sharp scissors, keeping it short. And books. He read while the daylight lasted, always outside. Books about anything at all. His one luxury in his otherwise spartan existence. When he visited Aviemore – the nearest hub of civilisation – to pick up supplies, he would buy five books. He didn't care what he bought particularly, as long as it was enough to prevent his mind wandering too far from the close confines of the shelter he had created.

The seasons came and went. Bitter cold in the winter. Just cold in the summer. He hadn't retreated to the north of Scotland for the warmth. But even the cold played its part, the discomfort another distraction.

Every two weeks, he made his sojourn to town. Eight miles

going the long way, seven of which were narrow trails slanting down from the Cairngorm mountains, cutting through forest, the last mile along a main road. It was the last mile he dreaded, and the inevitable interaction with other human beings. He kept his head down, bought supplies, packed them in a rucksack, scurried back to his haven in the hills.

It was Smith's fourth year of self-imposed isolation. It was the end of June. The sun had melted most of the snow off the mountaintops, trickles remaining like white teardrops on a weathered face, the great peaks sharp in a seamless sky. Smith set off on his journey into town, rucksack strapped to his back, not for one second realising how this day, and this journey, would spark a series of events both devastating and deadly.

# 4

———————

I t had just turned 8.20am. Paul Davidson had walked into town early to collect some groceries. He held a bag in each hand and stood in the kitchen doorway, silent, watching the scene unfold before him. A familiar sensation wriggled in his stomach. Dread.

"You know, I really don't get why you can't do the simplest thing."

A man sat at the kitchen table. Vincent Docherty. He toyed with the food on his plate, prodded his fork through a fried egg. He looked up at the woman who stood rigid at the opposite side of the kitchen, her back to him. Then he turned his attention to Paul, pointing at him with the fork.

"Your mother doesn't get it. You're just in time to see her learn her lesson."

*Learn her lesson.* Paul couldn't speak, words caught vice-like in his throat.

Docherty focused back on the woman. She hadn't moved. Both hands gripped the edge of the kitchen worktop. Paul watched her, saw the tremble in her shoulders, the profile of her face, lip quivering, chest moving – in, out – in short, terrified movements.

"Look at me when I'm talking to you."

Slowly, she turned. Turned her full body to face him. She didn't speak.

"Okay," said Docherty, voice soft, like it always was when the storm was brewing. "Thank you. Now that I have your attention, let's try to understand what's happened here. Yes? I asked you for a soft egg. Look what I've got. A piece of burnt crispy shit. You see the problem, Alison?" To demonstrate, he scooped up the egg on the end of his fork. It hung like a fragment of white rag.

She blinked. Paul stood, transfixed. Beside his mother, a block of kitchen knives. He saw, with horror, her hand creeping towards it.

"So I ask myself," continued Docherty, voice like silk, "what else can I do? I ask for something, and all I get is shit. You agree? Speak to me, Alison."

His mother said nothing.

"Speak to me!" He slammed his fist on the table. The motion was sudden. His plate rattled. The table shook. Paul jumped. His mother jumped. The situation had escalated to the next level. One which Paul knew only too well.

His mother spoke, her voice tight. "What do you want me to say, Vincent? Do you want me to make you another egg? No need to get upset. Please." She gave a small, frightened smile.

"Upset?" Docherty said. "Is that what you think I am? Wrong again. Disappointed. In fact, *fucking* disappointed. And when you disappoint, which is now becoming a regular thing around here, you need to learn your lesson." He turned again to Paul. "You get it, don't you, Paul? Your fucking whore mother needs to learn her lesson. Right? It's only logical."

Paul stood, unable to move, unable to speak. His whole world was diluted down to this moment.

"You get it, Paul?" roared Docherty suddenly. Paul gasped at the ferocity, stepped back, tongue clamped to the roof of his mouth. Docherty snapped his head to Alison. "Is your son mute? Maybe he needs to learn some lessons too."

Alison straightened, darted her arm to one side, grabbed a knife. An eight-inch stainless steel carving knife.

She spoke, her voice low, "You do not touch a hair on my son's head."

Docherty cocked his head, looked her up and down, examined her as if he was admiring a painting.

"Well look at you. Grown a backbone all of a sudden." He pushed his chair back. The wooden legs scraped on the hard floor tiling. Slowly, he rose to his feet. He was a big man. Six two. Heavy fleshed. Hulking shoulders. Hands like spades. Hands which could inflict pain, and often did.

With deliberation he unfastened the belt round his trousers, carefully pulled it free from the waist loops. He coiled one end around his hand, the buckle end dangling.

"Put the knife down, Alison, and come over here. If you don't, and I have to take it off you, then it's going to be bad for you. And the boy. I mean really bad. Like nothing you've had before. You understand what I'm saying?"

Paul watched as his mother took a small sidestep toward the doorway where he stood, knife poised.

Docherty shook his head, face creased in puzzlement. "Really?"

Still holding the belt, he put both hands under the tabletop, heaved it up and over. It clattered to the floor, plates rolling and smashing on the tiles. Alison screamed, tried to make for the door. With surprising speed, Docherty hurled towards her, grabbed her hair, slapped her hard. She staggered back, fell, knife skittering away. He loomed over, dangled the belt buckle over her face.

"Look what you made me do," he said. "This is what you

get, Alison..." He raised the belt, brought it down, lashing her shoulder. "...for being a stupid..." He raised his arm again, struck. "...selfish..." Once more up, down. "...whore."

Paul saw all this, acted before he really knew what he was doing. Instinct, perhaps. A boy protecting his mother. He dropped the shopping bags, ran towards Docherty. Docherty was hunched over Alison, absorbed in his violence. Paul was fourteen years old, small for his age, thin and bony. All elbows and knees. A minnow compared to Docherty. But he had momentum on his side. And rage. He pushed Docherty with his full weight, arms outstretched, catching him square in the middle of his back. Docherty lurched to one side, slipped on the grease from the spilled food, fell on his knees.

"You little cunt!"

He got to his feet. Paul ran, out of the kitchen, through the hall to the front door, Docherty lumbering after him. His fingers found the door latch. He glanced round. Docherty was within striking distance. For the briefest second, he glimpsed Docherty's face, set and mean. The door opened. He tumbled out onto the front path, took two steps. The buckle caught him on the back of the neck. He staggered, fell on his stomach on the slabs. He shook himself, tried to get up. More pain as the buckle raked the side of his head. He began to sob, body tensed, arms covering his face, waiting for the next blow.

It didn't happen.

He craned his neck round. At the end of the path stood a man. The man spoke.

Then everything changed.

# 5

---

The distance from Smith's cabin to Aviemore, keeping to the established trails, was about eight miles. There were shorter routes, but they met the road too early, and as such, were too public. The forest trail he used was a meandering path, snaking through trees and gullies in a wide looping route, until meeting the road a mile from the town. If he met hikers, he would politely nod and not stop, unless they were lost. He kept conversation to a minimum, his manner brusque, bordering on rude. Smith had come to the Cairngorms to forget. Not to converse with strangers.

Smith set off at 6am. The journey would take him about two hours, walking at a leisurely pace. He wore a lightweight running fleece, trekking trousers made of tough waterproof fabric, mountain boots. Strapped to his back, a bergen rucksack. The same type issued by the army. Dependable, hard-wearing. In it, a litre of water, a heavy jumper, a spare pair of dry socks, a woollen hat, a pair of gloves and nothing else. Highland weather was temperamental. Cold in the morning, freezing in the afternoon, deadly in the evening. People died in the mountains, usually because they were ill-prepared. Smith was making a relatively short trip to the shops, so there was little jeopardy. Nevertheless, old habits died hard.

He didn't carry food. Smith ate little, if anything, at breakfast time. He would buy a sandwich and maybe some fruit in the supermarket and eat it on the way back. The morning was bright, the air tinged with the slightest chill. At his back, the great Cairngorm mountain range, dappled golden-purple in the sun.

The way was quiet. Smith, when walking, tried to keep his mind clear, allowing in only the sounds and smells of the wildlife around him. Years back, in the badlands of Afghanistan, in the vast Hindu Kush, he'd walked plenty. Patrols. Daytime. Night-time. Anytime. But then, his mind was never clear. Always anticipating violence around every corner, behind every rock. Every second of every minute of every hour, mind sharp to danger. Until the mind switched off, numb with fatigue. And then the same thing the next day, and the next.

Which was why, when out walking, Smith made it his mission to keep things clear. To forget. To keep the shadows out. One shadow in particular.

He got to the main road at about 8.10am. Two lanes. It was twelve miles long, stretching from Aviemore to the funicular at the foot of the mountains. It was usually busy. In the winter, with skiers, heading to the slopes. In the summer, tourists driving to the lochs for fun on the water. The seasons in between were a mixture of both.

Smith made his way into town, another mile. He kept to a narrow pavement on one side, running parallel to a cycle lane. Beyond, houses sitting back a little from the road behind fences and hedges and stone walls. And beyond them, more forest. The road was quiet. Too early still for tourists. A cyclist passed him at speed, decked in skintight aerodynamic Lycra and wraparound sunglasses. He whizzed past, head down, taking little regard of Smith. No helmet. Smith wondered at the stupidity of some. All it took was a millisecond of bad luck – the front wheel nudged off course by a groove in the road, a motorist on his cell phone, a million things, and the cool cyclist with his cool aerodynamic suit and expensive wraparounds had his brains splashed on the concrete. A cheap way to die, thought Smith.

Smith walked on, got to a row of small terraced houses, each similar with dark wood cladding, high pitched slate roofs, each front garden separated by hedgerow. He approached the last one. A sound caught his attention. Unmistakable. A scuffle, a shriek of pain. The hallmarks of violence, to which Smith was well acquainted. Something was happening in the front garden. His view was blocked by a high wild hedge, growing front and side. He got to the gate, stopped, looked in. Before him, on the slabbed front path, lay a young boy on his stomach. Looked like he'd taken a tumble. His forehead was cut. Looming over him, a man. Large, not quite fat but well on the way. Hulking shoulders. His expression was one of detachment, almost businesslike. In one hand a belt which he was using as a lash, buckle end, without restraint. As Smith watched, he brought it down, striking the boy on the head. The buckle caught in the boy's hair. The man tugged it free. The boy screamed.

Smith reacted. It was automatic. Instinctive.

He spoke. "Stop it. Now."

## 6

P aul scrambled to his feet, scurried to one side. He stared at the man at the front gate. Docherty was six foot two, and Paul reckoned the stranger was about the same height, maybe taller. He was lean and deeply tanned. He wore a close-fitting running top, moulded around sinewy, knotted muscle. Face all hard edges – prominent cheekbones, rather gaunt cheeks. Striking, in a hard-bitten way. His eyes, thought Paul, were as cold as grey granite.

Paul looked back at Docherty. Docherty raised himself up, appraised the man at the gate.

"And who the fuck are you?"

The stranger kept his gaze fixed on Docherty. He opened the gate, entered the front garden.

Paul witnessed a new expression on Docherty's face. Uncertainty. Docherty hesitated, took a step back, the belt wrapped tight round his hand.

The stranger had a rucksack on his back. He loosened it off, dropped it on the ground, strode forward, stopped only inches from Docherty. Docherty was bigger, wider. But the other man looked strong and vital. Paul searched for the right word – *capable*.

The stranger spoke again.

"You like hitting kids?"

Silence. Paul held his breath. The air seemed caught, held in this moment.

Docherty attempted bluster, but Paul saw through it, plain as day. He felt a small spark of glee. Docherty, his mother's boyfriend, always heavy with his fists, was shit scared.

"What the hell do you think you're doing?" Docherty rasped.

The stranger seemed to consider the belt hanging from Docherty's hand, let his gaze wander up slowly as if sizing up measurements for a jacket, until resting on Docherty's face.

"I asked you a question," the stranger said quietly. "Do you like hitting kids? It's either yes or no."

"This is none of your business," muttered Docherty. "This is private."

The stranger leaned in close.

"I'm making it my business. Why don't you try to hit me? I'm game, if you are."

Docherty swallowed, took another step back.

"Let me tell you something, friend," continued the stranger, his voice still soft. "If I ever hear you hit this boy again, I'll break first your arm and then your neck. Here's the thing. I'll enjoy doing it. You understand?"

Docherty's face had paled. He licked his lips with the tip of his tongue, wiped his mouth with the sleeve of his shirt, blinked away sweat.

"You understand?" The stranger's voice didn't raise. Nor did it have to, realised Paul. It carried more menace quiet and composed.

Docherty cast a scathing glance at Paul. His lip trembled. "Fuck this," he said under his breath. He sidestepped the man, made his way to the front gate. Something glinted on the slabs. The stranger stooped, picked it up. Paul recognised it instantly. Docherty's key ring, a distinctive silver 'V'.

"That's mine," said Docherty. The stranger tossed it to him. Docherty tried to catch it, missed, bent to pick it up. His face burned with rage. He swept the stranger a baleful look, turned away, walking quickly in the direction of the town.

# 7

---

Smith regretted his actions as soon as he'd stepped into the front garden. He should have walked by, pretended nothing had happened. But there was the problem. Something *had* happened. Something *was happening*. Despite his self-imposed isolation, he was still a member of the human race. He was still a human being. He saw a boy being beaten. Maybe by his father, maybe not. It didn't matter. It was a bad situation. And he had been trained, for a major portion of his adult life, to deal with bad situations.

But he still regretted his actions. If he had a desire to join the human race, this was not the way he intended. The kid was looking at him. Smith reckoned he was no older than fourteen.

"You okay?"

"He'll come back," replied the kid. "With backup."

Smith digested this information. More bad news.

"Are you hurt?"

The kid's forehead was cut and swollen where he'd cracked it on the concrete. Also, a small smudge of blood where the buckle had torn away a clump of his hair.

"I'll survive. He hit my mum..." The kid raced into the

house. Smith's mind struggled with indecision. He didn't want to be here. He wanted to be back in his cabin in the mountains with nothing but fresh air for company. Instinct told him to get the hell away.

*With backup!*

But still. He read the urgency in the kid's eyes. Despite his misgivings, he followed him in. Through a hallway to a kitchen at the end. The table was overturned, food on the floor, broken crockery. A woman sat slumped against a cupboard door. She was disorientated. The side of her face was discoloured. The early blossom of a new bruise. She groaned, got to her feet, unsteady, the kid trying to help her up. Smith went over, put his hand gently under her arm.

"We need to get a doctor," he said.

She groaned, shook her head. "No doctor." She put her hands on the unit, finding her balance, spoke. "Did he hurt you, Paul?"

The boy blinked back tears. "I'm fine. But you're not. I'll call a doctor."

"I said no." She touched his head, his face. "The bastard did this?"

"It's nothing."

Smith stepped back, giving her space. She took several deep breaths as she gazed about, at Paul, the mess around her, then focusing on Smith. She narrowed her eyes.

"Who are you?"

"Nobody. I was passing..." Smith hesitated. He should leave, now. He didn't want conversation. He didn't want recognition. He didn't want this situation. He wanted to go. But she looked like she might need help. Another minute wouldn't do any harm. "I was passing. I saw... Paul... in the front garden. A guy was whipping him with his belt. I told him to stop. He's gone now."

She remained motionless. Smith wondered if she'd heard

him. Eventually she spoke. "That *guy* is my boyfriend. Vincent Docherty. A real piece of work, yes? Looks like you were passing at the right time. What's your name?"

"You're both hurt. I really think you need a doctor."

She gave a small, weary smile. "You think this is the first time? I only go to the doctor if he breaks a bone. This..." she gestured to her face, "...is just a scratch. He was being playful. But he shouldn't have touched Paul. He's crossed a line."

Smith said nothing. Her azure-blue eyes under dark lashes were clear and direct. Despite the bruising, she was not unappealing. Dark hair tied back into a ponytail. Her face, wide of forehead and cheekbones, slanted down to a small chin and a curving pink mouth. She kept herself in shape. She looked trim and agile.

"Thank you," she said. "You were kind to do what you did. Most people stay away from Vincent. He's... unpredictable."

Smith was unsure how to respond, but felt compelled to say something. Even as he uttered the words, they sounded lame to his ears.

"Unpredictable? That's an interesting way to describe him. You could report him to the police."

Again she responded with that small, sad smile. Suddenly, to Smith, she looked exhausted.

"That's part of the problem. Who would believe me?"

Smith said nothing.

"You don't understand," she continued in a dreary monotone. "He is the police."

# 8

Paul watched as the man graciously righted the kitchen table back on its four legs, and straightened the chairs. Then, after a brief 'goodbye', he made his way back through the hall and into the front garden. Paul followed him. A dull ache was spreading round the back of his head. Perhaps the stranger was right, he thought. Perhaps they should go to a doctor.

"Thank you," he shouted after him. The man was in the process of shouldering his rucksack back on. He turned.

"You sure you're okay?"

"I've seen you," Paul said.

The man gave him a quizzical look.

"You're the guy that runs. I've seen you in the mountains. You run round Loch an Eilein. I go there sometimes to fish."

The man nodded. "Nice place in the summer." He turned, got to the front gate.

Paul took a step towards him, hesitated, then made a decision. "Can I run with you?"

The man stopped, regarded him with his grey, burning gaze. "Get to a doctor. You're bleeding."

The man adjusted the straps of the rucksack, made his way out and along the main road to Aviemore, disappearing behind the high hedgerow forming the boundary of the front garden.

"What's your name!" shouted Paul after him, to which he got no response. He raced to the front gate. The man was heading away in long strides, raising a hand in farewell.

"Your name!" Paul shouted again, knowing he would get no reply.

He trudged back to the house. His mother was standing at the door. He bit back tears. She reached out her arms and held him in a tight embrace.

"He's right," she whispered in his ear. "We need to get you to a doctor."

"And tell him what?" he retorted. "The usual story?" He could barely contain his bitterness. "You fell down the stairs. I had a fall playing football. Or maybe we should think up a new lie."

"I'm sorry, Paul."

Paul swallowed back his tears. "It's not your fault."

"He's crossed a line," she said. "Things will change. I promise. You're safe now."

He drew back, regarded her. "Nothing will change, until he brings a crowbar and beats you to death. Because that's what's going to happen. And then it's too late."

"No," she soothed. "I promise."

"I saw something I haven't seen before. When the stranger confronted Vincent in the front garden."

"What?"

"It saw it in Vincent's face."

"What?"

"Fear."

# 9

Chadwick Purkis lived in a castle. Set in thirty acres of manicured gardens, it was a work of impressive and lavish architecture. Purchased in hard cash in 2008, in the wake of the credit crunch when prices had slumped. Two million pounds. The property was in poor condition, bordering on dilapidated. Riddled with dry rot, wet rot, a sagging roof, cracked walls. His original intention was to inject some money, renovate it on the cheap, ride out the depression, then sell when the sun had risen on the market again. But the more he spent, the more he grew to love it. Eighteen months later, and he'd spent another eight million bringing the place up to a standard way beyond even he had imagined.

Shining clay roof tiles, new marble and oak flooring, all rot eradicated. The walls were strengthened with metal girders. He had built another wing, housing a squash court, bar, gymnasium and sauna. At the back, a new glass extension, each pane imbued with floral art in the style of Charles Rennie Mackintosh. Inside, a heated swimming pool, jacuzzi and plunge pool.

Altogether, a thirty-room palace.

The gardens were of equal splendour. A myriad of paths formed from blue and yellow flagstones. Lawns flat and green as the baize of a snooker table. A pond shaped in a precise circle, over which spanned an arched Japanese moon bridge coloured coral pink. Everywhere, stone figurines, gazebos, arbours, swing benches. Purkis had installed soft lighting and net lights in all the trees. At night, the garden sparkled like a million jewels. Purkis called it his fairy garden.

And then the basement, running the entire length of the building, load-bearing pillars every twenty feet or so. Originally used for storing junk, inhabited by rats, the walls mottled blue and green with mould, the air cloying with decay. Purkis got it fixed up, creating rooms and passages. The mould was gone. The rats were destroyed. Now tapestries hung from silver rods. The floor was renewed and carpeted. In one room in particular – the biggest – a bar was installed, behind which, a gleaming marble gantry with every conceivable liquor. Toilets were built. The ceiling was painted soft blue. Chairs, sofas, divans, low tables were scattered in an apparent random manner, similar to a gentleman's club, which, in a way, it was. The pillars were encased with varnished wood.

In the centre of this room, Purkis had created a very special and unique feature. A structure measuring precisely twenty-five by twenty-five feet with no ceiling, and with a single door.

It had a name amongst those who were invited. The Glass Box. And like the Glass Box, the activities organised within its confines were special and unique. One evening at the end of every two months, it held a spectacle like no other.

Such were the thoughts running through Purkis's mind, as he sat in another section of his castle, in a room he liked to call his library, the walls comprising floor-to-ceiling glass cabinets, stocked with books, many of which were first editions, and none of which Purkis had read. Purkis was a collector, not a reader.

It was 8am. Purkis was an early riser. He usually got up at 6.10am. He liked routine. Breakfast consisted of blended carrots and spinach with some apple juice. He glugged down a half pint of the stuff. Then the gym. Part of the renovations included a training room, complete with machines, free weights, punching bags. Purkis spent an hour building up a sweat, then a shower, then some muesli and fruit. Purkis was forty-seven and was as fit as any twenty-year-old. He was lean, his stomach hard as wood. All sinewy muscle.

Then, at 8am, his workday started, when he did what he did well. Which was make money.

He sat behind a desk of solid oak, bare, except two cups of black coffee on saucers, a glass cafetière, and a letter delivered the previous morning. Purkis detested clutter. Sitting opposite was Jacob. Purkis had told him to come to the house for 8am sharp. *Told*, not asked. To discuss certain matters. He regarded the man opposite. Lean, like himself, but fifteen years younger. All sinew and tendon. A face chiselled by the elements into hard lines and angles. Calculating eyes the colour of blue agate. A man shrewd and resourceful. A man Purkis could rely on when darker paths had to be considered.

Pleasantries were ignored.

"The pen is mightier than the sword," Purkis said. "What's your thoughts on that?"

Jacob responded. "I immediately think cliché. And I wonder why you mention it."

"No cliché. A real-life example." He gestured at the letter on the desk before him. "I got this yesterday. It's causing me considerable concern. It's barely half a page, and yet, despite its length, it's cost me what? Fifty million? Maybe more? That's a lot of money, for such a short letter. The pen and the sword. I'm beginning to understand the weight in those words."

Jacob's eyes narrowed to slits. Purkis was reminded of a fox. Worse, he thought. A wolf. A hungry one.

"It's bad news, I take it."

"You could say that. Read it, please."

Jacob stretched over, picked it up, scanned it, replaced it back to its original spot.

"It's been rejected. Not what you were expecting."

"Which gives me a problem." Purkis lifted the cup to his lips, took a delicate sip. It was fresh and strong, felt sharp in his mouth, clearing the senses. Ground from Jamaican Blue Mountain beans, it was absurdly expensive, but it hit the spot. And if it hit the spot, its expense was an irrelevance.

He continued. "I paid our dear friend Mr French a hundred grand. In return, I was given assurances. Promises. The promises have not been delivered. That, in my estimation, constitutes a breach of contract, yes?"

"Not the type of thing you can go to a lawyer about."

"One thing I hate almost as much as losing money, is having to talk to a lawyer. Though they have their uses."

"But not in this case," said Jacob.

"No." Purkis fell silent. He was aware Jacob probably knew where the conversation was heading.

"Nevertheless," he said at length, "Mr French has reneged on our... arrangement. To make matters worse, he hasn't had the decency to speak to me. You would almost think he was trying to ignore me. Now that's plain rude."

Jacob nodded slowly. "He doesn't grasp the situation."

"No. Indeed." Another sip. "I need information. Mr French has to explain himself. Plus, provide a solution to our problem. And, of course, he has to compensate for my loss."

"Compensation. I understand."

"Suggestions?"

Jacob gave the merest of shrugs. "He won't come to us willingly. If we contact him, he'll get scared. He may even call the police. I suspect Mr French believes that if he keeps his head down, the problem will disappear." Jacob tapped his chin with the tip of his finger. "Let me think about this. I'll check his movements. We should let matters settle for a while, lull him into complacency. Then he'll be at his most vulnerable."

"Two weeks," said Purkis. "No longer. And when the time comes, and I get my compensation, I want to enjoy it."

"Naturally."

"I always like these little chats, Jacob. Our minds click together, yes?"

Jacob said nothing. Purkis wasn't expecting a response. He switched the conversation.

"And our 'gathering'?"

"Full house," replied Jacob. "Twenty-five seats booked."

"The Glass Box never fails to raise a crowd."

"It's unique."

"It's entertainment. Of the million dollar variety. Make sure there's plenty of champagne. Blood lust always creates a thirst, don't you think?"

Another sip. Then, "Thank you, Jacob."

Jacob was dismissed. He stood, offered a slight nod, left.

Purkis sat back. He tried hard not to display emotion before others. That way, he was unreadable, which meant it was near impossible to guess his intentions. But the letter had sparked a fury in his chest. It had been unexpected. And Purkis hated the unexpected. And losing money.

He picked up the letter, scrunched it in his hand, placed it back on the tabletop. He pulled out a plastic lighter from his pocket, lit it, brought the flame to the paper. It caught instantly. It would leave a mark on the oak, but Purkis really didn't give a shit. He watched the flames, initially taking hold, then dying to nothing, the letter reduced to fine particles of ash, drifting in the air.

People would burn over this. If you crossed Chadwick Purkis, such a consequence was inevitable.

Dark paths. Purkis had travelled many. And had no trouble doing so.

## 10

Smith went straight to the supermarket, his pace brisk. He kept his head down, avoiding eye contact, acting invisible. He cursed himself for his stupidity, his rashness. He should have walked on, ignored the situation. It was someone else's business. A private matter he should never have concerned himself with. A more sympathetic part of his mind answered back – that if he saw the events play out all over again, he would react just the same. A thousand times over, as inevitable as the rising sun.

Regardless, the facts were simple. He'd got involved and was now on the radar. Quite with who, he wasn't sure. The police possibly. If the guy really was a cop – and Smith had no reason to think the woman was lying – then he'd have resources. And power. A vindictive cop was a dangerous enemy. He might have friends keen to help, seeking a little playful revenge. Everybody knew everybody in a place like Aviemore. People talked. Gossip spread, sure as a virus. He'd embarrassed a guy in his own home, in his own goddamned front garden. The guy would be aching for a little payback.

The more he analysed it, the worse it got. So much for his grand retreat from the human race.

He reached the supermarket, nerves sharpened to a point. The car park was empty. The place was too early for queues at the checkouts. He half expected a police car to draw up beside him, doors opening and closing, uniform spilling out, hauling him to one side. Handcuffs. Bundled into the back. And then what? He didn't wish to speculate.

He got what he needed. Mostly tinned stuff. Some fruit. Shaving foam, razors, soap. Basics. The checkout assistant was a young man no older than eighteen. He looked pale and heavy-eyed, hair tied back in a tight ponytail, forehead dotted with a smattering of pimples. Possibly hungover. He didn't venture any conversation, for which Smith was glad. Smith would have preferred using the self-service kiosks, but he didn't own a bank card. He was strictly cash only.

He put the items in his rucksack and left the store. He skipped the bookshop and went back the way he'd come. The road was busier with traffic. He was about a hundred yards from the kid's house. He crossed over to a narrow path. He had no desire to see either him or his mother. He yearned to get back to the safety of isolation. He upped his pace, kept his head down, concentrating on putting one foot in front of the other. If he chose to ignore the world, hopefully it would ignore him back.

He sensed a looming shape over his left shoulder. A car slowing. He glanced up. A black Jeep Wrangler. Massive all-terrain tyres. It pulled in, bumped onto the path a short distance from Smith. Smith continued, nerves tingling. Three men got out and stood in a group, effectively barring Smith's way. Smith made to cross the road.

"Hey there, friend!" shouted one, raising a hand. Short and wide, barrel-chested, thick black beard, thick legs. Wearing a yellow T-shirt cut at the shoulder, revealing heavily muscled arms. Loose shorts. Bodybuilder. Smith stopped. If he crossed, it might inflame the situation. They were congregated at the side of the road. Traffic was getting busier. Nothing could happen. Or so he hoped.

They approached, each intent on Smith. Next to Blackbeard lumbered a man four inches taller, hulking shoulders, slit pale-blue eyes almost closed by bulging apple-red cheeks, sparse sandy blond hair. In contrast to Blackbeard, he seemed more puffy fat than muscle. A step behind towered the third man. Easily six foot six, a clear four inches taller than Smith. Tree-trunk torso. Twin columns of muscle arched up, supporting his jaw, giving the impression his bullet head was narrower than his neck. Splayed nose, dog-brown eyes, bald as a stone, revealing a tapestry of scars.

Smith waited. They stopped a yard away.

Blackbeard appeared to be the spokesman. "Hey. What's up?"

Smith gave him a bland look, all the while assessing each of the three, exactly as he had been trained. Their posture, mannerisms, idiosyncrasies. Blackbeard was bulked up and ungainly, restricting fluid movement. A man who spent hours preening before a gym mirror. He was all show. The man beside him was bordering on portly, and though big, was essentially unfit. A man who needed backup. He was gnawing on his bottom lip, blinking away sweat. The guy was twitchy and scared. The third, however, was a beast. Naturally powerful. The scars suggested he was a man of the fray. Hands like spades. Should one connect then game over. But he too was big, to the point of cumbersome. No match perhaps for a swift and agile opponent.

Smith assimilated all this in the space of the two seconds it took to respond.

"Nothing at all," he said. "Everything's good."

Blackbeard responded. "We were just passing. Saw you

striding along, like you were trying to get away fast. Like maybe something was wrong. Isn't that right, lads?"

He glanced at his friends. The one to his left – Sandy Hair – gave a nervous, lilting laugh, a little too loudly. "Sure. Like something was wrong."

The man behind – Beast – remained silent, like a chunk of stone.

"You sure there's nothing wrong?"

"Sure," replied Smith. "No problems."

"Because," said Blackbeard, "that's not what we heard."

*Here it comes.* His pulse quickened. He heard a sound in his ears – his heartbeat.

"We heard that a guy who looks just like you – a real weird-looking bastard – caused a scene. Attacked a friend of ours. For no reason. And guess where? In his own fucking front garden. What do you think of that?"

"I don't think anything," said Smith. "I just want to get on. I don't want any trouble."

"Whoa there, cowboy," said Blackbeard, raising his hands as if in placation. "We don't want any trouble either. Just clarification. Our friend is upset, you understand? I mean really upset. So this is like…" His face creased in puzzlement. Then, "…a *process of elimination*. You like that phrase? Fucking awesome, isn't it? We have to check every mangy, dirty-looking scummy bastard until we find the right guy. Because that's what our friend said." Blackbeard took a step closer, lowered his voice to a gravelly whisper. "The guy who attacked him was a scummy, mangy bastard. That's why we thought it might be you. You can hardly blame us, no?"

Smith said nothing. Cars were passing. People were walking. Would they attack here? Safe territory didn't seem so safe.

Beast suddenly spoke, his voice surprisingly soft. "I know you."

Smith looked at him, said nothing.

"You're the hermit who lives in the woods. In the old cabin. I've seen you running." He smiled a ghastly smile, his mouth a clutter of chipped teeth. "You're a fucking mad fucker."

"You hear that?" said Blackbeard. "My friend thinks you're a fucking nutjob. I think you're a scummy, mangy bastard. Guess you can't win today. What's your name, friend?"

Smith said nothing. As ever, in a situation of conflict, his mind was sharpened to a higher level of competence. It was fight or flight. If he fought, the repercussions were far-reaching. Flight was easier. He could outrun them no problem, lose them in the forest. But flight, no matter the circumstances, had always been a hard pill to swallow for Smith.

"I asked you a question. Now you're being rude. Which is just downright fucking unpleasant. Especially when we're being so polite and civil."

"Fucking rude," chimed Sandy Hair.

"Cat got your tongue?" said Blackbeard. He moved closer still, face only inches from Smith's. Smith could smell his cologne, cheap and pungent. Blackbeard's forehead wrinkled, as if he were about to impart deep wisdom. "You know what I think?"

Smith said nothing.

"I think you're shit scared. I think you're shitting in your pants. You sure smell like it." His lips curled into a sad droop. "You understand now what happens when you shove your nose into other people's business. People like Vincent Docherty don't like it. In fact, they fucking resent it. Do you know what Vincent wants?"

Still, Smith said nothing.

"Retribution."

Blackbeard stepped back. Suddenly the man behind him – Beast – jabbed his finger.

"We know where you live."

Blackbeard gave a small shrug. "You hear that? Bad news for you, my friend." His demeanour changed. His face split into a wide smile, revealing a row of gleaming teeth. "Best advice? Leave. Move out. Get far away from here. These mountains are bad. Bad things happen. Real bad. There you go. That's my good deed done for the day." He raised his hand. "Adios, amigo. Hope you enjoy the views."

The three men made their way back to the Jeep, got in, Blackbeard driving. The car bumped back onto the road, completed a U-turn, tyres squealing on the tarmac, and headed back into town.

Smith watched them go. He experienced a dreary feeling of foreboding. An innocent sojourn into town had ended in disaster. His brief but intense confrontation with the man called Vincent Docherty had triggered unpleasant consequences.

He tightened the straps of his rucksack, headed along the path, wondering if their threats carried any weight.

Smith could never in a million years have imagined the events to follow.

## 11

The incident with the stranger never left Paul's thoughts. He'd witnessed something in the man which had, somehow, ignited a spark. He couldn't quite define it. Courage. Strength. The ability to stand up and fight back. Something young Paul Davidson had wanted to do all his life.

Paul formed a plan. It was simple, and probably doomed to failure. But it was all he had.

He had some knowledge of the mountains. Born and raised in Aviemore, he knew many of the trails and paths, the lochs and lochans, where to go, where not to go. The place he liked best was Loch an Eilein. It was secluded. It was peaceful. It was perfect. A place to escape. Even in the warm summer months it was practically tourist-free. An occasional off-road cyclist. Hikers, sometimes. And one particular runner. The same runner who had entered Paul's front garden and scared off Vincent Docherty.

During the summer, Paul went to Loch an Eilein to fish. He had a spot. On a grassy verge, hidden in the shade of towering Scots pine, he sat with his back against a tree trunk, listening to music through headphones, and cast his line. Beside him, a basket of sandwiches, some chocolate, and a bottle of cola. There, he would while away the hours. He didn't care what he caught. Usually nothing. He didn't care if it rained, or if it was cold. Being on his own suited him fine. He was used to it. He preferred it. Better than dealing with the other shit going on in his life.

It was there Paul had seen him, months back. The same guy, running round the periphery of the loch. In itself, nothing unusual. But Paul remembered him. The guy had done something unexpected. He was on the opposite side, a distance of maybe two hundred yards, skirting the loch, dressed in shorts, a long-sleeved running top. Paul watched from the shadows as the guy, in mid-stride, suddenly dived into the water, fully clothed, then swam the length of the loch to a small beach of white sand at the far end. There, he left the water, dripping wet, and continued running as if the swim was a regular part of his run. Perhaps it was.

Since then, over the weeks, Paul had seen him several times, running along the line of the loch, though the swim had never been repeated.

Paul, by a process of simple deduction, assumed the guy lived close by. The essence of his plan therefore was that he would go to Loch an Eilein, and perhaps encounter him again.

Paul did this every day, armed with fishing rod and basket. Exactly a week after the confrontation, he saw him. On the opposite side, running to the far end of the loch. Paul dropped the rod and sprinted. He had a good start and reckoned, if he ran fast enough, they would meet at the beach.

Paul had never done any major exercise. When he arrived, he was breathing hard. He sat on the sand, gulping in deep lungfuls of air. He looked up. The man was approaching. He spied Paul, slowed to a jog. He seemed to show little outward signs of fatigue. Paul raised a hand somewhat feebly.

"Hi."

The man said nothing. He wore a pair of track bottoms and a dark-blue T-shirt stained at the chest and under the arms with sweat. He gave Paul a piercing stare.

"I'm glad I found you," Paul said.

The man spoke. "Why?"

Paul got to his feet. "I wanted to thank you. What you did was… awesome."

"What I did was stupid. Is your mum okay?"

"She's… okay. I suppose she gets used to it after a while."

"Used to what?"

"The beatings."

The man remained silent for a short spell, regarding him with a burning gaze. *The eyes*, thought Paul. *They look at you. But they do more. They look through you.*

The man said, "Does she know you're here?"

"My mum? She knows I'll stay safe."

"You haven't answered the question. You're in the mountains by yourself, miles from your house. I'll ask again, does she know you're here?"

"It's not an issue."

"Glad to hear it. What age are you?"

"I'm old enough."

"For what? Jesus, it's not easy getting a simple answer. I reckon you're no older than fourteen. You're too young to be here on your own. The weather can change. You could get lost. You could twist an ankle. You found me. You've thanked me. Mission accomplished. Now go home. And if you want to venture into the mountains, get permission, and go with some friends. Nice talking to you."

He made ready to commence running.

"That's the problem," Paul said, stepping forward.

"What is?"

Paul took a deep breath. The conversation was getting way beyond his control. Yet, he couldn't help himself.

"I don't have any friends." As soon as the words were uttered, he felt pathetic. Ashamed.

The man scrutinised him. Paul felt embarrassed.

"And?"

"I just thought I'd mention it. No reason, really."

"You want my advice?"

Paul nodded.

"Buy a dog. I don't know why you're here but whatever the reason, I can't help you. Go home."

"I think I know where you live," said Paul suddenly, trying to keep the dialogue going. "The old cabin. That's why you run round the loch, because it's close by. I'm right, yes?"

The man sighed, gave a faintly exasperated expression. "Goodbye, kid." He started to run across the small stretch of sand, towards a low grassy embankment.

"I still don't know your name!" shouted Paul. The man bounded up and onto higher ground, then disappeared into the shadows of the trees.

Paul sat back on the sand. *Complete disaster*. He'd made himself out a weakling. A victim. No wonder he'd been dismissed. He found a smooth, flat pebble in the sand, felt its clean texture in the palm of his hand, tossed it into the water. It landed with a plunk, causing a brief ripple, gone almost before it started. Like his life, he thought dismally. Amounting to not much.

He screamed in rage at the loch, a shrill sound echoing across the water, through the trees. A rage against Vincent Docherty, against his school, against his mother, against everything. He lay back on the sand and stared at the sky, an expanse of pale blue, fractured with thin slivers of cloud, and decided he would not give up. His mind turned back again to the confrontation in the front garden, the sheer power of the stranger, the fear in the face of Docherty, and thought, *I'll never give up.*

## 12

Smith didn't know what the kid expected of him, but he did know something. He was becoming way too popular. It seemed suddenly everyone knew where he lived, and Smith didn't like it one bit. First, the three goons who'd approached him a week ago, now this young boy. *Paul.* What was the kid thinking, wandering around on his own in the wilderness? Smith had been harsh, but if the kid had problems, these weren't his concern. All Smith wanted was to retreat back to his little comfort zone of isolation and pretend the world outside didn't exist. Was that too much to ask?

He got back to his cabin, a five-minute jog from Loch an Eilein, drank a bottle of mineral water, changed into jeans and a pullover, fixed himself a coffee and sat on the small front porch.

A stillness had settled, the trees solemn and quiet, the morning breeze died to nothing. It was at such moments Smith closed his eyes, regulated his breathing, relaxed, let the tension seep away. Sometimes it worked, sometimes it didn't. More often it didn't. Inner peace for Smith was as elusive as a will-o'-the-wisp. Memories always hovered close.

His training, rigorous and severe, had concentrated not only on the physicality of combat. The mind was just as important, if not more so. The ability to focus under extreme conditions. Then the ability to switch off, remain unaffected, and keep moving. To shrug off the experiences of war, like they didn't happen. Certain men possessed this ability and were hand-picked for missions dangerous and extreme. Smith, initially, had been one such soldier.

But the experiences did happen. He moved on, but they left their scars, and the scars got deeper and wider. Until one fateful afternoon deep in the Afghan badlands when the scars burst open, and Smith changed.

He sat on his small wooden porch, tried to unclutter his mind, concentrate on nothing in particular.

An image flashed in his mind. The same image. A room. Not any room. One which was both unique and horrific. A room unlike any other.

Chairs, a table. Walls. Shelves. A ceiling. A floor.

If he had been asked in the hospital if any one event had triggered his breakdown, he would have answered, unequivocally, the room.

He had entered, and his mind snapped.

Smith opened his eyes, shook his head, stood. He made his way to the small lochan, the size of a tennis court, surrounded by thick tangles of vegetation, only a hundred yards from his cabin. He stripped off, plunged into the freezing water. The cold struck him to the core. The distraction helped, chased away the memories. For a short period. He floated on his back, embracing the sensation, stared at the sky and wished, not for the first time, that he was dead.

## 13
---

The man called Jacob was meticulous and cautious when it came to performing tasks for his boss, Chadwick Purkis. Two essential skills in achieving success. And success was everything. It kept Purkis happy. It kept Jacob's bank balance in a healthy state.

The letter had thrown him. Not what either of them was expecting. Jacob was mildly amazed at Mr French's failure to grasp the situation. Perhaps French was stupid. Or naïve. Or perhaps he had balls of steel, a less likely scenario. No phone calls. No texts. No emails. No meetings explaining what had gone wrong. Nothing. And by doing nothing, he inflamed an already fraught scenario.

Jacob, in the first instance, had sent French a text. Innocuous, in itself.

Think we should meet.

No response. There was little doubt French would know the source of the message. Jacob sent an identical text the following day. This time, Jacob was watching.

French was a man of habit. He parked his car in a space in the staff car park, exclusive to the Head of Planning. He did so at the same time every morning. 8.45. He got out of his car – a coral-blue Lexus – and walked the short distance to the council building's front entrance. Once in, he got the lift to the fourth floor, and went straight to his office. He finished for lunch at 12.30. Sometimes he went to the canteen. Sometimes he had lunch with staff, or heads from other departments. Sometimes he went home. He lived in a plush penthouse flat in a new development a mile outside Inverness. He lived alone. Divorced. No kids. No girlfriend. He was always back at his desk for 2pm. Worked until 5pm. Never one minute later. Then straight back to his flat.

When Jacob sent the second text, he was parked on a road adjacent to the staff car park. It was 8.45am. He had clear visibility. He sent the text at the point French was opening his car door. He had picked this specific time for a reason. He wished to gauge French's reaction. The reaction would tell him everything.

French stopped midway getting out. He fished his mobile from an inside jacket pocket, pressed the keypad, read the message. Jacob watched. French pursed his lips in a frown, gave the slightest shake of his head, put the mobile back in his pocket.

*Irritation*, thought Jacob. No anxiety. No fear. The message had been dismissed, like a scam text. Jacob understood. French thought he was untouchable. Which indicated stupidity. Which indicated carelessness.

Every Saturday afternoon, at midday, French had coffee at the *Whistling Tomcat*. A bijou coffee shop selling exotic coffees at absurd prices in a town called Boat of Garten, about twenty miles from Inverness. Midday, without fail. Jacob knew exactly what French ordered. A caramel latte and a biscuit.

Usually shortbread. He read a newspaper. He spent about an hour there, then drove home.

Jacob waited, patient as a watching lizard. Three days. On the fourth, Saturday, he visited the *Whistling Tomcat*.

It was quiet. The place was compact, catering for eight tables. It was just after 12pm, the sun bright, but the interior was dark oak, shimmering with candles, creating a witchy feel. The air was tinged with the scent of sandalwood and coffee, which was not unpleasant. Soft classical music played, just on the periphery of the senses. At the far end, a counter, beyond which a gleaming, complicated-looking coffee machine and shelves of brown bags containing an assortment of coffee beans. A man in jeans and a white shirt – the barista, assumed Jacob – was preparing a coffee. The coffee machine rumbled and frothed. The man shouted above the noise, "Take any table!"

Jacob nodded and smiled. There were four vacant tables. Jacob, however, was interested in the table in the corner, occupied by a man reading a newspaper. Small, wiry. A thin, angular face, a nub of a chin. A dome of a forehead with a high receding mat of oil-black hair. Tony French.

"Do you mind?" Jacob gestured to the chair opposite French.

French looked up. "Sorry?"

"Thank you."

Jacob sat.

French made a show of looking around, obviously baffled. "This table is taken," he said, his tone sharp. "There are plenty of other places to sit."

"This is perfect," Jacob said. "How's the coffee? You recommend any particular type?"

French said nothing. He regarded Jacob with a brooding gaze.

Jacob caught the attention of the barista.

"Espresso?"

"Of course. Anything in mind? Peruvian organic is popular."

"You do decaf?"

"Of course. Five minutes." The barista started to work on the coffee machine. Jacob turned his attention back to French.

"I used to drink a gallon of coffee every day," he said. "Honestly. A gallon. No wonder I couldn't sleep. Now, it's only decaf. And guess what?"

French remained silent.

"I sleep like a baby. I hit the pillows, and I'm out. Ten seconds. Off to the land of nod. I don't even dream. Maybe that's a sign of something. Like... what? A clear conscience? Who knows?"

French sighed, began pointedly to fold his newspaper.

Jacob raised his hands in placation. "Sorry – I hope I haven't interrupted anything. But I thought you might like the company."

French shook his head, rather like the way he'd shaken his head when he got the text. Dismissive. Irritated. He started to shuffle sideways out his chair.

"Don't go," Jacob said. "Please. Mr Purkis sends his regards."

French stopped shuffling.

*I have his attention.*

French sat back. "Mr Purkis?"

"The very one."

"And you are?"

"His representative. When certain things need doing, I act on his behalf, if you catch my meaning."

"You have a name?"

"Jacob. My mother liked the biblical names. She was episcopalian. Lived for the church. She was... how can I put it... *devout*. Amazing memory. She could quote any part of the

Bible, I kid you not. Lucky I wasn't called Isaiah. What do you think of that?"

"And what can I do for you, Jacob?"

"As I said, I'm speaking for Mr Purkis…"

French leaned over, cut him off. "I'll not be intimidated. Not by the likes of Chadwick Purkis. I never made any promises. He paid me, things didn't turn out as planned, end of. I did my best. If he wanted a guarantee, he should have bought a toaster."

Jacob nodded thoughtfully. "A hundred grand buys a lot of toasters."

French continued, ignoring the remark. "I'm keeping the money. It's mine. And if you think you've got leverage…" French gave a short harsh laugh. "…I took a bribe. So what. Purkis supplied the cash. If he reports me, then we go down together, make no mistake."

"Mr Purkis isn't the reporting type," said Jacob softly.

"Then I think there's nothing further to say."

"Whoa there, Tony. May I call you Tony? You're way off the mark. Finish your coffee. Relax. Mr Purkis simply wants to say – *no hard feelings*."

"What?"

"Mr Purkis knows you did your best." Jacob shrugged his shoulders. "Sometimes you win, sometimes you don't. Mr Purkis is a reasonable man. And he's a businessman. He doesn't undervalue your importance. You've been helpful in the past. He wants to ensure you continue to help in the future. The money's yours. You don't need to worry."

"I don't worry."

"That's good to hear."

The man behind the counter came over with a coffee in a wide-lipped cup on a saucer and a small jug of hot milk. On the side of the saucer was a small wedge of chocolate fudge.

"Enjoy," said the man.

"Thank you." Jacob popped the fudge in his mouth. "Can't resist," he said. "But the heartburn. I read somewhere it's the sugar that causes it. Acid reflux, I think it's called. I'll pay for this later. Do you have that problem, Tony?"

French took a tentative sip of his coffee. "I'm pleased Chadwick has taken the reasonable approach."

"As I said, Mr Purkis is a reasonable man. This whole thing is just a... what? A blip. A wrinkle. Nothing to fuss over."

"I'm sure there will be other projects in the future, where we'll have more success. I'm always available to accommodate Chadwick's entrepreneurial spirit."

"Entrepreneurial spirit," said Jacob. "Now that's a mouthful. But, of course, you're right. Mr Purkis isn't one for sitting still." Jacob tasted the coffee, frowned.

"Not to your liking?"

"Bitter."

French stood up. "Pass on my regards. And if I was a little brusque, I apologise. I possibly overreacted."

"Don't you worry about a thing, Tony. As I said, just a blip."

French nodded, went to the counter, paid for his coffee, left the shop.

Jacob watched him go. French thought he was immune from any repercussions. If he had a shred of sense, he would run a thousand miles. But his ego was blinding him from the obvious. The chat over coffee had heightened his complacency, thus rendering him more vulnerable.

Jacob took another sip, pushed the cup and saucer to one side, deciding it was overpriced shit.

*A blip*. Hardly that. For Tony French, storm clouds were looming.

## 14

Smith got up at dawn. It was raining. Strangely, his first thoughts were of the kid. If he'd got back home okay. He couldn't have been older than fourteen, and it was a long trek back to Aviemore. And when he did get home, Smith wondered, what did he go back to? With a guy like Vincent Docherty hovering in the shadows, trouble was always close. He felt a flutter of guilt. What the hell could he do?

Smith boiled the kettle. The cabin had electricity, adequate for Smith's needs. He needed hot water for coffee and cooking, and a shower in the morning. Illumination at night was provided by a bedside lamp. He required little else.

He made himself a black coffee, courtesy of a jar of instant Nescafé. He doused his face in cold water in a tiny sink and shaved using a cut-throat razor. He shaved every morning. Another small but important habit instilled into him by the army. Shaving involved a degree of discipline. Discipline was the key to survival.

He changed into track bottoms, an ancient T-shirt, an equally ancient pair of running shoes. He went outside to sample the morning, coffee mug in hand.

Sitting on the porch was the kid.

Smith stared. The kid was sitting on the only chair, asleep. Smith took five seconds to take in what he was seeing. He went over, shook him gently on the shoulder, stepped back.

The kid immediately jolted upright.

"Morning," he said. "I must have dozed off."

"So it seems. What exactly do you think you're doing?"

"I knew you lived here. Didn't I say you lived here?"

"I'm glad we've established this. I hope you're happy. But you've not answered my question."

"Your house is pretty basic. Doesn't it get cold in the winter?"

"It's fine. You needn't worry. Does your mother know you're here?"

Paul yawned. "I had to leave the house at four thirty in the morning to get here. I'd say that was pretty good going, getting here in the dark in just over two hours."

"You're lucky you didn't get lost and fall off a cliff."

"Didn't I tell you? I know all the paths and trails."

Smith took a deep breath, sipped his coffee, trying to rationalise the situation.

"Okay. You know where I live. You walked through the night to get here. I get that. Why? Please just answer the question."

"Is that coffee?"

Smith bit his lip in irritation. The kid was wearing waterproof gear, but that wouldn't prevent him from being cold if he'd walked. Smith poured the contents of his mug onto the long grass at the side of the cabin, went back inside, made another coffee. When he came back out the kid was standing, looking out at the trees.

"You don't get much of a view."

Smith handed him the mug.

"Thank you," said Paul. "Any milk?"

"Nope."

"I don't mind black. My mum likes black coffee. With lots of sugar. Any..."

"No."

"Black's good."

"Pleased to hear it. Why are you here, Paul? It's not a difficult question."

Paul remained silent for a spell. Smith waited. Paul turned to him.

"Here's the thing. I don't really know. I mean, I do know, but I can't explain it in words. Does that make sense?"

Smith said nothing.

Paul sipped the coffee, grimaced. *Perhaps black coffee wasn't so good, after all.*

Paul continued. "To answer one part of your question, I'm going to be honest with you. My mum doesn't know I'm here. But that's okay. She never knows where I am. It's the summer holidays. I'm fourteen. I can do pretty much what I want. As long as I'm back for dinner time, which I always am."

"She lets you walk in the mountains by yourself?"

"I'm sure she would, if I told her."

Smith nodded slowly. "If you told her. And the answer to my other question?"

"What was that?"

Smith bit back his frustration, kept his voice neutral. "Why are you here?"

"Oh that. That's the difficult one. That's the one I'm finding difficult to put into words. Mum says I need to learn to *express myself*. But I'm not very good at it."

Smith sighed, said nothing, waited. He'd never had a more complicated conversation.

Paul hesitated. "I saw what you did. Obviously. That day in the garden."

"And?"

Paul took a deep breath, as if summoning up courage, and then he spoke, his words gushing out.

"It was amazing. Vincent Docherty is a bully and a monster. He hits Mum. And she just accepts it. Everyone's scared of him. Including me. *Especially* me. Because I'm a..."

Paul's eyes suddenly welled up. Smith said nothing. Paul turned to face the trees again. He spoke, his voice barely a whisper.

"Because I'm a coward."

Still Smith said nothing. The only sound was the soft drizzle of rain pattering on the leaves and the roof of the cabin. The sun was hidden behind rolling clouds. The beginning of a dreary day.

Paul turned once again to look at him, face pale and tired.

"I want to be like you. I want to be able to face people like Vincent Docherty, and..." He waved a vague hand, his voice suddenly fierce. "...I want to show them I'm not afraid."

"Them?"

Paul bowed his head, staring at the wooden decking of the porch. "Them. Guys in my school. Guys like Vincent Docherty." He looked up, took a small step forward. Smith didn't know whether it was the rain, or the tears, but the kid's eyes shone. "You could teach me. To be like you. To not be afraid. I know you can."

"You get bullied at school? Here's my advice. Take up karate. Or boxing. Docherty hits your mum. Here's another bit of advice. Tell her to go to social services. Or even better, a good lawyer. And here's the best bit of advice I'm going to give you. Stay away from me. I can't help you. Help yourself. That's the first step. But don't look to me. I don't help anyone, understand?"

"You helped that day."

"I was reckless, and it won't be repeated."

Another silence. Then Paul spoke again.

"Were you in army? You look fit and trained. Were you? I've read about men in the special forces. Were you in the special forces?"

Smith didn't answer. He went back into the cabin, put on a fleece-lined rain jacket, came back out.

"You'll be pleased to know you've interrupted my schedule," he said.

"You have a schedule?"

"I now need to get you home. Which means a long march back to the main road. We'll leave now. I don't want any chat. No conversation. I like silence. You understand silence?"

"So you have a schedule. Like a training schedule?"

Smith began to walk the path to the main road – an eight mile journey. Paul followed.

"I don't want to go home."

"I'm sure. But that's where you're going."

"I still don't know your name."

"Good. Let's keep it like that."

"But you know mine. It's only polite to give someone your name. What will I call you?"

Smith stopped, exasperated, looked down at the kid. "No names. You don't need to know my name because you're never going to have to use my name. Because after I've seen you to the road, we're never going to meet again. I hope I'm clear on this matter."

"I thought you liked silence," said Paul, smiling. "For someone who doesn't want to talk, you do a lot of talking."

"Fuck," muttered Smith, though he couldn't help smiling back, something he hadn't done for a long while. The kid was gutsy. He started to walk again, taking long strides, eating up the distance, the kid a step behind him.

The journey to the road took under two hours. Paul talked incessantly about anything that popped into his mind, or so it seemed. His father had died in a car accident when Paul was ten. His mother worked part time in the ski centre. She'd been a champion skier when she was younger, but had broken her leg and never got the strength back. Paul was good at English and history, hated maths. The teachers were okay. But he hated school with a passion. He had a theory. Some of the other kids picked on him because he didn't have a dad. School was a cruel place, he said. *Welcome to life*, thought Smith, who pretended not to listen but took in every word. And so it went on until they reached the side of the road leading to Aviemore, about a mile from Paul's house.

Paul made his way along the cycle path, Smith waiting in the shadow of trees. Paul looked back.

"Thanks for listening." He waved.

Despite himself, Smith waved back.

## 15

A circus marquee had been erected in Purkis's fairy garden. It was large enough to hold 200 people. Consisting of heavy PVC fabric around aluminium frames, it had taken a day to assemble. Inside, ivory pleated linings with swags and silver drapes and rose-red buntings. The ceiling was a thousand tiny stars. On the ground was a soft, dark carpet, spread on underlay. The exterior was coloured blue and white and emerald green. Soft light came from bronze box lanterns. Heaters had been placed in discreet places. There were two long tables, lined with food and drink. Purkis hadn't stinted. If you wanted champagne with lobster, it was there. Or beer with hamburgers. Or anything at all.

Along the inner wall of the marquee were lines of mobile wooden partitions, upon which hung 500 paintings. In Purkis's calendar, this was the Artists' Fair. He invited artists within a radius of a hundred miles to sell their work, a proportion of which went to charity. He didn't care which one. Tickets were sold at £100 each, all proceeds going to charity. Purkis always got a full house. Everyone wanted to visit a castle straight from Camelot, and everyone left happy. Food and drink were in abundance. Purkis supplied the taxis. Plus he donated a further £50,000. Everybody loved generous Chadwick Purkis; altruist, believer in good causes, philanthropist. Purkis himself flitted here and there, always polite, smiling his gleaming smile, never rude, never loud. His conversation was brief and humorous, commencing with a shake of the hand, finishing in the same manner. Today, he wore a soft black velvet tunic, black trousers, black suede ankle boots. A contrast to his pallid white skin. In one hand, a glass half full of wine which he didn't drink.

During the course of the afternoon, the soft-footed Jacob entered the marquee. He waited quietly at one of the pillars, until he caught Purkis's eye. Purkis nodded, finished his conversation, made his way over.

"I've had a chat with Mr French," said Jacob.

"Yes?"

"All is well. He thinks he's a god. Immune from mortal hand."

"He's a complacent fool. I expected no less. We'll reel him in soon. Are we prepared for this evening?"

"Of course."

Purkis moved off to join another group of people. More flippant chit-chat. Jacob left the marquee, a wraith, no one noticing his arrival, no one realising he had gone.

The afternoon wore on. All the paintings were sold. Over £200,000 had been raised. The day had been a success. Most had now left, except twenty-five men who lingered in the marquee, sipping wine. Purkis addressed them.

"Gentlemen, it's so very good to see you again. If you would like to follow me."

He led them out of the marquee, through the gardens, up a stepped marble landing, and through open patio doors into a large reception room. Here, Jacob sat at a mahogany bureau, an open laptop before him.

"Now, gentlemen," said Purkis, his expression calm, a serene, secret half smile twisting up the corners of his mouth. "To proceed, the usual 'entrance fee' is required. You have the details. Jacob will ensure the transfers are received. If there are any doubts, now is the time to leave."

Each of the men took out mobile phones, tapped the relevant digits. Ten minutes passed. Jacob looked up, nodded.

"Excellent," said Purkis. "Funds are all transferred. Please, have some champagne."

On a long dining table was a glittering array of bottles and glasses. The men became jovial, laughing and chatting, pouring drinks into long-stemmed crystal flutes. Several had cigars. Purkis laughed with them, his cool veneer gone. These men formed a very select and private club, indulging in a recreation both unique and forbidden, devised by Purkis, arranged by Purkis. The castle setting added that extra dimension, creating an almost surreal quality.

A soft gong sounded. Once, twice, three times. Purkis once again addressed the group.

"If you please..."

They followed him from the room, into a vaulted hallway, and onwards, deep into the interior of the castle, to a plain wooden door under a black beam architrave. He opened it. They made their way down carpeted stairs, their chat muted to respectful whispers. Fixed on metal brackets on the stone wall torches of real fire, casting shadows and orange light. They reached the bottom, to the basement where Purkis had lavished a fortune on redesign and reconstruction.

Here, to one side of heavy double doors, waited Jacob, unsmiling – a sombre figure, dressed in a dark dinner suit. Behind him, a set of closed velvet drapes.

Purkis kept up an easy smile. They gathered at the doors. He turned to them, his dark eyes aglow with excitement, like two pebbles caught in the sun. The group were hushed. Anticipation hung heavy.

He spoke, his voice, for effect, deep and brassy.

"Gentlemen, may I say again, it's a pleasure to see you all here. I'll be brief. I know you're keen for proceedings to commence. You've all been given details of the contestants. To remind you of the rules..." and at that, he gave a small rattling laugh, "...there are none. You can stand or sit where you want, provided you do not interfere, assist or aid. You must let the fighters do what they do until the end. Though if any of you are the squeamish sort..." and again the small rattling laugh, "... then do not enter. But if blood is what you want then enjoy. Now for the surprise. Let's see what Lady Fortune has in store for us tonight."

He nodded at Jacob. Jacob made a motion, pulled on a white silken rope cord. The drapes behind him swished open. Revealed on the wall was a large circle of sheer white metal mounted on a spindle. It was split into six equal sectors. Words were engraved in each sector. Above the circle was a simple red mark, daubed on the stone.

"Where will fate take us?" intoned Purkis. "What will it be, I wonder? Spin the wheel!"

Jacob acknowledged the command. He appraised the men watching, paused for dramatic effect, then with his right hand, took hold of one side and did as instructed. The circle spun. Not a word was spoken. Round and round, silent. It slowed, then stopped.

Purkis stepped forward, and read the words on the sector below the red mark. He turned, his face long and solemn. "Tonight," he said, "is axe and shield."

A sudden murmur rose.

Purkis had to raise his voice. "Gentlemen, if you would please come inside." With a grand sweep of his arms, Purkis opened the doors wide. Purkis entered first, then the others. Jacob followed, the last man in, closing the doors behind him.

They had entered a room requiring a three-million-pound entrance fee.

They had come to spectate on a sport unlike any other.

They had come to the Glass Box.

## 16

The Crafty Fox was one of many pubs in Aviemore. Because it was on the periphery, and because it was a shithole, tourists stayed away. But it had a late licence until 1am, and Vincent Docherty knew the owner, so lock-ins weren't uncommon, which gave it great appeal to Docherty and his friends.

Docherty sat on a high stool at the bar, a pint of lager and a whisky chaser before him, and a bowl of nuts. It was ten in the evening. Sitting next to him, lined against the bar, the three men who had confronted Smith a week ago – the squat bodybuilder with the black beard, the plump-faced sandy-haired man, the splay-nosed beast. They were all drinking. Had been for the last three hours. A group of men were playing darts in one corner. At a table, an old man watching European football on a television set on a wall. Otherwise, with the exception of the bartender, the place was empty. The wallpaper was dated and peeling. The carpet was stained and sticky. The furniture was plain. But it sold liquor and it opened late. Which suited Docherty fine.

He'd let his friends talk on for most of the night, contributing little, only half listening. He downed the whisky, slammed the glass on the counter. The conversation stopped. The old man watching the television jerked his head round. The men playing darts fell silent. The barman stopped drying glasses, frowned.

"It's a fucking liberty," muttered Docherty. An object glinted in his hand, which he slapped on the bar. His silver key ring in the form of the letter 'V'. Attached to it, two keys.

The man next to him – Blackbeard – nodded solemnly. "Too fucking right."

"You don't know what I'm talking about, you fucking moron."

Blackbeard took a gulp of his lager, said nothing. A second passed. Another. The pub resumed to normal frequency. The old man went back to watching. The conversation started up again amongst the darts players. The barman continued drying.

Docherty ran a hand through his hair.

"A guy like that – a fucking tramp – comes strolling in, like he owns the fucking place, and thinks he can do what he wants. Who the fuck does he think he is? It's fucking... what?"

The man with the sandy hair finished off his pint, gestured to the barman for another, then said, "A fucking liberty."

The incident had played in Docherty's head, rolling around like a loose boulder, scraping the walls of his mind, loosening more boulders, until he thought of little else.

"But it's much worse. It's *disrespectful*. That's something I will not abide."

The barman placed a fresh pint of lager on the bar before Sandy Hair, who immediately raised it to his lips.

"He's not coming back," said Blackbeard. "Not him. I know fear when I see it. The guy was shitting his pants, I kid you not. Shitting in his fucking pants."

This was not the first time they'd had this conversation. The dialogue was always the same. As if they were speaking lines in a play. But this didn't bother Docherty. It fuelled his rage, though the way he felt, the rage burned regardless.

"Disrespect," muttered Docherty. "It's an insult. He insulted me. In front of that bitch. In front of her son."

"She didn't stick up for you," said Sandy Hair. "If you ask me, she's as bad as him. Women. Who fucking needs them."

"This is true, Jasper," said Docherty. "She needs slapping down, hard. So she knows her place in the pecking order of life. Which is at the bottom. Fucking sublevel. And she spoils that boy. Wouldn't do him any harm either, a slap now and again. Just so he knows who's boss. Am I being unreasonable?"

He took a long draught of the lager, finished it, and like his friend, gestured to the barman for a replacement.

Blackbeard answered. "A fucking hard slap. She should have had your back. Like you say, Vincent, a fucking insult."

Suddenly the big man – the beast – rumbled into life. "I could have snapped his scrawny neck like a dry twig."

"Wish you had," said Docherty. "One less scumbag in the world."

"You said it," chimed the man called Jasper.

"He lives up there in the forest," said Beast. "A hermit. Living in a hut."

"Who lives like that?" said Docherty. "It's not civilised."

Blackbeard spoke out the side of his mouth. "Fucking animal."

"Give me the word," continued Beast. "Quick and easy."

"In time," said Docherty. He gave a sly look, picked up the key ring between his thumb and index finger, the keys dangling. "I still have her keys."

"She let you down," said Blackbeard. He gave a mirthless

chuckle. "I know what I'd do if a woman of mine fucking let me down. She'd need to be corrected. Big style, and no mistake."

"Corrected," echoed Jasper.

"Corrected," whispered Docherty. "Amen to that."

## 17

Night Terrors. Much worse than nightmares. The hospital had given Smith a detailed explanation of how and why they occurred. Which didn't make them go away. More common in children. Usually triggered by anxiety or trauma. Often forgotten in the morning, the recipient having no recollection, the events of the dream buried deep in the subconscious. A particular issue for those suffering from PTSD.

For Smith, they never went away. Nor were they forgotten upon waking. Sleep was something to dread. The theme was consistent, the details vivid and stark.

Always the village. Always the room.

He had never talked about it, despite the prying questions of both the military and the consultants. He vowed he never would. It was a terrible secret kept by himself and his small band of men, too horrific to articulate into words. Perhaps too horrific to be believed.

Smith woke at 4.30am. The darkness was complete. Almost a tangible thing, pressing against his body. He wasn't sure whether his eyes were open or closed. He was sticky with sweat. He lay for a second, disorientated, gripping the sheets, unsure where he was. The uncertainty brought a sudden strong ripple of fear. He lay, breathing deeply, in, out, felt the beat of his heart lessen, the tension subside.

He recited softly the litany of words taught by the specialist doctors assigned to his convalescence.

*The fear is in my mind.*
*The fear is not real.*
*It will not kill me.*
*It cannot kill me.*
*I control the fear.*
*The fear is nothing.*
*The fear is in my mind...*

And as ever, the fear diminished to lurk in the shadows, never quite vanquished.

Smith thought back. The regiment's answer to depression was considerably more simplistic: *Don't dwell on things. Keep moving.*

Keep fucking moving.

Which Smith had done, until the day he stopped.

He got up, sat at the edge of his bed, letting his eyes adjust, and as he did so, the dark reduced. Moonlight slanted through a window of the cabin. He recognised familiar shapes – the stove, the cupboards, a table, chairs. His home. Whatever that meant.

It was the morning after his encounter with the kid. He got up and did what he always did when the dreams were bad. He changed into waterproof trousers, fleece, jacket and boots and went for a hike, letting the land distract him from his thoughts.

---

Smith walked for two hours, skirting round the foot of the mountains, keeping to well-worn trails through the forests.

Even with Smith's skill and fitness, it would be foolish, bordering on suicidal, to attempt a climb. Nevertheless, in the dark, walking was treacherous enough to keep him focused. The morning was still, the sky clear, and as the sun rose, the dark softened to a reddish hue, like old wine, dappling the leaves bronze and gold. There was a chill in the air. There was always a chill at this time of day.

Smith got back to the cabin for 6.30am.

Sitting on the same chair on the front porch was the kid. Beside him, a small rucksack.

Smith stopped, stared.

Paul stood, returned Smith's stare.

"Before you say anything," he blurted, "it's a free country. No one says I'm not allowed to go for a walk."

Smith made his way towards him. "It's called trespassing when you sit on my porch. What the hell are you doing here? I thought I'd made myself clear."

"Look." Paul gestured to his feet. "Running shoes. Nike. I got them half price on the internet. Good for cross training. More grip on the mud. See the tread on them? The magazines say they're the best." At that, he raised his foot to show Smith the sole of his shoe. "I would have got the same make as yours, but I don't know what they are? Have you got Nikes?"

"Jesus," muttered Smith.

He walked past him, into the cabin. He took off his jacket, flung it to one side, took off his waterproof trousers, put on track bottoms, took off his boots, put on his trainers, grabbed a couple of over-ripe bananas, came back out. He tossed a banana to Paul.

"I wear New Balance," he said.

"Because they're good for cross-country?"

"Because they're cheap."

Smith unpeeled the banana, took a bite. Paul did the same.

"This is a one-off, you understand?" said Smith. He hardly

believed he was having this conversation. "You can run with me, but if you don't keep up, I leave you behind. Simple. I change the route every day. Keep the same route and the body and mind go stale, and suddenly running becomes something to be endured rather than enjoyed. Today, I'll run up to Loch Morlich, run round it, then further up to the foot of Ben Macdui. There and back, twelve miles, I reckon. Maybe more. No stopping. Lots of hills. Steep hills, but it's the way I like it. I don't take breaks. Straight run. If you want to learn to fight, then you need to learn to run. Running will give you fitness, and a bedrock upon which you can learn skills in combat. Without fitness, you'll fail. Twelve miles. You want to do this?"

Smith waited while Paul chewed on his banana, thoughtful, obviously processing. Smith suddenly realised he hadn't spoken this much for months, if not years.

"Twelve miles?" Paul said.

"Yup. What's in the rucksack?"

"Sandwiches. A bottle of water. A can of Coke."

"Ditch the Coke. It's equivalent to drinking liquidised shit. You can bring the water if you want, though you can drink from mountain streams. But you'll need to carry the bottle, and it's not easy running distance with a weight in one hand. Looks like it's going to be a warm day. You're going to sweat. Your skin will itch and chafe, and maybe bleed where it rubs against your top. I repeat, you sure you want to do this?"

Paul didn't answer immediately. His jaw worked up and down, slowly, as if the movement of his muscles reflected the movement of his mind as he pondered Smith's words.

"Stream?" he said eventually. "You can drink from a stream?"

"Sure. The water here is as clean and fresh as the water in your bottle, if not more so."

Another silence, then, "Bleed?"

"Yup."

Paul nodded, as if coming to some inward conclusion, placed the banana skin carefully on the chair, said, "I want to run with you. But please, tell me one thing."

Smith waited.

"Your name?"

"Jesus Christ."

"Really?"

———

Paul lasted a mile. Despite Smith's harsh words, he stopped when Paul stopped. He scrutinised the boy, bent double, taking great gasping breaths of air.

"Too much time on the computer, I think."

Paul didn't disagree. He straightened, hands on hips. His face was flushed, bright as a plum.

"You want to go on?"

Paul nodded, started a shambling half trot.

"Hold," said Smith.

Paul stopped, looked at Smith. "I'm sorry. I thought…"

Smith cut him off. "We'll stagger it. Interval training. We'll walk for five minutes, then start again. We'll reduce the pace, and run for five minutes, then walk, then run, and so on. We'll do a lap round the loch, then head back."

Paul didn't offer any complaint. They walked, no conversation, the dominant sound being Paul's laboured breathing, until gradually it lessened. The sun was bright, reduced to glints and slants through the trees.

"Don't you play football at school, or rugby?" enquired Smith.

Paul shook his head. "I fish."

They continued thus, neither speaking. The walking got longer, the running shorter. The forest thinned to a section of wild grass and gorse, and then to a narrow strip of white unblemished beach. Beyond, the flat calm of Loch Morlich.

They walked to the lochside, two sets of footprints in the sand. The water shimmered silver-grey, as still as Smith had ever seen it. In the distance, not far, the mountains, their scale and symmetry clear in the morning sunshine, the tops still speckled with patches of snow.

He squinted up into the sky, pointed. "Look."

A shape hovered, framed against the sun like a line of ink on a yellow page. It took shape, substance, as it glided closer. A massive wingspan. Maybe six feet, maybe more. Brown plumage, pale head, its tail feathers a splash of bright white colour.

"An eagle," breathed Paul.

"A white-tailed eagle," whispered Smith, afraid that if he spoke too loudly the bird might fly away. It swooped down, intent, talons skimming the surface of the loch, then a blur of movement, the silence broken by a spray of water. Something silver quivered in its grip. A fish. The great bird veered up and away on its great, ponderous wings.

"I've never seen that before," said Paul.

*Me neither*, thought Smith. The silence of the place resumed. The bird was now a speck, heading towards the mountains.

"Time to go back," said Smith.

"Everything changed when he died," said Paul suddenly.

Smith turned, but the boy's gaze was fixed on some indeterminate point on the water.

"I was ten. It was my birthday." He looked at Smith. "I'm not looking for sympathy, okay? I'm just trying to explain things."

"Who died?" said Smith softly.

"It was my birthday. He was coming back from work. He was a restaurant manager. He left early, with a birthday cake. It was a Sunday. A tourist, we were told. From Germany. Driving the wrong side of the road. Head-on collision." Paul wiped his face with a sweat-streaked forearm. He held Smith's stare with hard, shining eyes. Shining with what? Tears, thought Smith. And anger.

"He died instantly. That's what we were told. One second he was there. Next, he was gone. Like he never existed." He gave Smith a puzzled look. "And here's the thing. I'm beginning to forget what he looked like. How can that be? Why is that happening?"

"Your father," said Smith.

"If he hadn't left early. If it hadn't been my birthday, then none of it would have happened."

*He blames himself.*

Paul picked up a pebble, threw it into the water. It caused the tiniest ripple, then was gone, back to the flat calm.

*As if it never existed.*

"I'm sorry…"

"We should head back. Same interval. Five minutes walking, five minutes running. Let's go."

———

They got back to the cabin. The return route was easier, being mostly downhill. Smith increased the pace for the last quarter of a mile, and the kid kept up. When they reached the front porch, Paul collapsed on the grass, on his back, face to the sky.

Smith allowed himself a half smile. He went into the cabin. He had never bothered locking the front door. If anyone ever felt inclined to break in, then good luck to them. He had nothing worth stealing.

He got the bottle of water the kid had brought, tossed it on the grass beside him. He got a pork pie from a fridge marginally bigger than a shoebox, put it on one of two plates he owned, and put it on the seat on his porch.

"Eat," he said.

Paul sat up, drank half the contents of the bottle, somewhat stiffly got to his feet, went to the porch, devoured the pork pie.

Smith waited until he was finished, then spoke.

"I'll walk you to the road. And that's it. You've done well today. If you want to take it further, join a running club. But that's it. I can't help you. I'm not what you're looking for."

"Why not?"

*Because I'm broken.*

"Because I can't. I repeat – I'm not what you're looking for. Leave it at that."

Paul said nothing. They walked the few miles to the road in silence. When they got there, Paul said, "Were you in the army?"

"A long time ago."

"Have you ever seen anything like that before?"

"The eagle? No."

"That's good."

"Why is that good?"

"Because we both saw something amazing together for the first time. We've shared something important. It makes me feel good."

Smith sighed. "Go home, Paul."

"Can you tell me your name? It's a simple thing. Unless it's really weird, and you're embarrassed about it. Which I get."

Smith shook his head in exasperation. "You win. John Smith. There you are."

Paul wrinkled his nose. "It's not very glamorous."

"I'm not the glamorous type. Now go home and enjoy the rest of your life."

The kid took three steps in the direction of Aviemore. He turned and grinned.

"John Smith," he said. "It's cool."

"Sure, kid. Cool."

Smith watched him until he turned a corner, disappearing from sight. He retreated into the forest and ran, almost in a half sprint, back to his cabin.

The kid wasn't his concern. But the image of the eagle plucking the fish from the loch stayed with him, and would probably stay with him all his life. And he found he was glad too. Glad that the kid had seen it, and glad they'd seen it together.

That night, for the first time in what felt like forever, he slept a dreamless sleep. He awoke early the next morning, and went out to his porch.

The kid was there.

# 18

A week after the charity event held in Chadwick Purkis's back garden, Jacob got the call he had been expecting. From Purkis. The conversation was short, and entirely one-sided.

"It's time. Bring him in."

Saturday evening. North Kessock was a village just over two miles from Inverness, with a population of about eight hundred. There was little of significance about the place other than the North Kessock hotel, popular with tourists, and the Popinjay Tavern – popular, so it seemed, with everyone.

Also popular with Tony French. Saturday evening was 'live music' night. A band called The Steam Rollers played sixties hits from 8pm until 11pm. The pub closed at 1am. The music, and the late licence, meant the pub was packed.

Jacob had monitored Tony French's movements with care. He was, if anything, a man of routine. And a loner. Which helped. And Saturday evening signified his weekly excursion to the Popinjay Tavern. He got there by taxi and had a seat by 7pm. He drank Blue Sapphire gin with a splash of tonic. He sat on his own. He left at 11.30pm by way of a pre-ordered taxi. The journey back to his flat was at most fifteen minutes.

Jacob waited in a car a hundred yards from the pub. He had a clear view of the front entrance. There were no CCTV cameras. On one side of the road, fields. On the other, houses set well back, enclosed by high hedges. Accompanying him, sitting in the front passenger seat, was his colleague, Mr Halliday.

It was 7.15pm. French was in the pub already. They had watched him leave a taxi and enter.

"Now," said Jacob.

Halliday got out of the car, and made his way to the entrance. Jacob watched. Halliday walked like a man without a care – like a man going to a pub to listen to some live music, his manner giving no hint of the dark deeds ahead. Jacob pulled out a packet of Marlboro Reds, lit up. He lowered his window, blew smoke into the evening air. He reached over, got a paperback from the glove compartment, opened it, and began to read.

The pub filled up. Taxis came and went. At just after 8pm, noise blared. The band had started. People filtered in and out, stood in groups, sharing chat as they smoked by outdoor ashtrays. Jacob glanced up every minute or so. Still a little early. At 9pm he put the book away, focused on the front entrance. At 9.23pm, to the backdrop of 'Sgt. Pepper's', two men emerged, one the worse for wear, being propped up by the other much larger man. The large man was Halliday. The other was Tony French.

Jacob started the car, did a U-turn, parked a further fifty yards up the road, on the opposite side, now out of sight of the pub. He watched the two men approach in the rear-view mirror, Halliday practically carrying the other.

Jacob got out, went round, opened the rear passenger door, waited. French was mumbling, voice slurred and low, his head lolling on Halliday's shoulder. They got to the car. Halliday rolled French onto the back seat, where he lay, an arm and a leg drooped on the floor, motionless.

Jacob returned to the driver's seat, Halliday got in the passenger side.

"No issues?" said Jacob.

"Simple," replied Halliday.

Jacob eased the car away, heading south, to the home of his master.

---

Chadwick Purkis had decided the meeting should be held in the conservatory. In the strong morning sunshine it was the brightest and warmest room in the house, and as such, put him in a cheerful frame of mind. But then, he reflected, at such moments as these, he was always cheerful.

The conservatory, as per the norm, was constructed entirely of glass. The floor was marble the colour of burgundy, reflecting the sun in a warm glow, like old wine. It was large and at the far end, wide patio doors opened to his fairy garden. On one wall – the gable wall, to which the conservatory was attached – was mounted a collection of weapons. Broadswords, rapiers, scimitars, longswords, cutlasses. Different types of daggers – anelace, poignard and misericorde. Fifty altogether, blades glittering.

He sat on a grey velvet chaise longue. Before him, a low palisander Indian coffee table and placed on it, a silver tray with a blue teapot and three porcelain cups and saucers.

Opposite sat two men on high-backed rattan chairs. On one sat Jacob. On the other, Tony French. To one side, watching, the brooding presence of Mr Halliday.

French's head rested on his collarbone. His wrists were bound to the armrests of the chair by heavy duty sealing tape, his ankles bound tight to the front legs.

Purkis nodded to Jacob. Jacob leaned over, gently slapped French's face. French's head twitched, swayed. He cracked open one eye, closed it, wincing. He made a small, incoherent mumble. Jacob slapped him again, a little harder. French opened his eyes, shook his head, blinked, focused. His pallor was bone-white, his eyes dark and hollow in their sockets. He still wore the clothes from the evening before.

"Sorry for the inconvenience, Tony," said Purkis. "It's good to see you again. It feels like forever."

French licked his lips, swallowed. He worked his mouth, stretching his jaw. Eventually he spoke.

"What happened?"

"What happened?" repeated Purkis. "That's an interesting question, giving rise to a host of possible answers. Wouldn't you agree, Jacob? Is that an interesting question?"

Jacob said nothing, still as a waiting spider.

"What happened," Purkis repeated. "I suspect you mean, how did you get here, when doubtless the last thing you remember is sipping a gin and tonic and watching a band thump out some old Beatles tunes. I was never a Beatles fan. I preferred the Stones."

French stared at him, eyes reduced to bloodshot pinpoints, the bones in his face harsh and sharp.

Purkis continued. "The process was simple. Though Jacob is a master of making complex situations look simple. Your drink was spiked by a gentleman called Mr Halliday, Jacob's assistant in such matters. A dash of Rohypnol while you were in the toilet. The effect was swift. You were helped out of the pub and into Jacob's car. And now you are here. But that hasn't really answered your question – what happened."

He reached over and poured the contents of the teapot into the three cups.

"Please, Jacob. Let Tony enjoy his tea."

Without a word, Jacob unbuttoned his jacket, unclipped a small leather scabbard attached to his trouser belt, pulled out a short fixed-blade hunting knife, and cut away the tape round French's right wrist.

"I love Darjeeling," said Purkis, voice smooth as soft silk. "Referred to as the 'champagne of teas'. It still amazes me when I see people ruin it with milk and sugar. It's a... what would you say, Tony?"

French swallowed again, blinked, said nothing.

"A violation," said Purkis. "Please, drink."

Purkis lifted the cup, holding the handle with thumb and index finger, sipped, placed the cup back on the saucer.

"Not like Darjeeling?" he said. "Fair enough. You can't please everybody all the time. Now, back to your question – what happened."

He fixed his gaze on French.

"Please," said French. "I don't..."

"I'll tell you what happened," interrupted Purkis. "We had an arrangement. I gave you £100,000. In cash. In return, I was to get planning permission to flatten the Royal Hotel and build thirty luxury houses on the land. You gave me your promise, and you took my money. You can understand my puzzlement when I got a letter from your department telling me my application had been refused."

Again, he raised the cup to his lips, sipped, licked his lips with the tip of his tongue, savouring the flavour. Savouring the moment.

"And then when you didn't respond to my calls, the puzzlement turned to consternation. And concern. I thought perhaps you were ill. Or in an accident. No?"

French didn't respond.

"I didn't think so. Breaking our agreement was one thing. But to ignore me was just plain rude. Rude, bordering on disrespect. And that's something I cannot abide. Please, have some tea. No? You more of a coffee man? I understand."

"Please," mumbled French. "There was nothing I could do. It wasn't my fault."

"A hundred thousand is a lot of money. If you had doubts, you could have said no. But you said yes. As you always do when I pay you. Do you know what happens when I pay a person that type of money?"

"No."

"It means I own them."

French used his free hand to wipe away beads of sweat from his brow. In the strong sunlight his face shone, skull-like.

"Listen, please, Chadwick. The hotel is a listed building. Plus, because of its age, it's protected by Historic Scotland. It's... untouchable. I thought I could sway the planning committee, but there was nothing I could do. I did my best. I swear I did. Sometimes things just don't work out."

"Don't work out," echoed Purkis. "Not quite the response one expects after handing over a hundred grand."

"I can give you it back." His voice lowered. "Or some of it. If you give me time."

"You're missing the point, Tony. I don't want the money back. The money, to be honest, is irrelevant. But when you didn't return my calls. A bridge too far, I think. It's the disrespect that's the problem. How do you pay that back?"

French fidgeted in his chair. The drug had worn off, the dullness evaporated, and in its place, fear, sharp and cold. Purkis had seen it many times and saw it now. He was an expert in such matters.

Suddenly, French straightened his back, spoke in a louder voice, attempting bluster.

"I won't be intimidated. You wouldn't dare do anything.

Do you know who I am? I'm the chief planning officer. Let me go and it won't go further."

"Won't go further? I should think not. Do you know who I am? There's a cliché. Better to understand exactly who I am, Tony. I'm the one relaxing in my conservatory, sipping Darjeeling, rather enjoying myself. You're the one strapped to a chair, about to face some rather grim realities. Do you know what you need, Tony?"

French's voice had lowered again to a husky croak. "What?"

"Perspective."

Purkis gestured to Jacob with a delicate flutter of his hands, from which Jacob seemed to derive exact information. He raised the knife. The blade glittered. A swift movement. French shrieked, tried to twist away. Too late. Suddenly, from the side of his eye to the corner of his mouth, a thin crimson trail appeared, like slime from a snail, blooming thicker. Blood dribbled down his neck, onto the collar of his shirt.

Jacob casually cleaned his knife on French's trouser leg, then replaced it back into the scabbard at his belt.

French touched the wound with his free hand. Blood now was running freely. His bottom lip quivered.

"Don't cry, Tony," said Purkis. "This was inevitable. Surely you understand the situation you find yourself in. You take my money. You treat me with breathtaking arrogance. Surely you understand it was never going to end well. This is the fun bit. Me watching you squirm. A precursor before the main event." He finished off his tea and sat back. "I'm sorry, Tony, that it should end like this. But end it must."

He flicked another meaningful glance at Jacob, who again, almost telepathically, understood. He got up and went over to a mahogany side cabinet. He opened it and took out a roll of plastic sheeting. Halliday now began to shift furniture over to one side – chairs, couches, low tables. He lifted lamps and ornaments and placed them with care also to one side, forming a space in the centre of the room.

Jacob spread the sheet across the marble, flattening it out with his feet. Then he and Halliday gripped either side of the chair French was sitting on, lifted it, and carried it to the centre of the sheet, then placed it down. They both stood back, waiting.

French began to babble. "I'm sorry, Chadwick. We can work this out. I can't get all the money. Not right away. Give me a month. A week! I'll find it. I'll borrow it. A week!"

Purkis shook his head. "Tsk tsk. You've not been listening, Tony. The money is an irrelevance. It's the disrespect, remember?"

He stood up, made his way to the stone wall behind him, and gazed at the display of weapons, hands clasped behind his back. He swivelled his head round. "Do you like my collection?"

French stared back, blood drained from his face, skin ghastly pale, the wound in his cheek open and weeping.

"Please, Chadwick."

"These swords are all authentic," said Purkis. "They're not replicas. Do you know how difficult it is to obtain such items? And the cost! But worth it, Tony. I look at these and wonder whose hand clasped the grip, whose flesh did the blade pierce. These are so much more than sharp steel. They each have a history. A past. Forged in blood. They're *real*."

He reached over and gently lifted one from its silver brackets. "This is said to have been used at the Battle of Bannockburn. It belonged to the chief of Clan Cameron. It's 110 cm long. Light enough to be used in one hand. Fish-skin-covered grip." He held it in his right hand, stepped back, hefted it above his head, waving it through the air. From the sides, Jacob and Halliday watched silently. The blade was sharp and keen, shimmering in the strong sunshine, like a beam of light.

"But when used in a two-handed stroke, thus..." and here, expertly, Purkis switched the grip, arching the blade in great sweeps, to the left, to the right, "it could cut through textile armour and break bones through mail. It could even split hardened leather armour and dent metal plate. It's a killer. Isn't it beautiful?"

He stopped and with care placed it back on its brackets. "But it's not my favourite. Can you guess which is, Tony?"

French spluttered and coughed. "We can work this out. Please."

"You like to use that word – please. It's a shame 'sorry' doesn't appear as popular in your vocabulary."

French responded instantly. "Sorry, Chadwick. A million times, sorry."

"I like your style, Tony. A real joker. But you haven't guessed. Which is my favourite? No? Then let me show you."

He reached up, standing on his tiptoes, and removed a weapon somewhere between a dagger and a sword, the blade maybe eighteen inches long, the pommel encrusted with a cluster of tiny red gems, the grip bound in black leather, encircled by an intricate hand guard the colour of dull bronze.

Purkis slotted his hand into the guard, grasped the handle, held it up before him, angling the blade. It was thin, pointed, sharp as a needle.

"The misericorde," breathed Purkis. "Isn't she splendid? Of all the blades, this one is unique. It had a very special function, back in the day. The others were designed to maim and kill. This one, however, was designed to *relieve*."

He made his way over to French, sitting in the centre of the conservatory, on a chair, upon a plastic sheet, in the strong sunlight. *What a wonderful scene*, thought Purkis. He stood over him. Purkis spoke, his voice low, almost gentle.

"On the battlefield, in the aftermath, those who were seriously wounded would lie, screaming and howling.

Probably wondering, just as you are now, how things could come to such a pass. The priests would then pick their way through the carnage, seeking those who were dying, and use the misericorde. Maybe to stab a throat, or pierce a heart. Relieve them of their pain. Provide mercy. Really, such a weapon should never be feared but rather embraced."

He pressed the tip under French's right eye. "With a little pressure," he whispered, "I could pop out your eyeball."

"There's still a way," gasped French. "You didn't get the planning you wanted. But there's still a way."

Purkis waited.

French, perhaps sensing the possibility of reprieve, continued with enthusiasm, words spilling over each other. "The hotel is listed. Which means you can't touch it. But if it were to suffer an accident."

Purkis lowered the blade. "Yes?"

"What I mean is, if the hotel were to be destroyed in a fire. I mean totalled, where restoration was impossible. Then you could do what you want. It's the building that's listed, not the ground it sits on."

Purkis's lips twitched in a semblance of a smile.

"A fire. I hope you're not suggesting we break the law."

French licked away the blood trickling into the side of his mouth.

"Accidents happen," he said, eyes fixed on Purkis.

Purkis moved away, cast a meaningful look at Jacob. Jacob took four steps, leaned over French, slit his throat with a quick, deft movement. French gave a rattling croak, raised his hand to his neck, trying to staunch the sudden bright flow. He attempted to speak, his jaw flapped open and shut, but more blood bubbled out through his mouth. His face crumpled in a strange mixture of fear and bewilderment. He was choking to death, and he knew it but didn't want to believe it.

"And so!" hissed Purkis. He leapt forward, sword held

high, then down, the point puncturing the heart, the action swift. In and out. French spasmed. His hand dropped to his lap. His head lolled forward, his eyes lost focus as life left him.

Jacob and Halliday worked quickly. They cut French's bonds. He flopped onto the plastic sheeting. The chair was put to one side. They rolled him up in the sheet, enclosing him like a cocoon. They each lifted one end and carried it out of the room. Purkis had built an incinerator in an outbuilding not far from the main house. There, Tony French's flesh, organs and bones would be dissolved to ashes, then the ashes mixed with compost and sprinkled into the soil of Purkis's fairy garden.

Purkis sat back on the chaise longue, and poured himself another cup of Darjeeling. The affair had gone well. Not only did he feel rejuvenated, but French had imparted interesting information, which might prove advantageous.

He pondered. Arson held no difficulties for Purkis. If it meant getting his way, Purkis would burn the hotel down in a heartbeat.

If it meant getting his way, he would burn the whole fucking world down.

# 19

The days passed. July slipped away. For Smith, a strange and unexpected routine was forming. A routine he would hardly have believed possible. Every morning, early, Paul would be sitting on the cabin porch. Rain or shine. Smith had, long ago, given up remonstrating. Now, he accepted the situation. In fact, grudgingly, he was enjoying it.

There were no morning greetings, as such. Smith made the kid hot coffee. They ate a little fruit. Then they started running. Four weeks had passed, Paul was gaining confidence, getting fitter, stronger. Four hours every day. Smith now graduated the training to a different style.

"Your stamina is solid," he explained one grey morning, the sun swaddled in black cloud, his skin sensing a smir of rain. "But we need to escalate. Introduce a new dimension – resistance."

They had jogged ten miles, through the winding forest trails, the trees eventually thinning, then disappearing, until they reached the foot of the mountains, a great barren swathe of rock and wild grass.

Smith stopped, looked up. A mist had descended,

obscuring the higher ridges. But vision was good enough for what he intended. Before them, the incline was steep, formed of loose stone, grass and trickling streams. It rose maybe a hundred yards, then plateaued, then rose again, until lost in the mist.

He leaned against a boulder. "Now, I want you to sprint up the hill. When you reach the flat section, you do ten press-ups. Then you run back down. Thirty-second break, then you repeat the process. Only you do ten star jumps. You know what star jumps are?" Paul nodded. "Good. Then back down, thirty seconds, then back up, then ten burpees. You know…"

"Yes," said Paul. "I know what they are. What will you be doing?"

Smith grinned. "Watching. Relaxing. And timing."

"I thought you'd say that."

"After the burpees," continued Smith, "you repeat the process – press-ups, star jumps, burpees. Three sets. Then we'll see. Now go!"

The kid darted up the side of the mountain, digging his feet into the ground for balance, slipping and scrambling. Smith watched on, memories surfacing – *running up hills in full combat gear, a fifty-pound bergen rucksack and Heckler & Koch G3KA4 assault rifle strapped to his back. Basic training for men of the Special Air Service. Staff sergeant bellowing out commands. No respite. You stopped when you dropped. Then you dragged yourself up again, exhausted. On and on, until there was nothing left. But you still carried on until you thought you were going to die.*

The kid got to the top, got down, hammered out ten press-ups, ran back down, covered in mud. He reached the bottom, dropped to his knees, taking great, gasping breaths.

"Up," said Smith brusquely. "Stay on your feet." Paul stood, bent over, hands on his knees. Smith checked his watch, waited, then, "Again."

Paul completed the three sets. When he finished, he collapsed on the grass, face down, apparently unfazed about lying on wet earth. This time, Smith let him lie. Eventually, he spoke.

"Tomorrow," he said, "you'll do the same again. Only different. You'll be carrying a rucksack weighed down with a few stones. Something to look forward to."

"Is that what you did? In the army?"

"Something of the sort. Now, get up."

Slowly, Paul got to his feet.

"How do you feel?"

"Like my lungs are on fire and my chest is about to burst."

"Is that all? Then let's do it again."

---

They arrived back at the lodge around 2pm, the return pace faster than a jog. After the hillside exertions, Smith expected the kid to stop-start his way back. But he didn't. He struggled on, keeping up, face set like marble in determination. Smith was mildly impressed.

He fried some sausages and bacon on his tiny stove, put them in buttered rolls, made some tea, while Paul sat on the porch, hunched over, catching his breath. He put the rolls on a plate, placed them on a small outdoor table with two cracked mugs. He sat opposite. They ate in silence. The rain stopped, but the day was still shadowed by cloud, lending a gloomy cast. The forest beyond was dark and quiet. It seemed to Smith the world had become suddenly still, as if caught in time.

"How am I doing?" said Paul.

"How do you think you're doing?"

Paul blew through his lips. "I feel better. Fitter. And

stronger. And I feel more…" His brow furrowed, as if searching for the right word.

"Confident?" said Smith.

Paul nodded. "I think so."

"It's a natural progression. If you look after the body, the body looks after the mind. And the mind is everything."

"But I need more than that."

Smith said nothing.

"I need courage. You can't teach that. You either have it or you don't. I don't think I've got it."

"Courage can come from confidence. Provided you're not overconfident. Then it can lead to recklessness which isn't good for anyone."

"I want to be as confident as you."

"I'm like anyone else. I have my…" Smith hesitated, licked his lips as an image that would haunt him forever flashed in his mind. "…fears," he finished.

"Will you teach me to fight?" said Paul suddenly.

Smith smiled. "Fighting. Why does everyone want to fight?"

Paul's eyes opened wide. "It's a miracle!"

Smith regarded him quizzically.

"I've witnessed something impossible," said Paul.

"What?"

"You smiled."

Smith couldn't help smiling again. "Time to go."

"That's two," said Paul.

"Savour this moment. It won't happen again."

---

Smith walked the kid back to the main road, which had now also become part of the routine. During this stage the conversation was sparse, which suited Smith fine. He liked the silence. And he reckoned the kid did too. They reached the road. A hundred yards away, jogging on the grass verge, was someone they both recognised.

"Shit," muttered Paul.

Smith recognised her instantly.

It was the kid's mother.

## 20

Vincent Docherty had been a policeman since he'd turned eighteen, twenty-five years ago. He had never risen above the rank of constable, because he had no inclination to do so. It was simply too much like hard work. Too much admin. Too much responsibility. Too much everything. But the problem he faced was that a constable's salary, even with overtime, couldn't accommodate his lifestyle, which involved large amounts of alcohol and a serious addiction to cocaine.

Which, years ago, had led him to the path of Jacob Starling.

It was mid-afternoon. Just as Smith and Paul were making their way through the forest towards the main road, Docherty was sitting in the lounge of an obscure little pub called the Swan Inn in the village of Eaglesham, ten miles outside Glasgow. He had been instructed to get there for 2pm sharp, which he did. The type of people he was involved with, lack of punctuality could have serious consequences.

He had been working three consecutive twelve-hour shifts, and he now had four days off. He was exhausted. He had just driven three hours from Aviemore. For reasons unexplained. The message was simple. A place, a date, a time.

The pub was furnished in an olde-worlde style. Age-blackened rafters criss-crossing the low ceiling, the walls reduced back to bare stone, wooden flooring which creaked with every step. At one end, a wide hearth of grey flagstone in which, during the winter months, a real fire would smoke and crackle. The windows were small, allowing scant light, creating a close, gloomy feel. The place was quiet. A few locals, surmised Docherty. Men hunched at the bar, reading newspapers. In one corner, a group of four, sipping pints, chatting in low voices. On a wall, a television on mute, showing English football. No one appeared to be paying attention. A place like a million others, he thought.

He gazed at the glittering row of bottles on a mirrored gantry behind the bar. The temptation was strong. More than that. Irresistible. To Docherty, there was nothing quite like the allure of alcohol. He shook his head, looked away. Not today. Today was business. He had been called to this place by a man who wouldn't take kindly to seeing Docherty sitting with a large G and T.

His thoughts were interrupted. The very man entered the pub. Casually dressed. Leather bomber jacket, jeans. A man of average height, lean as a whippet, dark hair flicked trendily over, saturnine features, face all hard lines. Jacob. As ever, when he met this man, Docherty experienced a brief flutter of nerves. Jacob exuded an undefinable aura. A mixture of competence and menace – in his manner, his demeanour. And his voice – always soft and reasonable, which made it worse. A man to be taken seriously. A man, in Docherty's opinion, who was dangerous, bordering on psychotic.

Jacob spotted him, came over, sat opposite.

Docherty nodded. "Good to see you again, Jacob."

Jacob responded with a steely smile. "I'm sure. Is that coffee?" He was referring to the tall glass on the table.

"Double-shot latte."

Jacob turned his head, caught the attention of the barman. "Two more of these, please." The barman acknowledged him with a thumbs-up sign. Jacob turned his attention back to Docherty.

"I like the old-style village pubs. There's something civilised about them. Rooted in the past. Things change all around, shifting with trends and fads. *Here now, gone tomorrow.* But these old buildings stand constant. Don't you think?"

Docherty went through the motion of looking about, said, "I guess. Civilised. I get it. But why here? Why Eaglesham?"

"Because of its charm. Plus, from a practical perspective, it's a hundred and forty miles from Aviemore. Unlikely we should meet anyone who knows us. Which means we can enjoy a little privacy."

Docherty nodded his head solemnly, thinking, *Why the fuck did I drive three hours for a little privacy, when they could have met in a thousand other shitholes just as private and a lot damn closer.*

"Of course," he said. "Privacy."

"You understand," said Jacob, "that given the nature of our business, privacy is important."

The bartender arrived with two coffees, which he placed on the table, removing Docherty's empty glass. "Would you gents like to see the menu?"

"Thank you, no," said Jacob.

The bartender left. Jacob sipped his coffee.

"You know what else I like about these old pubs? They have real fires. Do you like real fires, Vincent?"

Docherty hesitated, not sure where the conversation was going. "I've never given them much thought."

"Then you might want to start," answered Jacob cryptically. They were sitting by a narrow window. Daylight, grey and dreary, slanted through. Jacob seemed to switch his attention to the view outside. The pub sat on one side of a long, steep road, along with rows of high, cramped, terraced houses. On the opposite side, a park stretching the length of the village.

"A place like this is nice to visit," he said softly, perhaps to himself. "But to stay here? I don't think this is meant for men like us. People come here to die, not to live."

Docherty didn't know how to respond, so said nothing.

Jacob flicked his eyes back to Docherty.

"We have a job for you." He put his hand in his inside jacket pocket, produced a white envelope, placed it in the centre of the table. It bulged. Docherty liked bulging envelopes.

"Four thousand," said Jacob. "Another four when the job's finished."

"Sounds reasonable," said Docherty.

"You haven't heard what the job is."

Docherty shrugged. "Does it matter?"

Jacob gave a cold smile. "The Royal Hotel. You'll know it, of course."

"Of course. The one which Mr Purkis..." He licked his lips, face assuming a neutral expression. "...acquired."

Jacob maintained his smile. "Acquired. That's one way of describing it. But yes. The hotel is owned by Mr Purkis."

Docherty waited. The envelope sat, full of promise. Already he was calculating how many lines he could buy.

"The Royal Hotel has to suffer an accident of sorts. It's an old building. A small fire and before you know it..."

"Before you know it, whoosh!" finished Docherty.

Jacob nodded. "Complete destruction. You understand what is required?"

"Easy." He leaned forward, lowered his voice. "A can of

petrol poured through the letterbox. A place like that would go up in ten seconds. I can go with a couple of guys. No problem."

"A couple of guys? I don't think so. You'll go with a friend of mine, Mr Halliday, who has some experience in such matters. I'll be there too. To ensure matters proceed as required. No petrol, no diesel, no paraffin. A little too obvious. The police will use sniffer dogs. You understand, yes?"

Docherty gave a sly smile. "I understand. Insurance job? Has to look good? I get it, Jacob."

Jacob stared at him, spoke with a metallic undertone. "You get nothing. We don't pay you to *get*. We pay you to *do*. Don't start thinking, Vincent. It's not your role in life. The best thing you can do is take the money, do what you're told, and shut the fuck up. You get that?"

Docherty, a little shocked at Jacob's change of mood, hesitated, bowed his head. "Sure, Jacob. Sorry. No harm meant."

Jacob's smile widened. "That's good to hear. That's why we trust you with these delicate matters. We know you're discreet. Loose lips and all that. Otherwise, the consequences are... how should I put it... *unpleasant*."

"Sure, Jacob."

Docherty cast a hungry glance at the envelope, reached across, placed his hand on it. Jacob did likewise, resting his hand on Docherty's. "We know we can count on you, Vincent."

"I won't let you down."

"Good boy."

Jacob lifted his hand. Docherty slid the envelope to his side of the table, tucked it in his jacket pocket.

"Three weeks," said Jacob. "Maybe four. I'll contact you. Be ready."

"I'll be ready."

Jacob said nothing further. He issued a curt nod of his head and left the pub. He had hardly touched his coffee. No wonder, thought Docherty. It tasted like shit. Docherty watched him cross the road, into the park, and was soon lost from sight.

He sat back. He had four grand in his pocket. More – much more – than he was used to. He'd been working for Jacob for five years. The jobs were usually routine, involving passive rather than active involvement. Essentially turning a blind eye. Ensuring there were no cops at a certain place, at a certain time. Or occasionally, something a bit more inventive. Planting drugs in a car, in a house. Giving false testimony. Easy work. This, however…

Docherty knew the Royal Hotel. An impressive building, standing solitary on a large area of land a few miles north of Aviemore, hidden deep in the countryside. He also knew the owner – ex-owner. Raymond Chesterfield. Chesterfield had a gambling problem. Then, out of the blue, Chadwick Purkis had taken ownership. Such was common knowledge. The details surrounding the acquisition were less clear.

Chadwick Purkis. A well-known name. Rich landowner, property developer, businessman. Generous with his money, donating fortunes every year to charity. Docherty was aware that Jacob worked for Purkis. Where there's light, there's always shade, he thought.

Four grand. The job was therefore important. Docherty was wise enough not to ask any questions. He knew his place in the scheme of things. Plus, he really didn't give a shit. He had cash in his pocket, and already he could feel it burning, like an itch.

And he had other matters to occupy his mind. One in particular.

He had a score to settle. Like the money, it burned and itched, to be eased by only one thing.

Payback.

## 21

When she saw them, she stopped. She was fifty yards away. Dressed in black leggings, black hoodie, red fluorescent training shoes.

"Paul?"

She started again, marching towards them. Smith sensed the kid tense. Her hair was tied back in a ponytail which bounced and bobbed with every step.

Paul essayed a lame smile, gave her a half wave. "Hi, Mum."

She stopped, facing them both. Her face shone with sweat and exertion.

"What's this?"

"You out jogging, Mum?"

She looked at Paul, then Smith, frowning. "It's you."

Smith had no answer to give.

"Can you tell me what's going on?"

"I've been running," said Paul, his voice decidedly sheepish, thought Smith. "With John."

"John? Explain, please."

Paul began to fidget. "We go running."

"You've said that."

"I asked him to train me. To get me fit."

"To train you. What does that mean? This is a regular thing?" They were speaking as if Smith wasn't there.

"Yes."

Now, she turned her attention to Smith. "This is a regular thing?"

"You never told your mum, did you, Paul?"

"Told me what?"

Smith heaved a deep sigh. Since the altercation in the kid's front garden, life was suddenly a tangled mess. If he hadn't stepped forward, had kept to his own business, stayed away, then his existence would have continued undisturbed But... the nightmares had diminished. The kid was growing stronger, a fact which gave Smith satisfaction. And something perhaps more. A reason. Something he hadn't felt for years.

"Paul comes to my cabin every morning. Early. He asked me to help him. He wants to get fit and strong. I agreed. No harm done. And certainly no harm intended."

She gazed at Smith, presumably processing the information. "Paul's been telling me he's been going to friends' houses. He tells me he goes to the loch to fish. He tells me everything but the truth. What's your name? Your full name?"

"John Smith."

"You live in the forest?"

"Yes."

"Like some sort of survivalist?"

Smith allowed the faintest of smiles. "I survive, yes. I'm not entirely sure what a survivalist is, to be honest."

"The type that hunts and lives off the land. The type you see in the movies."

Smith's smile widened. "I suppose I might have to, if it weren't for the fortnightly trip to Tesco. I'm not entirely sure how a survivalist would find bananas in the Cairngorm mountains. Or coffee, for that matter."

Her features softened. "I never really thanked you, John. For helping us that morning. And I want to apologise. Paul shouldn't be bothering you. It will stop, I promise."

"But I don't want it to stop!" blurted Paul. "I know John doesn't want me there, I know he thinks I'm a pain in the arse, but at least he takes an interest. Or at least he pretends to. And for the first time, I feel..." He blinked, raised his hands in a helpless gesture, floundering for the right words. "...good about myself."

Smith turned, regarded Paul for a long second, then turned back to his mother.

"I would like to keep the training up," he said gently. "Paul is doing well. It's good for him." *It's good for both of us.*

Now Paul looked up at Smith, but he said nothing. Nor did his mother.

"If that's all right," said Smith.

"I never really introduced myself," she said. "I'm Alison Davidson." She held out her hand. Smith shook it.

"Pleased to meet you, Alison Davidson."

"As you can see," Alison said, glancing down at her black leggings, "I'm trying to get fit again. I'm off work for a week. Getting the most of the summer weather."

Smith smiled. "Summer. It's a season Scotland likes to avoid."

She smiled back, hesitated, then said, "I think at the very least, I owe you a coffee. If that's okay?"

"You don't owe me anything."

"Then call it an act of goodwill. Plus, if you're taking charge of my son, I think it's only reasonable for me to get to know you a bit."

"That's a great idea," said Paul, suddenly. "Come for coffee, John."

Smith found he couldn't disagree. Yet again he was mildly amazed at how quickly matters moved beyond his control.

"How about tomorrow afternoon?" said Alison. "Come back with Paul. If you're lucky, I might even fix you something to eat." She grinned. "Or maybe unlucky."

Smith had no argument. "Okay. If it's no trouble."

"No trouble."

Smith watched them both head back the mile journey to Aviemore, and wondered, not for the first time, just what the hell he was doing.

*Nothing good will come of this*, whispered a voice in his mind. Perhaps. Perhaps not. Perhaps he had to take the chance.

Perhaps he had to join the human race.

## 22

Eaglesham was not entirely a random rendezvous. Jacob had chosen to meet Docherty there because it was close to somewhere else. Somewhere Jacob had to be. Two miles away was a place called Jackton. Originally a cluster of houses, to be passed en route to somewhere else. Blink and it was missed. But developers saw potential and built around it, creating a sprawling estate of buildings each as characterless and cheerless as the next.

The original houses remained. One such house, long ago, had been used as a blacksmith's. It had been converted into a detached living accommodation. White-stone walls, black-framed windows, slate-tiled roof, an unobtrusive driveway, the front garden slabbed, devoid of any shrubbery.

Immediately after his meeting with Docherty, Jacob drove the two miles to this particular house. He parked hard up on the pavement. He popped open the boot, and lifted out a sports bag. He made his way to the front door, past a bright orange Volkswagen Beetle parked on the driveway. He rang the doorbell. He sensed movement from inside. He saw a shape through the bevelled glass. It approached. A key turned, a latch slid, the door rattled open. An elderly woman stood before him. Maybe seventy-five. Tanned, leathery skin. Used to hotter climates. Trim, well dressed, wearing a dark satin skirt with a cream waistband, a matching dark top. Her hair was silver-grey, styled in a half halo braid. She saw Jacob, and her face became animated with a sudden beaming smile.

"Jacob!" she said. "What a lovely surprise. How nice to see you again."

The reaction was always the same, which amused Jacob. She knew he was coming. This was no unexpected visit. But he kept the pretense going.

"Lovely to see you too, Mrs Pritchard. You look radiant."

"Such a nice young man."

She stepped to one side, gestured him inside. He entered a narrow hall. The wallpaper was garish – blue and gold stripes, pale blue cornicing. On the wall, lots of miniature framed pictures of bland landscapes. "Can I take your jacket?"

"I'm fine, thank you."

She closed the door behind her. "I'm making coffee."

"I'm fine."

"A croissant?"

"Not today, Mrs Pritchard."

"With home-made jam? Strawberry?"

"Go on then."

"Wonderful. Cornwall's in the living room. Just go straight through. I know you boys like your privacy."

She led him to a closed door on the right. She continued on to the end of the hall, to the kitchen. Jacob entered the living room. It was of regular dimensions, running open plan to a neat dining area, and a set of French doors, beyond which, a compact back garden. The walls were pale pink. On one wall – the one facing Jacob as he entered – was a tiled fireplace, and above it, a large bronze framed mirror. In a corner, a television showing an old black-and-white movie. A Western. Purkis didn't recognise it. A lime-green suite comprising two armchairs and a couch. On one of the chairs sat the individual he had come to see. Cornwall Pritchard.

The man was massive. He filled the armchair. There was no excess fat. He was all muscle. Neck as wide as his head, deep-chested, broad-shouldered, arms like pistons, hands like slabs. Long black hair swept roguishly back behind his ears. His face looked like it was sculpted from granite. He wore a loose T-shirt, jogging bottoms, a pair of open-toed sandals. Even sitting, it was easy to see he was tall. Jacob knew his exact height – six feet six inches and one quarter. His weight too – nineteen stone and six pounds.

He smiled when he saw Jacob, displaying a perfect row of teeth. "My old friend Jacob Starling." He pressed a button on the remote on the armrest, killing the sound.

Jacob sat on a chair opposite. Between them was a low IKEA coffee table, upon which he placed the sports bag.

"You've had them fixed," said Jacob.

Pritchard licked his teeth with the tip of his tongue. "Three grand for one implant. But it looks rather nice, yes?"

"Dazzling. You lost a tooth. The other guy lost…"

"Everything," finished Pritchard, maintaining his smile.

"Quite so. Mr Purkis is very pleased."

"So he should be. I give them what they want."

"Yes you do, Cornwall. You're an artist."

He leaned over, opened the zipper of the sports bag, took out a transparent polythene bag, containing neat bound bundles of bank notes.

"A hundred and fifty thousand," said Jacob. "Plus another ten, as a bonus."

Pritchard gave a small, grateful nod of his head. "That's very civil."

"Mr Purkis can be a civil man."

"Mother loves her holidays in the sun. She has a hankering for Mexico. Have you ever been to Mexico, Jacob?"

"You can afford to go wherever you want."

"She loves the warm weather. What with her arthritis. All her aches and pains."

"I'm sure."

A silence fell. Pritchard stared at the bag. Eventually he spoke. "And…?"

"Of course. There's always an 'and'."

The door opened. Mrs Pritchard entered. Her perfume was strong, dominating the room. She held a tray and on it, delicate porcelain crockery. Two plates, two embroidered cloth napkins, a warm croissant on each, two knives with pearl handles, a miniature pot of jam, a miniature pot of clotted cream, two cups of coffee. Black. She knew how he liked it. *She ought to by now*, he thought. With deliberation, she placed each on the table beside the bag of money, giving it only a cursory glance.

"Such a pleasure to see you again, Jacob," she said.

*I'll bet.*

"I'll leave you men together," she said, smiling, her skin stretching oddly in the process, giving her an almost reptilian look.

"Thank you, Mother."

"Thank you, Mrs Pritchard."

She left.

"Your mother's looking well."

Pritchard gave a mirthless grin. "She ought to. Plastic surgeons. What a fucking racket. I should have studied harder at school."

"But then you wouldn't achieve the same sense of satisfaction."

"This is true, Jacob. You always have an answer. But yes, she's a beautiful woman."

Jacob carefully spread the jam and cream on the croissant, took a small bite. Sipped the coffee. Pritchard watched him, didn't touch his.

"Nice," said Jacob.

"I'm not going to put shit like that in my body. She knows. She's only being polite."

"I understand."

"So..."

"Where we... yes. The best bit."

He reached into the sports bag, took out a plain wooden box roughly the size and shape of a large cigar box, the lid held shut by a tiny gold latch. He stood, went over to Pritchard.

"With Mr Purkis's compliments."

He gave it to Pritchard, who took it with both his huge hands, holding it gently as he might a precious ornament.

Jacob returned to his seat, ate another corner of the croissant and watched the next scene unfold.

Pritchard gazed at the box. "There's nothing quite like this moment," he said, his voice hushed. "The anticipation."

"Like Christmas."

"Better," said Pritchard.

With thick fingers he unfastened the latch, opened the lid. Inside, resting on purple velvet cushioning, was a human hand. Severed cleanly at the wrist. Pritchard took a deep breath, his great chest rising.

"Beautiful." He closed the box, put it on the armrest of his chair. "I don't like to look at it too long," he said. "I think, if you look at something too long it gets spoiled. You understand, Jacob? Important things like this should be treated with respect."

"It's a trophy," replied Jacob. "The hand of a man who tried to kill you should be treated with reverence. To be enjoyed sparingly. Otherwise it loses its wonder."

Pritchard nodded solemnly. "Wise words."

*Bullshit*, thought Jacob. *The man before him was a dangerous psychopath. But it was exactly the type of man Chadwick Purkis needed.*

"You must have quite a collection," he said.

Pritchard's blunt features creased into a small, secret smile, but he remained silent. Jacob thought back. *Eight? Nine?* He'd lost count.

"When is the next one?" said Pritchard.

Jacob dabbed the corners of his mouth with the cloth napkin. "Keen?"

"Restless. I like to keep busy."

"Of course. We're looking for suitable candidates. It can take time. Like your trophy, the Glass Box is something very special. Too much, and it loses its appeal. We'll contact you when we need you."

"The Glass Box. It's a name that sticks."

"For a very select few. Mr Purkis loves his games." *And the seventy-five million he collects each pop.*

Jacob stood, zipped up the sports bag. "Thank your mother. Her strawberry jam was delicious."

"I'll tell her. She's very fond of you. Goodbye, Jacob. Be sure to keep in touch."

"Undoubtedly."

He glanced round to the television. The movie was still showing.

"I didn't know you liked old black-and-whites."

"Randolph Scott. It doesn't matter how many guys he fights, he kills them all. You know he's never going to die. He's like me. He's invincible."

*But he did die*, thought Jacob.

Jacob made his way back into the hallway. Mrs Pritchard was standing at the far end, leaning against the open kitchen door.

"See you soon, Jacob my love."

When Jacob left the house of Cornwall Pritchard, he felt the familiar sensation. Relief. Not that Jacob feared him. Jacob feared few men. But Pritchard was a beast. And volatile. Plus, Jacob had seen him perform in the Glass Box and as such, knew what the man was capable of.

He drove off, heading back north.

There were things to plan. In particular, the Royal Hotel.

———

Cornwall Pritchard remained where he was. The box was before him on the coffee table, next to his untouched croissant. His mother came in and sat on the same chair Jacob had been sitting on.

"How much?" she asked.

"One hundred and fifty. Plus a bonus of another ten."

"Miserly cunts. Jacob comes waltzing in as if he fucking owns you. You deserve far more, Cornwall."

Pritchard shrugged his hulking shoulders. "I like what I do. I get respect."

"If they respected you, you'd get twice what they give you." Her eyes rested on the box. Without asking she reached over, opened it. She showed no reaction.

"I'll put it with the others." She snapped the box shut. "Next time ask for something a bit more interesting. And useful."

Pritchard frowned. "Like what?"

"Like a fucking cock."

They both laughed. She got up, went over to her son, kissed him on the forehead.

"You're a good boy, Cornwall. You know Mother loves you. You know that, don't you, Cornwall? You know Mother loves you very much."

"I know."

She straightened. Her face hardened.

"Now prove it."

## 23

As Smith had promised, he strapped a rucksack onto the kid, filled it with a couple of hefty stones, and told him to run up and down the same section of mountain. All to the tune of Led Zeppelin, playing from a portable CD player Smith had bought in a charity shop in Aviemore. In particular, 'Stairway to Heaven', which Smith thought, somewhat sardonically, was appropriate for the occasion. The kid had never heard of Led Zeppelin, which saddened Smith, realising he wasn't getting any younger.

Fifteen times. Up and down. Twenty-second breaks. And the kid did it. Uncomplaining, face set with determination, gasping, spluttering. Retching. But he did it.

Then Smith showed him some rudimentary moves in basic unarmed combat, all the while the music played and the wind whistled, the sun hidden behind billowing cloud.

"Ko-uchi-gari and tomoe-nage," Smith explained. "Inner reaping and circle throw. Foundation moves in judo. The first is appropriate when your opponent is standing with his feet wider apart than normal, which would be an enemy's standard pose. You push and pull. Push with the right side of your chest, pull his right sleeve down with your left hand. Then pull his right foot from under him using your right foot. Thus…" and Smith used the technique, rendering the kid to the ground.

"The circle throw is a neat trick," he went on. "Good for a larger opponent. I push you backwards. Instead of resisting, drop down slightly. I lose balance. I stagger. I'm leaning forward. Place your left foot between mine, your right foot on my abdomen, fall back, use your hands to throw, thus…" And to the kid's astonishment, he'd hurled Smith onto the grass. They practised the moves for well over an hour. Again and again.

"It must become instinctive. Almost like breathing."

"And if I'm attacked by a guy that's twenty stone?"

Smith gave a wry chuckle. "Kick him in the balls. It never fails."

The kid laughed. "And if it's a woman?"

"They're much tougher. Only one thing you can do."

"Which is?"

Smith grinned. "Pray."

Smith had grave doubts. He and the kid were at the main road to Aviemore. The usual departure point where they went their separate ways – the kid back to civilisation, Smith back to his self-imposed wilderness. He felt that if he were to join him on the road to town, to Alison's house, to coffee and lunch, to idle conversation, he might never go back, and he might lose something. A piece of himself. His resolution to remain isolated. Which, so far, had kept him sane.

Or he might gain something. The spark of human contact. Whatever, he had a choice. Perhaps this was the time. Perhaps this was a sign. Of what, he had no clear idea. His salvation?

Doubts plagued his mind. The kid's mother had a boyfriend

– or perhaps ex-boyfriend – who was both violent and volatile. A dangerous combination. Smith had no desire to inflame a situation.

He hesitated, held back.

"What's wrong?" said Paul.

*Fuck this*, thought Smith. *It's only lunch. What could go wrong?*

*Everything*, whispered the voice of his doubt. He buried it deep, chose to ignore it.

He and the kid made their way towards town, to Alison Davidson's house.

---

The front garden looked tidier than Smith remembered. The incident with Vincent had occurred weeks ago. The grass had since been cut, the weeds between the stone path removed, the hedgerow trimmed. A hanging basket had been put up either side of the front door, bright flowers trailing.

Again, Smith hesitated. It wasn't too late to turn back, flee to the mountains.

The kid opened the door. Smith, despite himself, followed him in.

The house was not large. He remembered the corridor, the walls white and fresh. He went through to the kitchen, to the clink and rattle of food being prepared, the kid in front. They went in. On his last visit, the kitchen table was on its side, food splattered on the floor, broken crockery. Also on the floor, the kid's mother, dazed and beaten.

The scenario he faced was entirely different. The place was neat and orderly, and bright with daylight streaming through a back window. Clean white tiling on the walls, cherry wood work surfaces. On one wall, several unframed paintings of the Cairngorm mountains, the colours wild and vivid. Three places had been set. In the middle, a large wooden bowl of mixed salad. Something was cooking in the oven. After a morning outside, the aroma was mouthwatering.

Alison stood before him, offering a somewhat lame smile.

"I hope you like lasagna?"

"You shouldn't have gone to any bother."

"You're avoiding the question. You hate lasagna."

"Love it," said Smith.

Alison laughed. "The love affair might end when you taste it. Please, have a seat. Anywhere."

Smith sat, facing the door. *Christ*, he thought. *Old habits never really die*.

She wore pale blue jeans, a plain bottle-green sweatshirt, white tennis shoes. The kid had said she was once a ski champion, that she worked in the ski centre. Her poise, her physical confidence was apparent. It struck Smith that athletes – even ex-athletes – possessed an indefinable grace in their movements, regardless of how small or casual. She was slender, clean limbed. Smith could envisage her skimming down the snowy slopes, fast and sure. Her hair was tied back. Her face was slightly flushed with the heat from the oven.

"Would you like something to drink? A beer?"

"Beer's fine."

Paul got a bottle of Bud from the fridge, opened it, placed it on the table.

"Pour it in a glass, Paul."

"Honestly, straight from the bottle's good."

Smith sipped. Alcohol hadn't passed his lips for five years. Its absence had never really bothered him, as it had never formed an essential part of his life. It had never formed any part of his life whatsoever. Unlike many others in the regiment.

With a dish towel wrapped round her hands, she took out a dish from the oven, placed it on a table mat.

"It might need salt," she said. "I don't like to salt when I cook. You okay with garlic?"

"No problem." It occurred to Smith he hadn't tasted garlic either for the last few years. Indeed, the last time he'd had a proper cooked meal was a distant memory, living on tinned stuff heated in a pot over a single ring.

She dished a healthy wedge onto his plate. "Salad?"

"Sure."

She used two wooden forks to transfer salad onto his plate.

"I have dressing, if you want."

"This is perfect," said Smith.

Paul sat next to him, Alison opposite. Alison dished food onto Paul's plate, then her own.

Alison also had a beer, drinking from the bottle.

"Please start."

"John taught me some judo," said Paul through a mouthful of food. "Ko-uchi-gari, and… another move. I can't remember what it's called."

"Tomoe-nage," said Smith quietly. "Basic moves. I hope that's okay, Alison."

"Judo?" replied Alison. "When I was younger, the big thing was karate. Probably still is, for all I know. Where did you learn it, John?"

Smith had no real desire to open up about his past to a relative stranger. His past was something he wanted to forget.

"Here and there. Picked it up along the way, you could say. Paul said you were a skiing champion. Now that's a real talking point."

"That was another time, another world."

"Tell me."

Alison laughed – a light, infectious sound, thought Smith. "Seeing as you've twisted my arm. Alpine Skiing. I was decent in the giant slalom."

"Decent?"

"Mum came in second in the Europa Cup," said Paul.

"Over twenty years ago," said Alison, dismissing the matter with a flutter of her hands. "As I said, another time, another world. You've probably never heard of the Europa Cup."

Smith had, but he chose to say nothing.

"It's a season, over three months. I had to compete in thirty-three races, starting in Switzerland, finishing in Austria. Do you ski?"

"When I was younger. Nothing to speak of." Which was the truth. He'd been trained in Arctic warfare, to survive and fight in extreme conditions. He'd learned to ski in Mittenwald. Not to win cups. Rather, to help him kill people. But as Alison had said, another time, another world. He chose not to elaborate on that aspect of his life.

"I'm impressed," he went on. "Really. The time and dedication to accomplish such a thing."

Alison gave a modest shrug. "It's easier when you're young. But then I broke my leg. After that, I had to change direction. Stopped competing and started instructing. Which I have been doing now for twenty years."

"You work in Aviemore?"

"Yup. Born and bred here. Might as well work here. How's the lasagna?"

"Excellent."

"John lives on tinned food and fruit," said Paul. "Sometimes, when we're lucky, he might cook me a sausage on special days."

"You live in the old cabin in the forest?" said Alison. "God. I mean, wow. I mean…"

Smith allowed a small smile. "That's okay. It's basic. It has running water and electricity. It keeps me dry when it rains. Sometimes. But it's not as bad as it seems. It could be worse."

"Really?"

"I could have moved to a cave."

"Who could live in a cave?" said Paul.

*You'd be amazed, kid*, thought Smith. *The fighting men of the Taliban destroyed countless enemies from such places.*

"You moved there recently?" asked Alison.

"Four years ago," answered Smith.

"Four years. I had no idea. That would have been a big change?"

"Pretty much. But it's funny. I don't have a television, or a computer, or an internet connection. I don't even have a radio. Or a mobile phone. I only recently bought a CD player. I think most people would imagine that without these items life would be intolerable. And yet, you quickly realise they're not essential. In fact, for me anyway, they were an obstacle."

"An obstacle?"

Smith felt perhaps the conversation was getting a little too deep. Still, he'd started.

"These things are a distraction from what's important. At least, important to me. Silence. Reading. Walking. Breathing fresh air. The sound of rain, the wind. Which must lead you to an obvious conclusion."

"Which is?"

Smith gave a wintry grin. "That I'm stark raving mad."

Alison smiled. "At least you don't live in a cave."

"Not yet."

Paul stood. His plate was clean. "Can I go upstairs?"

"No more than two hours," said Alison. "I'm serious."

"Two hours."

He left the kitchen. The house shook as he bounded up the stairs, presumably to his bedroom.

"He gets two hours on his computer," explained Alison, apologetically. "Games and stuff. I'm just grateful he's getting outdoors and getting a bit of exercise. Which I have you to thank for."

"As long as you're okay with it."

She nodded but said nothing. They finished lunch in silence. Smith knew she had a million questions. Who could blame her? A man she hardly knew spending time with her son every morning. It was a bizarre situation, and most people didn't like bizarre.

"Coffee?" she said eventually.

"Sure."

She got up, switched the kettle on.

"These are interesting pictures," he said, referring to the paintings on the kitchen wall.

"My attempt at a bit of art. Basic and amateurish. But I'll take *interesting* all day long."

"You've caught them right," he said softly, and he meant it. "The Cairngorms. Their wildness. Raw and unpredictable. You've captured their…"

"What?"

"…soul."

She was blushing.

"I'm sorry if I've embarrassed you."

She had her back to him. A tremor, almost imperceptible, rippled through her shoulders.

"Don't apologise. You don't know how nice it is to get a compliment. Really." She got the dish towel from the kitchen unit, used it to dab her eyes.

Smith said nothing. She concentrated on fixing two mugs of coffee.

"What do you take?"

"Black's fine. Just as it is."

She put two plain white mugs on the table, sat back down.

"Sorry," she said. "I love to paint the mountains."

"I understand that."

A silence fell between them. Smith waited for it to come, and then it did.

She took a sip, said, "What is it you do, John? Or what did you use to do?"

Smith likewise took a sip. It tasted bitter. Or perhaps it was old memories leaving an aftertaste.

"I was in the army," he said simply. He thought, *Skim the surface, don't linger on the substance, move on quickly.* "I joined when I was seventeen. Much to the horror of my parents. They had other plans. Like university, graduation, a safe job. Accountancy or law, or something. Their plans and mine didn't quite dovetail. My father was an accountant, my mother was a teacher. The army wasn't quite on the agenda. They came round, after a while. Grudgingly. What else could they do?"

"Why the army?"

"I'm amazed you ask. The cool camouflage gear. Obviously."

She smiled. "But seriously."

Smith took a deep breath. The truth was, looking back as he often did, he never really had an exact answer to the question. Restlessness? Boredom? Rebelliousness? A testosterone-based decision? Perhaps a combination of a whole lot of things.

"If I said I wanted to see the world, please don't treat me as a cliché."

She laughed. "You're definitely not that."

Smith moved on quickly. "I got to captain, took early retirement at the ripe age of forty-one and thought, time to do something radical again."

"And so you..."

"...decided to move sticks, and live in a hut in the mountains for five years. Isn't that what anyone would do? Which has a big advantage."

Alison looked quizzical. "Like not having to meet people?"

*There was that.*

"Like the saving on heating bills."

She nodded. *Skimmed the surface*. She still had questions. But Smith reckoned she was too polite to delve further. He'd given her a morsel. And the truth. He changed tack.

"And how are things?" he asked gently.

She gave a small, tight smile. "I'm sorry for what happened. It was… horrific." She took a sip of her drink. "My husband died. Perhaps Paul told you. Four years back. It was difficult. I started seeing Vincent six months ago. He'd stay over occasionally." She hesitated, took another sip.

"You don't need to…"

"But he likes the drink. I mean *really* likes the drink. And he has a temper. He's violent. Basically, he likes to hit women." She blinked back tears, lowered her voice. "Basically, he likes to hit me." Another sip, then, "Like he's got a fucking God-given right."

Smith said nothing.

She straightened. "But he's gone. I haven't seen him for six weeks. I don't want to see him. Ever again. I want to forget."

*Join the club*, thought Smith.

"He's not likely to trouble you?"

"He knows better. He crossed the line. He's stupid, but he's not that stupid. If he comes back, I'll report him, and he knows it. Then he loses everything."

Smith, knowing intimately the nature of violent men, wasn't entirely convinced, but he let the subject drop.

"Are you married?" she asked suddenly. She laughed again, that light tinkling sound. "Living in the Cairngorms?"

Smith allowed a grim chuckle. "I can see it now. Married bliss, living in a tin-roofed shack in the mountains. Not quite an ideal situation for married life. No. Unmarried. I think perhaps I'm not the marrying kind."

Alison gave the slightest shrug, her expression unreadable.

Another silence, then she said, "You don't mind Paul

coming? If it's not convenient or if you're fed up with it, I get it, and I'll make it stop."

"No," said Smith. "It's good." *Maybe for both of us.*

"You're sure?"

"He's a nice kid."

They chatted for another half hour, far longer than Smith had intended. Eventually, Smith made his farewells.

"You'll come again, I hope," Alison said. "Perhaps next time I'll offer you beer from a glass."

"Heaven forbid."

Smith made his way back through the forest paths to his little cabin, and to his surprise, found he was smiling.

---

He'd parked his car a hundred yards from her house on the opposite side, in a spot a little back from the road, rendered unobtrusive by foliage. Depending on shifts, he parked here either day or night. He had a clear view. She'd cut the front hedge. He could see the garden, the front door. He watched as Paul and the guy entered the house. Disbelief turned to rage, deep, a slow burn. He felt violated. As the minutes dragged to hours, his rage intensified. He watched as two hours later – *two fucking hours* – the front door opened. The guy was leaving. She stood at the doorway, talking. A lot of talking. He scrutinised her movements. She was too far away for him to be sure, but he was damned certain she was smiling. *Flirting.* The guy left. He watched. She still stood. She was waiting. Then the guy turned and waved. *And she fucking waved back.*

Docherty had seen enough. His suspicions were confirmed. She was a whore. She would pay.

As would her new scumbag boyfriend.

## 24

---

The property portfolio of Chadwick Purkis was impressive. He owned over two hundred flats and houses, dotted up and down the length of Britain. Some in the best parts, from London to Edinburgh. Others more squalid. But they were all rented out, generating sizeable income. Few people fell into rent arrears. Chadwick was an unforgiving landlord. Plus, he owned commercial properties, ranging from petrol stations to restaurants, office blocks to nail bars. He bought, he renovated, he sold. Those he kept, he rented, and always got a good return.

He had formed his own construction company, and had recently entered the development game. Buying plots of land, building luxury houses, making small fortunes. One such project was the Royal Hotel, sitting on roughly fifty acres of land. Nestled by the River Spey and in the near distance, the sweep of the Cairngorm mountains. Only a ten-minute commute to Aviemore. A developer's dream. He could build thirty houses and name his price. A short while ago he thought his dream had been crushed. Now, however...

He sat outside a bijou restaurant under a green-and-white

awning. Here, the walkway was cobbled, and beyond shiny black chain fencing flowed the Water of Leith, twenty-two miles long and Edinburgh's main river. Purkis liked to sit here. The whisper of the river was therapeutic. Also, he owned the restaurant and as such, was always guaranteed a seat.

On the table before him, a single glass of Malbec and a glass ashtray. People strolled by; dog walkers, cyclists, joggers, couples hand in hand. It was midday. The sun was bright, the tranquil scene around him a surreal contrast to the many different scenes he'd faced throughout his life.

Currently, things were good for Chadwick Purkis. There were occasional blips – like Tony French – but he'd experienced worse. He was a wealthy man. Wealth born from a violent past. His thoughts drifted to another time, to another place. To the opium poppy fields in Afghanistan. When Purkis was a younger man. When Purkis made his fortune in the heroin trade.

And inevitably, as inexorable as the flowing water only yards from where he sat, his thoughts ran to the village.

And in the village a room. A room like no other in the world.

His room.

His reverie was interrupted. A man approached, dark suit, silk open-collared shirt, sleek as a seal. Jacob. Punctual as ever. He sat opposite, gave a perfunctory smile.

"How was our friend in Jackton?" asked Purkis.

"Eager."

"Of course he is. He has an itch. We provide the means to scratch it."

"In a manner of speaking."

An elderly couple passed, stopped at the chain fencing to gaze down at the river below. They spoke in German. Tourists. At this time, the place swarmed with them. Which pleased

Purkis. Tourists didn't mind paying ridiculous prices. Which meant the restaurant would maintain the rent.

"How are things at the hotel?"

"Perfect," responded Jacob. "Two weeks from today." He reached into his inside pocket, produced a packet of Marlboro Red, and fished out a cigarette. From his trouser pocket he took out his silver Zippo lighter. He lit up and blew smoke into the air.

"Do you know why I like it here, Jacob?"

Jacob gave a sardonic grin. "The company?"

"The sound of the river. It's like a million soft whispers. They're telling me all their secrets, and I imagine only I can hear them. Which gives it intimacy. And with intimacy comes a sense of... peace. Don't you think, Jacob?"

"I haven't given it much thought, Mr Purkis."

"The Glass Box has its intimacy too."

"Of sorts, I suppose."

"We're set up?"

Jacob nodded. "Two from America. One from Iceland. Transport's been arranged. They'll be in the UK by the end of the month."

"Treat them well. They have much to endure."

"Of course."

"And our friends?"

"Keen as ever. Didn't hesitate. Twenty-five invitations. Twenty-five acceptances."

"The appetite for blood never seems to diminish."

"So it would seem."

"Thank you, Jacob."

Jacob stubbed out the cigarette in the ashtray, barely smoked. He put the lighter back in his pocket, gave another brief nod and left, shoes clicking on the cobbles.

Purkis sat back and closed his eyes, and listened to the whispers of the river.

## 25

---

P aul religiously visited Smith early every morning. He was taught further basic combat moves. Plus strength exercises. It was exhausting, but exhilarating. It seemed to him John Smith was taking a genuine interest, which bolstered his confidence and increased his enthusiasm. Now that his mother was aware and had approved, Paul trained with zeal. To augment his training, and in an effort to impress, he went to bed early and got up at dawn, and ran three miles before starting the journey to Smith's cabin in the woods.

For the first time in as long as he could remember, he felt good. About himself. About life. Summer holidays were ending soon, but he no longer felt the dismal dread in the pit of his stomach. The harsh training imposed by Smith had somehow rendered his old anxieties inconsequential.

At 1.30am, one week after Smith had visited for lunch, he was awakened by a noise downstairs. Sleep drifted away, his head cleared. He raised himself up. Silence. Had he imagined it? He waited. One second... two... There! The noise made him start. Someone was pounding the front door. This time it didn't stop. He slid out of bed. He went into the hallway. His mother was there in her dressing gown. He switched the hall light on. She looked pale and fragile. And scared. The pounding continued, the door rattling at the impact.

"He's not going to go," she said.

"We should call the police."

She shook her head. "That would only make it worse."

She straightened. She made her way downstairs. He followed. She turned, said, "Go back to your room. Please."

"No."

She said nothing, continued down. She got to the front door, Paul behind her. She slid the latch open. The pounding stopped. Silence, which, somehow, felt more frightening. Paul waited, heart beating fast, chest constricted. It seemed the moment between his mother turning the handle and opening the door was caught, frozen in time.

Then the moment was over. She opened the door.

Vincent Docherty stood there. He reeked of alcohol. He swayed on his feet. He was clutching keys attached to a key ring that was instantly recognisable. A silver 'V'.

"You changed the locks."

"What did you expect?"

"Where is he?" he said, his words slurred. "Where the fuck is he?"

He pushed her back, entered the house. Alison spoke, her voice calm.

"What do you want, Vincent?"

"I want you to tell me you're a fucking whore."

Paul stood with his mother in the hall, facing Docherty. He was six foot two, a slab of a man, and even drunk could inflict a lot of damage. He saw the tremble in his mother's shoulders. Same as the tremble in his hands.

"Is he here?"

"Is who here?"

"Don't fuck with me. The guy. Your new lover."

"You need to go home, Vincent, and sleep this off."

Docherty's lips curled back, his face contorted as he gave a snarling response. "Is he fucking here?"

Alison replied in a quiet, steady voice. "There's no one here except us."

"Liar!" he hissed.

He lurched forward, swung an arm. The movement was uncoordinated. He staggered, lost balance, fell against a side table, rolled to the floor. A lamp and a marble vase clattered round him.

With difficulty he manoeuvered himself onto his hands and knees, staring at the ground.

"I'm going to fucking kill you," he muttered. He raised himself up further so that he was balanced on one knee, as if he were ready to be knighted. Paul stared, transfixed. His mother darted to the kitchen, came back, a broad carving knife grasped in her hand, stainless steel with a keen blade.

Paul watched. She approached Docherty, her face set. She crouched down, level with him, pressed the tip of the knife against his throat below his Adam's apple, brought her face close to his.

"If you don't get out, you piece of fucking shit, I swear I'll rip your fucking neck open."

He stared at her, eyes wide and blank, face expressionless. To reinforce her point, she drew blood. Something registered. He blinked, licked his lips. Slowly, he found his feet, Paul's mother remained close to him, connected by a knife to the throat.

"Move," she said.

He swallowed, the act causing the knife to bob. But she held it close. He backed off, one unsteady foot after the other, Alison stepping with him in a weird, deadly dance.

"The door, Paul."

Paul stirred, got to the door, opened it wide.

Alison kept going until Docherty was outside.

"You come back here," she said, "and I'll kill you." She kept the knife raised, stepped back into the house, slammed the door shut, slid home the latch.

She turned, faced Paul, her face gaunt and ghastly pale. She dropped the knife. Her body shook. Paul went to her, held her tight.

A voice boomed from outside. "He's a dead man. You hear me! He's a fucking dead man."

They heard erratic shuffling footsteps recede down to the front gate, to disappear into the night.

"He's gone," whispered Paul. She held on to him.

"He's never gone."

———

Alison knew she wouldn't sleep. The confrontation had shaken her. Knocked her off balance. Plus, she was terrified he might come back. She hadn't seen him for weeks and had dared to hope. But hope wasn't realistic with a man like Docherty. Hope was a fool's dream. And she was the perfect fool.

Paul had gone back to bed, reluctantly. He, too, would find sleep impossible, and she couldn't blame him. He'd seen his mother threaten to slit someone's throat. Not an everyday occurrence. But then, violence stuck to Vincent Docherty like a disease. Come too close, and you got infected.

She went to the kitchen, poured herself a small neat whisky, downed it in one, poured another, and left it. Better to keep a clear head. She sat and stared at the wall, tried to stop the tremble in her body, tried to straighten her thoughts. She knew Docherty. He was the type of man who would keep coming back. The type of man who lashed out, regardless of consequences. Always, her thoughts veered back to Paul. Docherty would have no compunction in hurting him because hurt was in his nature. Whether drunk or sober. Tonight, she reckoned she'd been lucky. He was too pissed to do any damage. Maybe not the next night though. Or the night after. Or an afternoon. Or a morning. Or any damned time Docherty chose. Because this was Docherty's world, and she and Paul were hostages to his anger.

Nerves sharpened to a needlepoint, she expected the door to rattle and burst off its hinges. But the only sound was silence, save her breathing, the thump of her heart, the turmoil in her head.

*He's a fucking dead man.* His final words, dripping with intent. Referring to the man called John Smith. Another innocent who had the misfortune to stumble into Docherty's world. An innocent who had spoken up to protect her son. And she knew, the way Docherty was, with bitterness and anger bubbling in his heart like pus, he meant every word.

She maybe drifted into a sleep of sorts, sitting at the kitchen table, her mind a jumble of shapes and shadows. A noise started her. Paul was in the kitchen. She gave a weak smile. He was dressed like he was always dressed at this time, ready to go out and into the forest to see Smith. He looked pale, eyes heavy.

"Maybe you shouldn't go today," she ventured.

"I must. He's expecting me."

"Have some breakfast first."

He nodded. He looked half asleep. He went to a cupboard.

"Let me," she said. He sat at the table. She fixed him a bowl of cereal.

She sat opposite.

"You sure you should go?"

He nodded. He gave a wan smile. "I'm sorry."

"For what?"

He stared into the bowl of Rice Krispies. They snapped and crackled, exactly as advertised.

"For what?" she repeated gently.

"For not helping you."

"But you did help."

He looked up, frowned.

"By just being there," she said.

He gave a small, derisive laugh. "That's no help." He gave her a plaintive look, eyes shimmering. It broke her heart. "What if he comes back? What if I can't help you? What am I supposed to do?"

"First, you don't waste your thoughts on him. You've got school soon. You've got more important things to worry about. Please."

He shook his head, just a fraction. "Not easy under the circumstances."

"Not easy. But we can't let him hold us back. People like Vincent..." she rummaged her mind for the right words, "... they tire easily. They give up, and move on." *Bullshit*, she thought.

"Sure, Mum. They give up." *And he knew it was bullshit.*

"Why don't you give John a miss this morning. You owe yourself a rest."

He became indignant. "He expects me there every morning. I don't want to disappoint him. It's like a code."

"A code?"

"Yeah. Like a code of honour."

She smiled. He smiled back. "Cheesy, I know. But it's true."

"A warrior's code," she said solemnly. "Sounds serious."

He said nothing, concentrated on eating. She knew it really was serious for Paul. She didn't push it.

He finished, got up, and made to leave.

"Don't worry," was all she could think of saying.

"Sure."

She stood at the front door and watched him trudge down

the front garden path, then turn left, heading towards the forest, satchel strapped to his back with some fruit and a bottle of water.

Docherty's words played and replayed in her mind, like a never-ending echo.

*He's a fucking dead man.*

One of the few advantages in having lived in a small town like Aviemore all your life was that everybody knew everybody. A relative, a friend, a friend of a friend, an acquaintance. Or perhaps it was a disadvantage, depending on your outlook. But at that moment, Alison needed it to work.

She made a call. It was early, but she didn't give a shit. She might be worried about nothing, but instinct told her trouble was in the wind. And Vincent Docherty and trouble were joined at the hip.

## 26

Smith wasn't annoyed. He was surprised. He had been training the kid relentlessly for something approaching seven weeks. The kid had appeared at 7am every morning. As regular as sunrise. It was now approaching 8am. It suddenly occurred to him that maybe school had started. Smith gave a wry chuckle. He forgot there was a world outside his own, where people did normal things. Like going to school.

He sat on his porch with some hot tea. He would wait. And if the kid was a no-show, then fair enough. Smith didn't possess a mobile phone, but it wouldn't have mattered. If the kid had other places to be, then it was the kid's business, and Smith had no complaint. And if the kid decided he'd had enough, that was okay too. Smith would click back to his old solitary regime, and play out his old solitary life.

Still... Smith sipped his tea. It was a typical Cairngorm morning for this time of the year. Grey clouds, a sense of rain, sunlight pale and brittle. Despite himself, he felt a niggle of worry. Was the kid all right? Perhaps he'd fallen. Perhaps he was ill. Perhaps a million things. Smith grudgingly admitted to himself he was concerned.

At 8am the kid appeared. He looked drained, hollow-eyed, his face gaunt. He made his way towards Smith, dragging his feet, shoulders slumped.

"You made it," said Smith. "I wasn't sure."

"Bad night."

"You ready to run?" The rucksack Smith used was lying on the porch decking, loaded with a couple of chunky stones. Smith picked it up, tossed it over to Paul. It landed on the grass at the kid's feet. Paul stared at it dolefully.

"I don't know if I can do this. I don't feel in the mood."

"Mood?" Smith expressed bewilderment. "Mood? You think mood's got anything to do with it? In any battle situation do you think the enemy will cut you some slack if you tell him you're not in the mood? Moods are a luxury, ill-suited for someone learning to fight. Which is what you want, yes?"

"Yes," mumbled the kid. "Of course. But there was trouble last night. I haven't slept."

"Trouble?"

"Can I sit down?"

Smith said nothing. The kid made his way to the porch, sat on the steps.

"He came back," he said.

"Vincent?"

The kid nodded. His eyes glistened. He took a small shuddering breath. "He was drunk. He threatened mum." He fell silent.

Smith said nothing.

"He came in. Mum got a knife from the kitchen."

Smith's heart leapt to his mouth. *A knife!* He waited.

"She held it to his throat. She told him she would kill him if he didn't leave. She was amazing."

"And he left?"

Again, the kid nodded. "She was a lioness." He looked at Smith, angry, defiant.

"You know what I did? When she was forcing him out at knifepoint, you know what I did, John?"

Smith held the kid's stare, waited.

"Fuck all! Fucking nothing! What I'm good at. It doesn't matter how much you train me, or how fit I get, or how strong. I can't do this. Vincent came to our house last night, and I froze. I did nothing. You know why?"

Still, Smith said nothing.

The kid spoke in a whisper. "Because I'm a coward."

Smith responded in a measured voice. "You're a fourteen-year-old kid. You were faced with an impossible situation. Your mother did well to react the way she did. Most couldn't do that. Don't look at this the wrong way, Paul. This isn't your fault. No one's judging, because there's nothing to judge. This is all down to one guy. Vincent Docherty. Don't allow his actions to bring you down. He's not worth it."

"He might come back."

Smith found he had no answer to give.

"There's something else," said the kid.

*Of course there is.*

"What?"

The kid hesitated, then spoke, a quiver in his voice. "He said you were a dead man. He thinks you and mum are… together." Now a tear trickled down his cheek. "This is all my fault. I'm going to get you into big trouble. Vincent's an animal. He said you're a *dead man!* And it sounded like he meant it."

Smith gave a wintry grin. "I've heard worse."

"He doesn't stop. He's dangerous. He's out of control."

Again, Smith had no answer to give. He suspected the kid wasn't wrong. That a man like Vincent Docherty was someone who bore a grudge and was good at showing it. For the millionth time, he cursed himself for getting involved. But in his heart, he was glad he had.

"You don't need to worry about me," he said. "No one's likely to come all the way up here…"

He stopped in mid-sentence.

Three men emerged from the woods.

## 27

For all his bulk, Cornwall Pritchard was supple and surprisingly fast. Almost twenty stone of hard muscle. He'd boxed. He'd wrestled. He trained with heavy weights. Had done since the age of eleven. He could run a half marathon with ease. He was proficient with knife and sword. He was thirty years old, and in his mind was at his peak. Shedding blood did not faze him. Quite the opposite. He enjoyed it. He had a psychotic personality, or so the doctors claimed. Narcissistic, lacking empathy, incapable of remorse. Which were advantages, given the demands of his new employer, Chadwick Purkis. But these were hardly demands. He got supremely well paid for doing something he loved. It seemed to Pritchard, at this stage of his life, he'd arrived. Was living the dream.

Behind his house was a double garage, which he'd converted into a gym equipped with machines, free weights, punch bags, a treadmill. He spent a lot of his waking day there. He started early. Trained until mid-morning, ate, trained until midday, ate, trained until mid-afternoon. Ate. Then a rest until evening, and then another two hours. He ate like an animal, he trained like an animal. All the time, waiting for the email to ping on his computer. With the ping came a subsequent payload of one hundred and fifty thousand. Payable in cash, delivered in a sports bag by the man he knew as Jacob. Payable only if successful, for obvious reasons. If he wasn't successful, he'd be dead. And no one pays a dead man.

But the thought of death never occurred to Pritchard. He'd visited the Glass Box on eight occasions, and nothing could stop him. He had been christened a name. *Titan*. Titans were indestructible.

He was performing his third set of bench presses. The door opened. He caught the silhouette of a figure from the corner of his eye. With a grunt he heaved the bar back onto its stand. He sat up. When he trained he wore only shorts and training shoes. His torso was slick with sweat and white as marble. He swivelled round.

"You've got a letter."

His mother called his emails 'letters', which he thought was cute. She was of a vintage who thought computers and anything connected with them were strange and alien. Things unfathomable.

"I heard it beep," she said.

"Okay, Mum."

He got up, grabbed a towel, wiped his face and chest, padded over. At six foot six, he towered over his mother, rendering her a miniature doll, tiny and fragile.

They made their way into the house, into the dining room, where the computer and printer sat on an old-style writing bureau. He sat facing it.

His mother stood behind him, rubbing the back of his neck, his broad shoulders.

"What's it say?"

He guided the mouse with thick fingers and with a click, opened the email.

August 30th. Pick-up at 10am. Is Titan
ready?

"Tell him you're ready, son." Her voice barely contained
her excitement.

"Yes, Mother."

Titan's ready.

"Tell him you want more money."

Pritchard turned, confused.

"What?"

"Tell him."

"What if he says no? I don't want to upset them. They're
dangerous."

"You're dangerous, and don't forget it. A lot more
dangerous than those lily-livered fuckers. You're pure gold to
these people. They run a business, so we have to run a business
too. Ask for another fifty."

"You sure?"

"You trust me, don't you? Do it."

He typed in the response, slowly, one click at a time, the
keyboard absurdly small in his massive hands.

His finger hovered over the 'send' button.

"You sure?"

"Do it."

He pressed.

Two hundred.

He waited. He felt the sharp dig of her nails, which he
liked, causing a ripple of excitement. But suddenly he was
anxious. The money was an irrelevance. It was the act of

killing that was all-consuming. If his mother's greed jeopardised this, he would find it difficult to forgive her.

A minute passed. Another. Her hands felt like claws.

"He's not impressed. He's going to say no."

"Have faith."

It came. The *beep*. He opened it.

```
Agreed. Details are being sent.
```

He took a long, slow breath, felt the tension seep from his skin.

"What did I say? They know what you're worth." She kissed the top of his head, turned his head round, kissed him on the lips.

"You know Mum loves you."

"I know."

"I'll fix you something to eat."

She floated away, humming a tune he didn't recognise. She was happy, which made him happy.

Another email came through, with an attachment. He opened it, printed it out. Photographs of the other contestants. Plus details: weight, height, history. He thought about the trophy, to add to his collection. Maybe a head. He laughed out loud. What would mother say, a fucking head in the cupboard?

Mother would hug him.

———

When Jacob got the email, he immediately contacted Purkis, explaining the situation.

"He's getting greedy," said Purkis.

"It's not him. It's his mother. She controls him. They have a *special* relationship."

Jacob guessed the answer before he heard it.

Purkis didn't miss a beat. "Pay him. They love him. The things he does. Such things are difficult to replicate."

Purkis disconnected. Jacob had to agree with the sentiments of his boss. Cornwall Pritchard – aka Titan – created a spectacle with his love of gore. *The things he does.* Those things were beyond imagination. Pritchard was adept at inflicting suffering. Gifted, almost. And the audience – those billionaire select few – paid the big bucks for it.

He gave it a couple of minutes before he answered. *Let the old witch squirm.* Then he relayed the message.

Agreed. Details are being sent.

## 28

Smith stood, faced the three approaching. The kid frowned, turned, and stood as well.

"I know them," he said.

"I'm sure everyone does," said Smith.

They were the same three men Smith had encountered weeks back, after the incident in the kid's front garden. Blackbeard, Sandy Hair, and the big guy – Beast.

They stopped a short distance from Smith's front porch, spread out, so they stood in a line about four feet apart. They were dressed lightly – track bottoms, trainers, each sporting branded tops. The big guy – Beast – had a small rucksack on his back. Sticking out were three objects easily identifiable. Baseball bats.

Blackbeard smiled a beaming smile, raised a hand affably, arm sculpted with muscle.

"Hello again!"

Beast shrugged off the rucksack, crouched, pulled free the Velcro straps, pulled out the baseball bats, tossing one to each of his friends.

It looked like Blackbeard was to be the spokesperson. He

took four casual steps forward, the bat behind his neck, hands drooped over each end.

"Is that you, Paul?" His smile never wavered.

"They're Vincent's pals," whispered the kid.

Smith said nothing.

"What you doing up here? I hope this nutjob isn't causing you a problem."

"He's my friend," responded the kid.

Blackbeard flicked a glance either side to his two chums.

"Hear that? Friend?" He directed his attention exclusively at Smith. "What you doing with a fourteen-year-old kid, nutjob? Doesn't seem right to me." Again, a quick look on either side. "Does it seem right to you, boys?"

"Fucking weird," said Sandy Hair. Beast remained still, implacable as a pillar of stone.

"Do you remember our conversation?" continued Blackbeard. "The one where we told you to leave. To *fuck off*. You remember that?"

Smith said nothing.

Blackbeard took another eight steps forward. Smith counted them. The others followed. Now, the three stood about ten feet from the porch, square on.

The kid looked from Smith to the three men, confused. "He's done nothing wrong. What is this?"

"Shut the fuck up." It was Sandy Hair who spoke, his voice a rattling wheeze. The walk had tired him. He was undoubtedly unfit, and hence the weak link. A man who needed the numbers.

"Do as he says," said Blackbeard. "Stay out of this."

Fuelled possibly by the anger from the evening before, his judgement possibly clouded by lack of sleep, the kid strode off the porch, straight up to Blackbeard. Blackbeard wasn't tall, but he was a clear six inches over the kid. His arm was as wide as the kid's waist.

Smith watched. The situation was growing worse by the second.

Blackbeard looked down at the kid, his lips twisted in condescension.

"You have to listen – when my friend says 'shut the fuck up', you've got to *shut the fuck up!*" One arm darted out, hooked round the kid's neck, drawing him close. The kid gasped. Smith stood, breath held, faculties heightened, the world and everything in it diluted to this moment in time. The kid squirmed. But it was useless. Blackbeard had him in an elbow lock. An inch, and he would snap the kid's neck between bicep and forearm. As if sensing the imminent danger he was in, the kid relaxed, went limp. He stared at Smith, eyes wide and fearful. Suddenly, Smith's options were vastly reduced.

Sandy Hair and Beast nonchalantly approached the porch, holding their baseball bats. Each right-handed, noted Smith. Sandy Hair was slapping the end gently onto his left palm, an age-old mannerism indicating intended violence. Beast just let his hang. The guy was big. The bat looked as irrelevant as a twig in his hand. When he stood on the porch, the timbers creaked.

"What you got in there?" said Sandy Hair.

Smith said nothing.

Blackbeard, the kid still locked in his arm, shouted, "Go in and see what's what. Bet nutjob's got all sorts of shit squirrelled away."

"What you got in there?" said Sandy Hair, round face broken by a gap-toothed grin. "Bet you got kiddy porn. You got kiddy porn?"

Smith met his stare, face expressionless. He said nothing.

"Can't you fucking speak?" said Sandy Hair. All the while Beast stood motionless, gazing at Smith with brooding intensity, eyes like black beads.

"Go on in, Jasper," shouted Blackbeard. "Let's see what he keeps in that shithole. You don't mind if my friend takes a look, do you, nutjob?"

Smith had a name. *Jasper.* He said nothing.

Jasper laughed, a harsh sound. "I don't think he minds, Pat."

Another name. Careless. Or perhaps their lack of discretion indicated something more sinister. Perhaps their intention was to go way beyond intimidation. His mind churned in overdrive. With the kid folded in Pat's arms, Smith was hamstrung. Violence was brewing. The last thing he wanted. If they pushed...

Jasper entered the lodge. Beast stepped forward, taking Jasper's place, facing Smith.

He rested the end of the baseball bat gently on Smith's shoulder. "You do not move a fucking muscle, you understand?"

"Leave him!" the kid cried. Blackbeard – the man called Pat – tightened his grip. "Hush now. Enjoy the show."

Sounds came from inside. The sound of Jasper's heavy footsteps. Things smashed. He was using his bat to inflict damage. Suddenly a window broke, shards of glass sprinkling the porch. Jasper reappeared.

"It's a fucking mangy shed. Fucking dogs live better. Nothing but books and shit."

"Books?" said Pat. "Books burn, don't they?"

"They sure do," responded Jasper. "Think your books will burn, nutjob? Shall we see?"

Jasper went to where Beast had left the rucksack. He opened it, took out a plastic canister, trotted back to the porch. He unscrewed the top, sniffed the contents. He looked at Smith, eyes bright with mischief. "You think this'll do the trick?" He stood at the doorway, started to slosh liquid into the interior. The unmistakable smell of petrol wafted through the air. Beast remained standing, the bat still resting on Smith's shoulder. Things were getting way out of hand. Smith glanced at the kid, ten feet away. The kid was trapped. Even if Pat didn't mean to, if matters got physical, in the heat of the moment, he might snap the boy's neck as easily as a dry stick.

"You don't need to burn it down," Smith said.

"It speaks!" shouted Pat. "And here's me thinking you were brain-dead. Because you look fucking brain-dead."

Beast loomed closer. "I didn't give you permission to open your mouth."

"Let him talk," said Pat. "It should be fun."

Jasper, meanwhile, brought out a box of matches from a zip pocket in his trousers, opened it, took out a match.

"You want me gone," said Smith, his voice flat, deadpan. "Fine. I'll go. Let the kid loose. I'll pack my things, and I'll be gone in an hour." He turned to look directly at Pat. "You'll never see me again."

Pat's face creased theatrically, as if deep in thought. "You promise? I mean, pinky promise?"

"Let the kid go. Then it's over. I disappear."

"But that's a little too easy," Pat said. "We've walked all this way. We're owed a little entertainment. A bit of R 'n' R. Aren't we, boys?"

"Sure are," Jasper said.

Beast remained motionless. He could have been carved from wood. Then he spoke

"Say it like you mean it. On your knees, nutjob. I want you to beg. I want you to beg us to let you run away, like the fucking coward you are. On your knees."

Jasper hovered in the background, swaying from one foot to the other, gleeful, enjoying the moment, match ready to strike.

Smith nodded slowly. It had come to this. Decision time. He felt the familiar tremble in his hand, perhaps a nervous reflex. Something he experienced seconds before intense violence.

Jasper turned to Pat. "Do I light her up?"

"Hold on, Jasper. We want to see him beg, like a mangy cowardly scumbag."

Beast raised his bat a fraction, rubbing against the side of Smith's neck.

"On your knees. I wanna hear you beg."

The man called Jasper stepped closer, eyes shining like black gloss.

"Give it to him, Eddie."

Another name. Now he had the set – Jasper, Pat and Eddie. Men who didn't care. Men used to casual violence.

Smith stared at the big man, the man called Eddie. Smith was six foot two. This guy was four inches taller and possibly forty-five pounds heavier, arms thick with corded muscle, broad shoulders and back. Head like a bullet, neck wider. He wasn't like his friend, Pat, who was bulked up with steroids. This guy had a natural raw strength.

Smith had faced far worse.

He'd made his decision. Kneeling wasn't part of it.

He spoke, his voice barely above a whisper.

"Best that you go on your way. I am a dangerous man."

Eddie's eyes glittered. He leaned forward.

"What did you just say?"

Smith held his stare, face impassive, said nothing.

Pat's laughter rang out, a tinny sound. "What are you two lovebirds chatting about? Tell him to get on his knees. We want to see him beg!"

Eddie's eyes narrowed to dark pinpoints. A flush was rising up his face. A vein in his neck bulged. He was angry. Which was advantageous. An angry man was a careless man.

"You heard my friend," he growled. "You've got to grovel.

And you've got to mean it. Or else things are gonna get bad. Really bad."

"Do I fucking burn this shithole down!" shrieked Jasper. "I want to see the flames!"

A silence fell. It seemed to Smith even the forest was quiet, as it, too, waited to see what he would do. As if the world was on pause and everything in it was holding its breath. It was at such moments Smith felt an inner calm, his senses notched to a higher level of competence, his mind lucid and sharp. The moments before the killing zone.

But then the kid…

He returned Eddie's stare, who, unlike Jasper, wasn't smiling. He was as grim as stone, features set, slit-eyed. This wasn't a show for him. He wanted blood.

"We have a situation," said Smith.

Eddie's forehead twisted into a frown. Jasper now turned. Pat, a little back, shuffled forward, the kid still clamped in his arms. "What's he saying?"

Smith remained focused on Eddie. He could feel the grain of the baseball bat against his neck.

"The problem you have is location."

"What?"

"We're in the middle of a forest, in the middle of nowhere. How long do you think it's going to take?"

"How long's what going to take?" broke in Jasper, stepping closer, still smiling but the smile just not as certain. Eddie remained still. Smith felt the bat twitch as the big man clenched his fingers tight round the grip.

On the periphery of his vision stood Pat with the kid, at the foot of the porch. All were looking at him.

"Answer the man," barked Pat.

Smith spoke, his voice quiet, and as such, all the more menacing. "How long do you think it's going to take to find your bodies?"

They stood, motionless, like figures in a picture.

Still staring square with Eddie, Smith continued, keeping his tone level, almost conversational. "Because I'm going to bury you deep, make no mistake." He flicked a glance at Jasper. "You, fatso. Yours will be the deepest because I have to take account of your fat arse." He squared back up to Eddie. "I'll make yours deep too, because we don't want your fucked-up face frightening the woodland animals."

Now, he turned to Pat, gave him a burning gaze. "But you, brother. I'm going to have fun and games with you." He lowered his voice. "I'll need to dig several graves for all your body parts."

Pat stared back. For the first time, no response. The kid suddenly wriggled free, dodged to one side. Pat didn't react, his attention focused entirely on Smith. Smith gave a steely smile, focused back on Eddie.

"You want to dance, fuck-face? That's fine. Because I'm in a dancing mood."

Eddie's jaw muscles bulged. The tension was wire tight. Electric. If Eddie swung the bat, it would be the last thing he would ever do. And Smith had the feeling the big man knew it. Eddie licked his lips, his stony face suddenly expressive with a range of emotions. *Hesitation. Doubt.* And something else. Something Smith had seen a thousand times. *Fear.*

"Bring it on," whispered Smith.

The big man didn't move.

"I said bring it fucking on."

Then, a sound broke the moment. From the trees. The sound was a voice.

And then everything changed.

## 29

"What's happening here!"

Two men appeared from the trees, the same way Pat and his friends had come. Both uniformed in matching brown hard-wearing trekking trousers, brown pullovers, light rain jackets bearing an emblem on the right shoulder. Park wardens. The tension, so alive and sharp a second before, drained to nothing. Smith relaxed. Eddie quickly shifted the baseball bat from Smith's shoulder, and tucked it down by his side. Jasper put the matches back in his pocket. Pat turned, and said, "Everything's fine. Just having a friendly chat."

"That's right," said Smith, brushing past Eddie, making his way over to the kid. "Just a friendly chat. I was warning them about how dangerous the mountains can be."

Pat shot him a venomous look, but said nothing.

"The gentlemen were just leaving," continued Smith. "Heading back to Aviemore?"

Pat gave a forced smile, spoke with a metallic undertone. "I'm sure we'll bump into each other again."

"I'm counting on it," replied Smith. "Your conversation was stimulating. Next time, we'll pick up from where we left."

Pat made a curt gesture. "You can be sure."

The park warden who had spoken – short and stocky, weathered face, a white, tightly-curled beard – nodded knowingly. He addressed Pat.

"You know your way back? Just follow the path." He jerked a thumb in the direction he and his colleague had come.

Pat gave a polite assent, waved for Jasper and Eddie to follow. He gave a final bow of his head to Smith, and the three made their way back through the forest.

"We'll follow you, to make sure you don't get lost!" shouted the warden after them. He appraised Smith and the kid, while his partner – skin like tanned leather, coarse dark hair – kept his eye on the retreating figures.

"I got a call from Alison. She asked me to come and check up on you. Seems it was lucky that I did."

"Lucky for who?" said Paul.

The warden frowned. Smith spoke quickly. "No problems here. Everything's fine."

"Those three are troublemakers. Best you be careful." He squinted at Smith. "You're the guy who moved into the old cabin?"

"Yes."

He gave a friendly grin. "Must get damned cold in the winter."

"Bloody freezing."

"I'll bet." He smiled at Paul. "Tell your mum, hi."

Paul nodded.

The two wardens headed in the same direction as Pat and his friends, disappearing into the embrace of the trees.

Before Smith could speak, Paul blurted, "You don't need to say it."

Smith waited.

The kid kept his attention fixed on the forest where the men had gone, eyes averted from Smith. He tried to speak, stopped, lip quivering, shoulders trembling. Smith said nothing.

He turned, on the brink of tears. "I can't come back, can I?"

"It's over," Smith answered gently. He gave a small, sad smile. "It's too dangerous. For you and your mother. I'm..." *A fucking leper.* "...a liability. I'm no good for you. They'll come back. Who knows what damage they'll do. Best I leave. Best you never come here until I'm gone. You know that's the only way."

The kid nodded, eyes fixed forward again. Seconds passed, then he spoke, a tremor in his voice.

"Thank you, John."

Not looking back, he walked quickly to the trees, then turned one last time.

"You were awesome, by the way."

Then he, too, disappeared, swallowed up by the confines of the forest.

Smith remained still, mind churning with a swirl of emotion. The kid had entered his life, and for a brief time, given him the humanity he'd thought he'd lost. And something more – the kid had made him remember. That living was important. And now the kid was gone.

Smith went back to his porch and sat on his wicker chair. The place reeked of petrol, but he hardly cared. Tomorrow, maybe the day after, he would pack up his things into a rucksack and head off. His possessions were minimal. Nothing he needed particularly, save a toothbrush and a bar of soap and a change of warm clothes. He rented the cabin and had paid well in advance. He could leave, quiet as a whisper, and no one would notice the difference. Except the kid. And maybe Alison.

Where then? He would drift from one place to another, like tumbleweed on a sand plain. The future seemed bleak and uncertain. But he had little choice. He adjusted his thoughts – he had *no* choice. Where he went, chaos followed. And death was always close. He thought of Pat and his friends, how close he'd been to inflicting a whirlwind of violence.

And how he would have enjoyed it.

---

That evening Smith built a small fire, and slept outside in a clearing by the lochan near his lodge. The moon was unobscured, surrounded by a million stars.

The dream came back after a long absence, and as such, possessed a sharp, terrifying clarity.

*A village shrouded in silver darkness; shadows spoke to him softly, their voices indistinct; in the centre of the village, a structure; four walls, a flat roof, a door. One room. In the strange silver darkness, it gave a polished gleam, as if possessing its own inner radiance; he stood at the entrance; he watched his hand turn the door handle; the whispering persisted, urging him on. One step, two. He entered into darkness. Then, as if a veil had been drawn back, he confronted a scene unlike any other.*

*The whispers fell silent. In their place the sound of his own voice, screaming. He turned, but the door was gone. He was trapped. He fell to his knees. His screams continued, as the horror around him pressed close.*

## 30

As Smith lay under the stars, plans were being enacted.

Jacob, as ever, was methodical. He met Vincent Docherty and Halliday at 3am in a secluded parking area, a mile and a half outside Aviemore, designed as a starting point for tourists hiking the myriad of paths through the Cairngorms. There was no CCTV and it was unlit. They came in separate cars. They transferred into the car Halliday was driving. A black Volkswagen Polo. Paid for using counterfeit ID, from a dealer in England. After the job was completed, he would take it fifty miles away to another prearranged destination, burn it, then leave in another car.

The three sat in silence, Halliday driving, Jacob in the passenger seat, Docherty in the back. He had his portable radio and was thus able to monitor police activity. The hotel was approximately three miles outside Aviemore and approximately two miles from the car park. At that time, the road they travelled was deserted. After five minutes, they arrived. They made their way in through a gravel driveway, Halliday keeping slow for two hundred yards until reaching the front of the building. It was cocooned from the main road by high trees, set close, rendering it invisible to any passing onlookers.

Chadwick Purkis had never intended to use the hotel since his acquisition. Such a program would have been a needless drain on resources. He immediately arranged to have the doors padlocked, the windows boarded with sheet metal plates. *How quickly decrepitude sets in*, thought Jacob. Neglect takes its toll. Over the last few months gutters had become heavy with vegetation, sagging under the weight. Weeds grew in cracks in the flagstones, hanging baskets were overgrown with withered plants. Graffiti was emblazoned across sections of the front wall. *A great dead beast*, thought Jacob, *a carcass rotting under the Highland skies. Soon to be cremated.*

Halliday killed the lights. The hotel became a hulking shadow. They got out, switched on torches. Halliday had a sports bag. He placed it on the ground and took out heavy-duty bolt cutters, which he used to snap open the chains looped through the handles of the double-arched front doors. Next, he produced a crowbar, wedged the doors open, splintering wood. Jacob pushed. They were stiff, scraping the floor, the sound like a dying man's cough echoing through empty rooms. The smell of damp was strong. Furniture still remained, as did paintings and mirrors on the walls, wreathed in cobwebs. They were in the main foyer, torches kept low. At one end, the reception area. Along a passage to the right, a short distance, the lounge bar, where not so long ago he and Halliday had a memorable dialogue with the then owner – Raymond. He wondered, fleetingly, what Raymond was doing now, whether he had found another job. Probably grateful his kids were still alive. The thought lasted a second. Jacob really didn't give a shit. It was not in his nature to dwell on the past.

They moved past the reception area. Next to it, a wide staircase, leading to the rooms upstairs. Once grand. Now a blot of shadow. They kept moving, Halliday still holding his sports bag. They opened another door, and entered the dining area. A large room, tables, high-backed wooden chairs, a lofty ceiling. On one side, a long unit with glass-topped metal trays. Presumably the buffet. They kept moving, Jacob first, then Halliday, Docherty at the rear. A short passage connected the dining room to the snug bar. Much smaller, more intimate for late-night drinkers. On one wall, a wide, empty hearth surrounded by an oak mantlepiece and above it, staring down at them, the head of a stag mounted on a wooden base, resplendent with long, curling antlers.

"Creepy," said Docherty.

Jacob ignored him. He cast a meaningful look to Halliday. "This is where it starts."

Halliday nodded, put on a pair of heavy gloves. He positioned his torch on top of the mantlepiece, so it acted as a floodlight. He began to remove items from his bag. First, a tin box about the size of a kid's pencil case. Things rattled inside. He opened it and carefully removed ten syringes, complete with needles, which he placed around the room. Then, four litre-sized vodka bottles. He smashed each against the wall, spreading the glass about the carpet with his feet. Suddenly, the smell of damp was gone, replaced by the marginally more palatable smell of cheap booze. Then, another smaller box full to the brim with cigarette butts, which he scattered about like morning bread for the birds. Then, two cans of spray paint. He tossed one to Docherty, who fumbled it, dropping it to the floor. He picked it up, puzzled.

"Show off your artwork," said Jacob. "Do the walls in the dining room. Let your creative juices flow." Halliday was already spraying the walls in looping random letters.

Docherty frowned. "I mean, what's the point? There'll be nothing left in the fire."

Jacob responded in a flat tone. "Maybe. Maybe not. The fire may not catch everything. A syringe, a cigarette butt, a broken bottle. We're presenting a picture. Creating a scene. A dosshouse for junkies, wired out their skulls. Why wouldn't they start a fire? It's exactly the type of thing people expect them to do. Including your brothers in the police. You understand? A tactic of diversion."

Docherty shrugged. "If you say so."

"I do say so."

Docherty went back into the dining room.

Jacob often wondered at his boss's insistence at involving Docherty for certain jobs. He was a drunk, a bully, and lazy. But he also saw the logic. Draw him in deeper. And the deeper he got, the more compliant he would become. Nothing like having a bent copper on the payroll. Somebody who could work the inside. A useful asset. Until the usefulness stopped.

Two minutes passed. Halliday was finished. Docherty came back in. The empty cans were discarded on the carpet.

"Time," said Jacob.

Halliday went over to the far wall, to heavy velvet drapes covering a window. From a pocket he produced a box of matches.

"Here we go," said Docherty in a hushed whisper.

The edge of the drapes caught quickly. Halliday stepped back. They watched the flames grow, creeping up towards the ceiling. Jacob allowed himself a smile. Chadwick Purkis hadn't spent any money on the hotel, except for padlocks and metal sheets. Plus, replacing all the fire-retardant curtains for an old flammable variety. *Now that was thinking ahead.*

Without speaking he made his way out, the others following. They got to the front entrance. He glanced back. Already, smoke was billowing from the dining area into the main foyer. He felt the prickle of heat on his skin.

"Piss easy," said Docherty.

"Don't get complacent," retorted Jacob. "Things can change in a second."

"I think sometimes you worry too much, Jacob."

"I get paid to worry. It keeps us alive. And remember something, Vincent."

"What?"

"I really don't give a shit what you think."

They got into the car, again Halliday taking up the driver's seat, Jacob in the front.

"All quiet?" he asked.

"Nothing happening," replied Docherty, referring to the staticky voices on his police radio. "All is quiet in Aviemore."

"This is good," said Jacob. "Now if you don't mind, Mr Halliday, let's get the hell out of here."

# 31

---

Paul struggled to get to sleep. When bad things happened, they happened swiftly. Weeks had passed while he'd trained with John Smith, and it seemed to him they were the best weeks of his life. But in the space of a few hours, life had unravelled. First, the confrontation with Docherty. Then, the confrontation at Smith's lodge. Now, everything had changed. Everything was upside down, inside out. A deep swell of sadness filled his chest, crushing. He could never visit Smith again. He would never see him again. The one person, other than his mother, who took an interest. A real interest. Smith would disappear, doubtless to another remote place, gone forever, as if he'd never been.

And what made it such a bitter, shitty pill to swallow was that Paul knew Smith had no choice. The situation was brutal in its simplicity. If Smith remained, he and his mother were in danger. Smith had to go. It was a hard fact. And life had a way of rolling out hard facts.

Paul got out of bed, drew aside the bedroom curtain, gazed at the darkness outside. The sky was cloudless, the moon bright. The woods at the back of his garden were silent and still. No breeze stirred the leaves. The world was quiet. He checked the bedside clock. 4am.

The best cure for depression was exercise. Smith had told him that. *Keep moving.* When you think the world has turned to shit, and you feel the black clouds descending, *keep moving.* Activity lightens the load. If the body gets distracted, the mind gets distracted. That's how Smith put it.

*Keep moving.*

Paul switched on his table lamp, pulled on a pair of dark track bottoms, a sweat top, his trainers. He went through to the bathroom, quiet as a cat, splashed cold water on his face. He went downstairs, careful to avoid the creaks on the steps, got to the hallway. He glanced in the mirror, saw a face pale and pinched, tousled dark hair. Carefully, he unlocked the front door, slipped out into the night, a shadow amongst shadows. It was colder than he had expected. Possibly his body's reaction to the lack of sleep. The front garden was illuminated by a street lamp, casting a trembling orange glow. He loosened up, jumping on the spot, shaking his arms, rotating his neck. Stretching was overrated, according to Smith. Rather, get the circulation going, the blood moving. That way, far less chance of a snapped tendon, a pulled hamstring, or a dozen other afflictions.

*Keep moving.*

He knew his route. Altogether, five miles. Two along the main road, heading away from Aviemore, towards the mountains, then a further half mile, then back again along a tarmacadamed cycle track through the forest running parallel to the road, heading back to the house. The first two miles of the road and track were fairly well lit. After that, for the next half mile, darkness and shadow. But at this time, there was no traffic. And he kept to the road, which was smooth and flat.

The chances of a stumble or a twisted ankle were slim. He could do it in under thirty-five minutes. Two months ago, he'd be lucky to do it in an hour. Thanks to John Smith.

He looked up at the sky. A full moon, clear and stark, casting a pale witchy illumination. He set off.

# 32

Chadwick Purkis slept little. He wasn't an insomniac. He was simply capable of functioning on less than five hours sleep. It was after 4am. He was in the conservatory – the room where he had pierced Tony French through the heart, all vestige of his existence gone forever. Purkis was sitting at his desk, the only light from an antique tortoiseshell table lamp. He was reading. A rare occurrence for him. The book was a first edition of Walter Scott's *Ivanhoe*. Published in 1820. Only ten thousand copies were released on the first run. This one was in pristine condition. He'd bought it at auction and paid over £20,000. A trifle, he thought, for such a rare thing.

The only other item on the desk was his mobile phone, which suddenly buzzed into life. He checked the caller. Jacob. Only he had this number. The call he was expecting.

He picked up, answered, waited.

"It's done," said Jacob. "We're leaving now."

Purkis disconnected, sat back, stared into the darkness of the room. With the hotel reduced to a crisp, the wheels of business could turn again. He would get his planning, clear the land, build houses for people with money. And he in turn would make a small fortune. And life would go on. Or not, for some. The demise of Tony French had been unfortunate, but unavoidable. The equation was not complicated – if someone crossed Purkis, the consequences were swift and conclusive.

He got up, faced the display of weapons on the wall behind him. In the single light of the table lamp, the blades gleamed. He touched one, felt the keen edge with his thumb, always experiencing a vague sense of wonder that such simple constructions of metal were designed for an exclusive purpose. To kill. When it came to killing, Purkis was adept. He had perfected it down to an art. The kill had to mean something. The kill had to deter others.

And as ever, when his mind touched on such matters, he thought about the past. Five years ago. Another land, another world. So distant, it could have been a dream. But it was no dream. It was as real as the book in his hands.

A room, fashioned in a unique and terrifying manner. A room he had built in the centre of a village. A room designed to convey a message.

A room unlike any other.

His room.

## 33

The plan was to drive back to the car park, disembark, then each go their separate ways. A journey of just over two miles. Jacob did not predict any issues. The chance of other traffic on the road at that time was slim. Even if they did pass a car, big deal. By the time anyone noticed the fire they'd be long gone, melted away into the predawn darkness, by which time the hotel would be burnt and broken. Halliday, the consummate professional, kept his speed low. Not too low. A steady thirty-five mph. Docherty, sitting in the back, kept his ear to the police radio. All was quiet. Jacob sat back, relaxed. His mind was already running through future events, to plan, to coordinate. One event in particular.

The Glass Box.

In one week, twenty-five members of a rather elite club would congregate in the baronial hall of Chadwick Purkis's castle, each having deposited their three million entrance fee, and after partaking in expensive champagne served in fluted crystal glasses, they would be escorted to the lower section. The basement. Or the dungeon, as it was known. And then to the games, and the Glass Box.

The invitations had already been sent. Not by email. By couriered delivery. An invitation on Medioevale ivory paper, handmade, imported from Italy. Gilt-edged. To all sections of the world. Russia, Australia, USA, Britain, Europe. Written by Purkis himself using a fountain pen, the nib fashioned from rhodium-plated 18-carat gold. Jacob allowed a wry smile. How his employer loved the theatrical. The drama. But the admin side was less glamorous. Jacob arranged flights, accommodation, drinks, food. Plus, he located and brought those suitable enough to perform in the spectacle. But then he possessed a flair for organisation. Planning…

Jacob was startled from his thoughts. An image flashed in the glare of the headlights. A figure. A sudden glimpse of a face, white and stark, frozen in shock. Halliday, usually so calm, swore under his breath. The car swerved, hit something, jolted to a stop in the middle of the road.

Docherty lurched forward, the radio tumbling from his grasp.

"What the fuck!"

Halliday remained still, both hands on the wheel. Jacob took a second to collect his thoughts.

"What just happened?"

Halliday took a deep breath. "Shit just happened."

He pulled onto the side verge, killed the lights, got a torch from the glove compartment. There were no street lights. They were still on the periphery of wilderness. They got out. Darkness pressed in around them. Only yards away, the thick bristle of shadow which was the Cairngorm forest. Halliday flashed the torch to the other side of the road.

There! A figure lying still in the long grass, face down. The three men approached. In the full glare of the torch beam, details were clear. A runner. Jogging trousers, sports top, left arm twisted at an ugly angle. Dark hair, one side matted with blood.

"Why the fuck would someone be running at this time?" muttered Docherty.

Jacob shot him a burning glare. "That's hardly relevant."

"What now?" said Halliday.

Suddenly, the figure groaned. The three men stood, still as stone, watching as the figure stiffly turned to one side. Now, in the light, the face was distinct.

Docherty gasped.

"Jesus Christ."

Jacob snapped him another look. "What?"

Docherty said nothing.

"What?"

Docherty's voice was low, barely audible.

"I know him."

Jacob waited.

"He's Alison's son. Paul. Paul Davidson."

"So what do we do?" said Halliday.

Jacob fixed his attention on the boy. The pain hadn't set in yet, he thought. For now, shock. But pain would follow, rapidly. No wonder. His arm was the wrong way round. Blood was streaming from a head wound. He was a wreck. Jacob watched in fascination as the boy somehow raised himself up on one knee, where he remained, swaying.

"Help me."

"What the fuck do we do?" said Docherty.

The boy peered into the light. He took a struggling breath. *Broken ribs*, thought Jacob. Then the boy spoke, voice tremulous and reedy.

"Vincent?"

Docherty stepped away, back from the fringe of torchlight, merging with the shadows.

"Vincent," said Paul. "I need help."

"What the fuck do we do?" hissed Docherty.

"Shut up," said Jacob. *The best laid fucking plans.*

He turned his back on the boy, experiencing a mixture of anger and frustration, and made the call.

———

Purkis was surprised and disturbed when his mobile buzzed again, so swiftly after the first call. He hesitated for the briefest second, then picked up.

"A snag," said Jacob.

Purkis said nothing.

"We've hit a kid. Looks like he was out jogging. He's in a bad way."

The flutter of anxiety he'd felt dissipated to mild irritation.

"He's alive?"

"Yes," replied Jacob.

"Did anyone see you?"

"No."

"And why are you calling me?"

"Guidance."

"Please. You know exactly what to do."

He disconnected. Failure to exert independent thinking exasperated Purkis. Jacob was an efficient and pragmatic employee. Logical and brutally cold, which were useful tools in the sensitive tasks he asked Jacob to perform. The response to the situation should have been obvious. Purkis was disappointed.

He brushed it from his mind, and made his way to the gym. The thought of a kid out running gave him motivation – he would hit the treadmill, and pump out 5k. And then a sauna.

———

"And?" It was Vincent Docherty who spoke.

"You know the answer. You knew the answer as soon as the boy recognised your voice."

"Jesus Christ. This is fucking serious stuff."

"You're in a serious business," said Jacob tonelessly. "You took the money quick enough, Vincent. Risks of the job."

Paul was still on one knee. His breath came in a rattling wheeze. He fell back onto the grass, semi-conscious. *Maybe a punctured lung.* It hardly mattered.

He nodded at Halliday. "Find something."

Halliday understood. He lumbered off, almost casually, torch flashing in the undergrowth.

"What's happening?" said Docherty.

"We need to maintain consistency. When he's found, it has to look like a hit and run. He's half dead anyway. Another head wound won't make much difference. You understand, Vincent?"

"Yes," said Docherty in a resigned monotone.

*Of course you do. Rather the death of a young boy than the prospect of prison.*

"Here," said Halliday. Jacob went over. Halliday handed him the torch, then crouched and picked up a large moss-coated stone about the size of a football. Both men returned.

Jacob shone the torch on the boy, who stirred, eyes flickering open.

"I'm thirsty."

Jacob smiled down at him. He sensed Docherty watching from the shadows. Halliday loomed in, back arched, the stone in both hands raised above his head.

"Make it quick," said Jacob.

Halliday brought the stone down, crushing the boy's head.

Jacob scrutinised the result. The top of the skull was a tangle of blood and hair. A small rippling spasm. Then the boy fell still, lungs silenced.

"Again," he said.

Halliday repeated the process.

"Three's the charm."

A third time. Up, then down. Three ferocious blows, rendering face and head to pulp.

Jacob gestured to Docherty. "We'll put him in the trees."

Docherty wordlessly grabbed the boy's ankles, while Jacob hooked his hands under the arms and hoisted him up. They carried him to the dense dark of the forest, and tossed him into the shadows.

They got back into the car, Halliday driving off at a sedate thirty-five miles per hour.

"Just a blip," said Jacob.

Halliday, as was his way, said nothing, but kept his eyes on the road ahead, his composure unaffected. Docherty was silent too. Jacob swivelled round. Docherty sat in the centre in the back. In the glow of the dashboard illumination, his face was the colour of wax.

"You look a little pale, Vincent."

"I'm fine," he muttered. "The little brat had it coming. His fucking fault for being out at this time in the morning."

"That's the spirit, Vincent. Blame it on the boy. You cool with this?"

"Yes."

"Because when he's found, the shit will hit the proverbial fan. Maybe you should take some leave. Maybe develop a debilitating illness that'll keep you off work for a couple of weeks. You don't want to get too close to this one, Vincent."

"I can handle it."

"Sure you can. Because you don't have a choice. Mr Purkis likes his men to keep a level head. Like Mr Halliday here, who never gets flustered. The last thing we need is a loose cannon. Remorse can do strange things to a man. The need to confess. We would like to think you wouldn't stray down that path."

"Is this supposed to be a threat?"

Jacob gave a tinny laugh. "Merely a statement of fact."

"You'll get no trouble from me. As I said, the little fucker had it coming."

Jacob settled back in the passenger seat. "Of course he did, Vincent."

# 34

Smith woke to weak sunlight casting a dreary charcoal taint to the forest. Clouds converged, dark and heavy. The air stirred with the slightest breeze. Rain was coming. He checked his watch. 5.45am. The fire he had made was reduced to a pile of ash and cinder. The air felt damp, edged with cold. Summer was dying.

He had slept fitfully. The dream he had experienced – the same one, over and over – was fresh and vivid in his mind. He thought he could still hear its echo on the periphery of his senses. But it was the rustle of leaves and the creaks of the forest he heard.

He got up, shook away the fog in his head. He had work to do. He had to gut out the lodge, cleanse away all vestiges of the petrol poured into his living room from the day before. Then he had to pack and leave. Not that he had much to pack. He had lived a spartan existence, bordering on the extreme. Perhaps some prescient part of his brain knew a day like this might come around; hence no attachment to material goods, except the basics. A bar of soap, toothbrush, a change of clothes, all packed neatly in a bergen rucksack.

The circumstances provided a grim irony. Just as he was beginning to explore a life beyond his self-imposed exile, it was pulled away, like a rug from beneath his feet. Perhaps that was just the way of it, he thought. Perhaps he deserved no more.

Perhaps there was a god. And after what had happened, back in time, back in Afghanistan, perhaps this was God's retribution. For his sin.

Regardless of how he felt, he had no choice. He had brought danger to Paul and Alison, both directly and indirectly. If he remained, the danger would escalate. He would go, and few would notice the difference. And even then, those who knew him – Paul and Alison – would forget in time, until his existence faded to a half-remembered shadow.

He would bathe in the lochan for the last time, clean the place up, pack, have a final frugal meal, a final coffee and leave. North, he decided. Always north. To the mountains. Maybe get on a boat, and go where? He had no earthly idea.

---

9.30am.

Smith was sitting on one of the stairs leading up to the porch. He'd scrubbed the place clean, though the smell of petrol remained. There was little else remaining in the lodge. He had piled his collection of books in a corner. He suspected the landlord would have little interest in them and would doubtless consign them to the bin. Smith would never know, nor did he care.

He was ready to leave. A last half hour to savour the gentle silence of the Cairngorm forest. The prospect of rain was ever present. Clouds had thickened. He sat, a cup of black coffee cradled in his two hands.

A figure emerged from the trees. A figure he knew. Paul's

mother. She'd been walking at speed, her skin flushed, her face set and stern. There were no smiles. Her gaze fixed on Smith. Smith felt a flutter of worry.

She strode towards him, speaking as she moved.

"Hi. Is Paul here?"

Smith stood. "I haven't seen him."

She stopped, nodding to herself, as if she were debating.

"You haven't seen him?"

"What's wrong, Alison?"

"I woke up at six this morning. I couldn't sleep. I went through to check on Paul. He wasn't in his bed. His trainers aren't there. I waited until eight thirty, then I drove about. Then I came here. Now you're telling me you haven't seen him."

"I'm sure he's fine." The words sounded lame, but he had no other response to give.

"Fine?" she replied, her voice shrill. "Maybe. But I can't take that chance. I waited two and a half hours before I left the house, and there was no sign of him. Call me paranoid, but I don't care. Paul's missing, and right now we're not on the top ten favourite list of Vincent Docherty." She lowered her voice. "And Vincent Docherty is a fucking wild animal."

Smith answered in a level tone. "He could be back at the house. Have you tried the mobile?"

"He didn't take it with him."

"Have you tried his friends?"

She looked at him, her expression a mixture of pain and anger.

"You were his friend."

Smith could think of no direct response to her statement. "Let's go back. I'll come with you."

She gave a curt nod of assent, turned, made her way back towards the forest path. Smith went with her. The flutter he had experienced had sharpened. She was right. Docherty was a man spurned and insulted. That, coupled with his penchant for hitting women and kids, made for a toxic combination. He pondered her description – *a fucking wild animal.* He reckoned she'd got it spot on. Which increased his unease.

"Did Paul tell you?" she said.

"Yes."

"I let Vincent in, because I thought I could reason with him." She gave a hollow laugh. "He's not a man you can reason with. I should have known."

"There's nothing to know. Paul will be fine."

"Sure."

She'd driven the back road to Smith's cabin, cutting the walking distance through the forest path to a mile. *Road* was a misnomer. More a single lane track, rarely used, pitted and gouged. Like the surface of the moon. She drove an ancient pale blue Subaru four-wheel drive, all bumps and scrapes. But useful for off-road.

The track wound through the forest, three miles in all, the car bouncing and lurching, then it met a proper narrow-laned road, much smoother, then another three miles. They passed cyclists and a couple of hikers. They waved as she passed. Neither she nor Smith reciprocated. They reached the main carriageway, just on the periphery of Aviemore. She turned and drove the final quarter mile back to the house. She parked hard up onto the pavement. They got out. Smith followed her along the garden path to the front door. A brief image flickered up in his mind. A boy being whipped by a man with the buckle end of a belt. There on the path. How it all started.

She got a key from her pocket, opened the door.

"Paul!"

Silence.

The house felt empty.

"He might be in his room. On his computer." She bounded up the stairs, two at a time. Smith waited in the hall. The unease in his chest was blossoming into something else. Dread.

He heard a door open, then close. Then other doors opening. She came back down.

"He's not here."

"He had his training shoes on?"

She didn't answer. She went through to the kitchen, opened the back door, shouted his name. Nothing.

"He had his training shoes on?" repeated Smith softly.

She sat on a chair at the kitchen table, ran a fretful hand through her hair.

"Vincent has a temper." She looked up at Smith, eyes wide and scared. "He can be a vicious bastard. What if…"

"Check to see if his track bottoms are there. And his running top. If they're not, then we know he went for an early run. And if he did that, I know the route he would have taken."

She blinked, as if only just computing what Smith had said.

"Okay," she murmured. "He wears a Nike top. I'll check."

She went back upstairs. Smith waited. She came back twenty seconds later. "The Nike top's gone. Which means…"

"…he went running," finished Smith. "I know his route. He told me he was doing it early every morning before he came to see me."

Alison regarded him, her look disbelieving. "He told you that? I had no idea."

"It's about five miles there and back. Along the main road towards the mountains, then straight back but using the cycle track. Could be he fell, twisted an ankle."

"Could be," she replied in a hollow voice.

"Alison." She focused on him, her face tight and scared. He kept his voice level. "We'll find him. I promise."

"And what if we don't?"

Smith said nothing.

"Maybe I should phone the police."

"Maybe you should. But they won't do anything. Your son's fourteen years old. He went for an early morning run.

He's not been gone long enough for them to take an interest. Not a real interest. Also, we don't know who'll get called out. Maybe Vincent."

She turned away, gazed at the hall, at the front door. "Vincent," she said quietly. She turned back, anger in her voice. "I could tell them what Vincent's done. How he liked to beat me on the arms and legs. How he was skilful in his aim so the bruises didn't show. How he beat Paul. How he tried to thrash my son in the front garden with his belt. Perhaps they'll listen then!"

She cried hot tears when she spoke. Suddenly she leaned forward. Smith instinctively held her in his arms. Held her tight. She sobbed into his chest. He felt the tremble of her body.

"I'm so scared," she whispered. "I don't know what to do."

He held her, not speaking, until the sobbing subsided, the trembling stopped.

"Telling the police about Vincent isn't the answer. If anything, it might make things worse. More complicated." He drew away gently, faced her.

"Let's find your son."

She nodded, determined.

"Let's." She rubbed away her tears. "This is ridiculous. He's probably in town. In the library. He likes it there. Since he met you he reads about sports. About running. Or maybe he's in the bookshop. I should have checked." She hesitated. "Sorry, John. I'm not thinking straight."

"Take the car, go into Aviemore. Go to where you think he might be. Right now he's probably having hot chocolate, hunched over a book about marathon runners. He told me he likes hot chocolate."

The corners of her mouth lifted into a small, wan smile.

"He loves it. What will you do?"

"I'll follow the route he takes. I might meet him on the road, coming back."

"Take his phone. My number's in it. John?"

"Yes?"

"Thank you."

*Don't thank me yet*, he thought.

## 35

Alison took the car into Aviemore. Smith headed along the main road to the mountains. After a quarter of a mile the pavement stopped. On one side of the road – the opposite side from Smith – the forest loomed, dense and dark, hard up to the edge. On Smith's side was a grass verge, maybe six yards wide, then a low drystone wall, beyond which, thinly scattered trees and foliage. Beyond that, a path formed of compacted granite dust, winding its way up and down, following the contours of the land. Created for off-road cycling. Once smooth, time and use had taken its toll, the path peppered with ruts and grooves. A twisted ankle in the dark wasn't inconceivable. But still... the dread he felt thickened. He swallowed it back.

He walked the cycle path, scanning either side. Some cyclists were passing. Smith stopped them, asked if they'd seen a boy, maybe out running, maybe in distress. They shook their heads in unison. Nothing. Every half minute he called Paul's name, his voice sounding small and inconsequential in the midst of the forest. But he called anyway.

Smith kept walking, keeping a solid pace. He thought back. He'd asked Paul why he went running at such an extreme time.

*Because I want to be as fit as you,* he'd answered. *So I don't embarrass you. And it feels good. I feel...*

*Feel what?* Smith had asked.

The kid had smiled. *Free.*

Smith hadn't responded when the kid had said that, which he regretted deeply. *Too dangerous*, he should have said. *Too dangerous to be running in the dark at that time. Crazy.*

But Smith had said nothing. Perhaps he was overthinking the situation. Perhaps the kid really was sipping hot chocolate somewhere. But the doubt niggled in his mind. He knew trouble. Trained to see the signs, almost akin to a second sight. He was an expert in anticipating the worst and acting accordingly. As such, he had a keen scent for all things bad. He pushed it from his thoughts, concentrated on the landscape around him.

He felt a smattering of rain. The sky was a patchwork of cloud, like old bruising, masking the sun, tainting the day with a deep gloom. The cycle track, snaking through the forest, was never far from the main road, the farthest point only about thirty yards. Smith heard the passing cars, heading for a day out on the mountains or the lochs. At this time the road was always busy. But early in the morning, the road would be quiet. Smith's despondency deepened.

The rain, in a matter of a minute, got heavier. Thunder rumbled. Smith reached the two-mile mark, give or take. Here the road took a sharp turn. The low drystone wall had disappeared, giving way to pine trees and clusters of thick bushes. The kid, he reckoned, would have run another half mile before turning back, if he'd stuck to his routine. A big if.

His eyes roved the trees and vegetation to his right, at the verge of the road. He stopped, heart rising to his mouth. Something lay huddled at the foot of the bushes, concealed by long grass and bracken. At first glance it could have been mistaken for a black bin bag carelessly dumped.

Smith stared, fixed to the spot. Horror yawned wide. He knew what it was. No bin bag. The rain got heavier, drowning out all sounds save the beat of his heart which felt louder than the thunder above.

Step by step, his feet like concrete, he went over to the bushes, took a deep, shuddering breath, crouched. He remained motionless, eyes resting on the pale, broken figure cradled in the long grass. *He could be sleeping.* Only he wasn't. Smith had seen death in all its manifestations and saw it now. His head was crushed. His bones were broken. Tenderly, with the tip of his fingers, he touched the kid's pale cheek, stroked his face. He glided his hand down to the side of the kid's neck, feeling for a pulse. But he knew the answer. He knelt beside him, head bowed, gently smoothed the kid's hair, and as the thunder rumbled for a second time, and as the rain came down in great lashing sheets, Smith wept.

———

Smith remained at Paul's side, time rendered meaningless. The rain had washed away the blood, skin cleansed and shining like ivory. The kid lay like a discarded mannequin, no longer concerned with such mundane things as the weather. Smith knew his next task, but the thought filled him with such bleak sorrow he wished it was he lying on the grass, dead, and someone else who had the burden.

He took another deep breath, took command of himself, adjusting his mind, assuming cold rationality. As he was trained. Beside the kid was a stone tucked under the low leaves of a bush. Smith carefully pushed the leaves to one side. The stone had been kept dry. It was spattered in blood and matted with the kid's dark hair. Smith was careful not to touch. The conclusion was not difficult to reach. The idea that Paul had slipped and maybe struck his head on the stone was never going to fit. His bones were broken, which suggested he'd been hit by a car. Perhaps after impact he hit his head on the stone. But this was unlikely too. To Smith's mind, Paul had been placed there, camouflaged by the undergrowth, virtually impossible to detect for a casual observer. The stone? Dumped beside Paul. Possibly used to finish the matter. To ensure the kid wouldn't talk.

Something caught his eye near the kid's feet, glinting in the grass of the verge. Smith stood, squeezed through the bushes, went over. He stooped, squinted at the object. He was in the middle of a crime scene. Touching anything was forbidden. But this was way too personal. He picked it up, felt its texture in his hand, tucked it in his pocket.

He'd seen enough. Time now to do the unthinkable. He pulled out Paul's mobile phone, found Alison's number.

And made the call.

## 36

The fire had taken hold, as expected, reducing the hotel to a blackened carcass of stone and ash. Situated remotely, encompassed by high trees, the fire had quietly raged for over two hours before someone noticed a pall of smoke in the light of the dawn sky. When the fire engines arrived at just after 6am it was too late.

Chadwick Purkis was given the news by the police later that morning. He visited the ruin in the afternoon, displaying anger and outrage. He arrived back at his castle in time for dinner. He was famished, and delighted. After he'd eaten he summoned Jacob, who arrived exactly on time. They sat, the two of them, in the library, by a wide hearth. Summer was ending. The rooms, by their sheer size, were always difficult to heat. He ensured a real fire always flickered in the evenings, as it did so now. Jacob sat opposite him, patient as a rock, the flames reflecting in his eyes, giving him a wolfish look. As ever, his expression was one of cool detachment. Which was why Purkis employed him. Everything was business for a man like Jacob.

"Books are written to be read," said Purkis. "Do you read, Jacob?"

"On occasion."

"I have no idea how many books I have in this room. And I've only read a handful. That's not quite true. I haven't actually *read* any. Not cover to cover. I've dipped in, sampling a page. Feeling the texture of the paper, the cover, the binding. Sometimes the outside is more important than the inside. If something looks good on the exterior, then one assumes the interior is of equal measure. Reading the damn thing becomes almost… inconsequential."

"An interesting take."

Purkis stared into the flames, the heat bringing a glow to his skin.

"Of course," he said quietly, "looks can be deceiving. I went to the hotel today. Or what remains of it. A thorough job, Jacob."

"They'll suspect arson. Which it was, of course. But they'll look in the wrong direction. I have no doubts. Drugs, alcohol, kids. A perfect combination."

"That's reassuring. I like it when you speak with such confidence, Jacob. You have an almost prophet-like gift."

"I like to see plans completed successfully."

"And the other matter?"

Jacob made a small, dismissive gesture with his hand.

"The boy was found earlier this afternoon. Vincent is on the inside track. It's a hit and run. The car will never be traced. No one was seen. The police have given up before they started. We can move on."

"I already had," replied Purkis in a dry voice. Another short silence, the only sound the crack and sputter of burning wood in the hearth. Then, "We're all set for the end of the month?"

"All invitations have been answered. As ever, the Glass Box is popular."

"Everybody loves blood sport, whether they wish to admit it or not."

Jacob nodded. "I'm arranging transport and accommodation. The contestants arrive three days before the event."

"And our friend Cornwall Pritchard? He's primed and ready?"

"He lives for the occasion. He'll be ready."

Purkis stared into the flames. "He livens things up, make no mistake," he said softly, speaking more to himself than Jacob. He turned suddenly. "Would you ever visit the Glass Box? As a contestant?"

Jacob sat back in the chair and like Purkis, watched the flames dance.

"A place to be avoided, I think. It takes a certain type of man."

Purkis was intrigued. "A desperate man?"

"Some are desperate. They need the money. But then there are others, of an entirely different sort."

Purkis understood. Men like Cornwall Pritchard. Men who revelled in the kill. Psychopaths.

"Thank you, Jacob."

Jacob stood, allowed a polite tilt of his head, left the room. Purkis settled back in his chair. The hotel was destroyed. He would wait a respectful time – three months or so – and then make his application to planning to build his luxury development. The hotel would then be erased from existence. In time it would fade to a distant memory. And the boy? Collateral damage. Sheer bad luck. Purkis was unconcerned. In the great journey he had taken to make his fortune, Purkis had overseen the deaths of many. And as he was prone to do during these moments of introspection, he thought back to where it had all started.

To a village miles from anywhere.

To a room he had built.

His masterpiece.

## 37

Paul's funeral took place three days after his body had been discovered. Smith's perspective had altered. He no longer felt compelled to leave his cabin. In fact, he felt the precise opposite. The death of the kid had given him a reason to stay.

He attended the church service. The place was full. Schoolkids and teachers sat on varnished pews. People stood at the back, including Smith. He glimpsed Alison at the front, face etched with exhaustion, her posture stiff and fragile. Pamphlets had been distributed, containing photographs of Paul throughout his life, and in each, Paul was smiling. It broke Smith's heart. The kid had a middle name – Martin. Smith had been unaware.

The coffin was brought in. Smith struggled with the notion that the kid, once so vital and alive, lay inert and lifeless in a wooden box. An image formed in his mind – a white-tailed eagle, great wings spread, skimming the surface of a loch. Smith hoped the kid's soul soared high, free and wild like the eagle.

The coffin was placed on a raised platform. The minister

spoke, his words careful and tender. Smith, like everyone, listened and prayed. It was at the end, when the service had finished, that Alison caved, her shoulders trembling, her tears echoing. Defeated.

Paul's coffin was lowered. They played the kid's favourite song – Meat Loaf's 'Bat Out of Hell'. Smith allowed himself a wintry smile. He had no idea the kid liked it, but was glad he did. It was Smith's favourite too. An odd but touching coincidence.

The service was over. Smith left quietly, without anyone noticing.

---

The following day, Smith made the journey from his cabin in the mountains to Alison's house. It was late morning when he arrived. The sun was swaddled by cloud, giving a brittle, cheerless light. The air seemed heavy and listless, as if the day had been sucked of life. Smith knocked on the front door. He had no idea if she'd be in. If not, he would wait. For as long as it took.

He sensed movement inside. The door opened. Alison stood before him, gaunt, her cheekbones harsh, her eyes devoid of any spark. She didn't speak. She turned back into the darkness of the interior, leaving the door open. Smith entered, closing the door behind him, and went through to the kitchen. She was sitting at the table. Before her a school photograph of Paul, giving his broad, toothy smile for the camera. Beside it, a saucer adapted as an ashtray, a packet of cigarettes, a cheap plastic lighter, an empty glass, and a bottle of red wine. Smith sat opposite. She poured wine into the glass, almost to the brim, and drank half the contents. She pulled a cigarette from the packet and lit up. She took a deep drag, the tip of the cigarette glowing bright orange. She blew smoke up into the air above her.

"I don't smoke," she said, her voice deadpan. "But thought I'd start."

Smith nodded but said nothing. He put his hand in his pocket, took out an object which glittered in the light. He placed it on the table.

She gazed at it, inhaled the strong nicotine, exhaled.

"Where did you get that?"

"I found it beside Paul. It's distinctive, don't you think?"

She reached over, picked it up. A silver key ring, shaped as a 'V' attached to which was a single key.

"This is Vincent's," she said. "He tried to use this to get into the house. But I'd changed the locks."

"He's a persistent man. Do you want my take on this? It's blunt, but I believe it's what happened."

"Be as blunt as you want."

Smith met her eyes, spoke in a level voice. "Vincent was in the car that hit Paul. Either driving or a passenger. He decided to hide Paul's body to gain more time, presumably to ditch the car somewhere far away. At that hour in the morning, at that particular stretch of road, the place would be deserted. You want to hear this?"

She nodded, kept her attention fixed on Smith.

"He dragged or carried Paul's body to some thick undergrowth. I suspect he was carried. I didn't see any drag marks in the grass or the mud. Which to me indicates Vincent may have had help. During the process he lost his key ring." He chose not to mention the rock coated with her son's blood.

Alison responded with a thoughtful nod, placed the key ring carefully back on the table, stood, went over to the sink, and retched. Smith said nothing. There was nothing he could say. He waited.

She remained hunched over the sink, splashed her face

with cold water, straightened, dried herself with a kitchen towel, returned to her chair.

Smith remained silent. She took another gulp of wine, then another deep drag.

"You should have left it for the police to find."

Smith shrugged. "Is that what you would have wanted?"

"No."

She stared at the key ring. "Take it away. It disgusts me."

Smith put it back in his pocket.

"What do you want, John?"

She spoke in that flat, listless way. Weariness and heartbreak, thought Smith. Her soul was crushed. Her eyes, once vibrant, were dead.

"Permission," he replied.

Again, a thoughtful nod as she considered his response.

"You have it," she said.

"Thank you."

A final drag. The cigarette was finished. She stubbed it out on the saucer, where she left it along with several other cigarette ends. She didn't look at him when she spoke.

"What will you do?"

"Kill everyone who had a hand in Paul's death. Without exception."

"You can do this?"

"Yes."

"You have this… ability?"

"I have."

She nodded, as if coming to some inward conclusion.

"Starting with Vincent?"

"Yes."

She took a deep breath. "Good. Kill them all, John. Without exception."

"With pleasure."

## 38

Cornwall Pritchard received the call at 9am. He would be picked up from his house at midday and then driven to a hotel on the outskirts of Perth. Pritchard knew the hotel well. Woodland House. Luxury resort and spa. He would spend two nights there, all at the expense of Chadwick Purkis. He would relax, train lightly in the hotel gym, get mentally prepared. Then, on the morning of the third day, he would be taken to Purkis's castle. To the lower level. To the Glass Box.

His mother was fussing, hovering about like a wasp. She'd done his packing, folding things neatly in a small hard-shell travel case. Pritchard didn't object. If it pleased his mother, then it pleased him. Also, it was part of the ritual. To change might bring bad luck.

He had a light mid-morning snack of fruit and yoghurt and a glass of full-fat milk. His mother watched him as he ate.

"You come back to me in one piece, you understand?" She said the same thing every time.

"I'll be fine, Mother. Don't fret. I'll be back before you know it."

"Make it quick. You know how you like to show off. Don't be over-elaborate. Kill the fucker, then go."

"But they don't pay me to be quick." He shovelled a spoonful of fruit into his mouth, swallowed, "They like it to be…" His heavy brow furrowed as he searched for the right word. "…theatrical. That's what they come for."

"Theatrical. Maybe they do. But in theatreland people don't die."

"No one can beat me," he muttered.

Suddenly she stepped forward and slapped him.

"You're flesh and blood. You can die like any other man." He looked at her, his expression one of shock and confusion. Pritchard was sitting, she was standing. She pulled him towards her, cradled him against her chest, kissed the top of his head. "I love you, son," she whispered. "But you can't be complacent. These people you fight. They might get lucky. Then what? I don't want Jacob knocking on my front door telling me my son isn't coming back. Like I said. Make it quick."

Pritchard said nothing. She released him from her embrace, stepped back, scrutinised him.

"Did you hear me?"

"Yes, Mother."

She smiled. "I have good news for you."

"What?"

"I've booked a three-week stay in Cancún. Luxury, all-inclusive. Just the two of us. Wouldn't you like to see your mother all nice and tanned?"

Pritchard nodded.

"You're a good boy. You know how to look after me." She leaned in again, kept her voice soft and low.

"And I know how to look after you."

Transport arrived at 12pm precisely. A black Range Rover. The driver was unknown to him. He got out and took Pritchard's case, which he placed in the boot. Pritchard got in the back seat. His mother stood at the front door. She blew a kiss and waved, and mouthed *love you*. Pritchard waved back. The car drove off.

Pritchard settled back and thought of the journey ahead, and his visit to the Glass Box. He would ignore his mother's advice. He would ensure the death of his opponent was both prolonged and agonising. *Theatrical*. That's what they wanted. And that's what they'd get.

# 39

Smith had as much information as he needed. Docherty lived in a rented flat in a village called Kingussie, twelve miles outside Aviemore. A village like a thousand others in Scotland. Instantly forgettable.

Alison had also told him that when he wasn't working, Vincent Docherty would be found in a particular pub in Aviemore. The Crafty Fox. He spent most of his evenings there, accompanied by his cronies. He liked it, apparently, because he knew the manager, and the manager had no trouble with lock-ins. When the pub was shut to everyone except Docherty and his friends, they would remain at the bar, often until three or four in the morning, getting shit-faced drunk.

Smith didn't know the pub, but it was easy to find according to Alison. Just off the main road, a short walk from the bank. Aviemore wasn't big enough to make anywhere difficult to find.

Smith left Alison's house, returning to his cabin. He changed into dark jeans, dark top, mountain boots, a dark rain jacket. He had a hunting knife, kept tucked away in a cupboard in the bathroom. A relic from the special forces. Seventeen inches from the top of the grip to the point of the double-edged fixed blade, the blade itself eleven inches. Since leaving the army, Smith had never drawn it from its leather sheath. He drew it now. It gleamed. A perfectly honed piece of steel. To kill a man with a gun was one thing. To use a knife, however, changed perspective. Death became intimate in such situations. Smith was well acquainted with such intimacy. He slid the blade back in its sheath, and clipped it to the belt of his jeans.

He had time to kill. He walked in no particular hurry to Loch Morlich, to the spot he and Paul had witnessed the eagle swoop down to catch its prey. He sat on the stretch of sand. Nothing had changed. The sand was soft and seamless, undisturbed. The loch was as still as glass. Here, thought Smith, time seemed caught, the moment constant. Things around it moved at a frantic speed. People were born, people lived, people died. But here, in the heart of the mountains, on the shore of a blue loch, a stillness existed, unblemished by events.

He sat cross-legged and just breathed. He felt the tinge of rain, the stir of a cold breeze. He had no idea if he would survive the night. Possibly not. Death did not scare him. He had lived with it for many years. His time was overdue. Like a library book. A late return to be brought back at last, and tucked away with a million trillion other books. To be forgotten.

A feeling blossomed in the pit of his stomach. A feeling he hadn't experienced in years. The sensation before battle. The quiet thrill of the kill.

Death did not scare him. He was death. And death was coming to supper.

## 40

Most of Aviemore had attended Paul's funeral. Vincent Docherty was one of the few who didn't. He had chosen to stay away. Not through any feelings of guilt. Guilt, for a man like Docherty, was a wasted emotion. He had been told – *ordered* – to keep his distance. *Keep your head down*, Jacob had said. And Jacob was not a man to be ignored.

Docherty had taken sick leave. Stomach bug. He stayed put in his somewhat squalid flat in Kingussie, drinking beer and wine in the afternoon, snorting cocaine in the evening. He watched porn, and box sets on Netflix. He gave Paul little thought, other than a vague worry as to the consequences should the car be traced, or if a witness had seen them. But the prospects of being caught were remote. Jacob and the man called Halliday were clever and careful. Plus, he'd kept his ear to the ground. The cops were clueless. Other than slivers of black metallic paint embedded in the boy's skin, they had sweet nothing to go on. Vincent knew he was in the clear. And he toyed with the idea of paying Alison another visit, when everything had settled down. She'd humiliated him. He wanted to humiliate her right back.

Sick leave did not entirely restrict his movements. At midnight, like clockwork, a taxi picked him up, and took him into Aviemore. Specifically, to the Crafty Fox. There, waiting at the bar, his friends, including the bar manager, who kept the pub open until 3am. Sometimes later, depending on when they ran out of stamina. Then, a taxi back to his flat to collapse into bed in a stupor.

Such was the routine of Vincent Docherty, every evening. The night after the funeral was no different.

At 12.30am the taxi dropped him off. He kept to the shadows, sidling his way to the front door of the pub. He was absent from work through illness and thus wished to slip in and out unnoticed. The door was bolted shut. From the outside the place looked devoid of life, a single window at the front blanked out by heavy drapes. He knocked at the door gently, three times, then hung back. The lock rattled, the door opened three inches, revealing a column of light from inside. Someone peered through. Docherty stepped forward. The door opened wider, the manager letting him in.

They made their way through to the main bar. There he found his three friends, all sitting on high stools, hunched over pint glasses. Otherwise the pub was empty.

The manager, a man called Owen Henderson, didn't need to ask. Docherty was a man of habit. A pint of Carlsberg with a whisky chaser. Henderson whistled as he poured the drinks. Sounded a bit like 'Three Coins in the Fountain'. He was big and burly, sleeves rolled up to his elbows, revealing a tapestry of tattoos, thick-framed spectacles wrapped round his face, hair cut to a dark bristle.

Docherty sat on a high stool next to his friends. Henderson placed two glasses on the bar.

"Enjoy," he said.

"Sure will." He downed the whisky in one, sipped from the pint glass.

His friend sitting next to him, the big man called Eddie, clapped him on the back.

"How's the invalid?"

Docherty clenched his stomach, assumed a pained expression.

"Fucking agony. Alcohol's the best cure."

A ripple of laughter.

Jasper spoke up. "The only fucking cure!" To endorse his remark, he took a healthy swig of lager.

"If only it was true," Henderson said. "I might turn a profit one day."

"A lick of paint might help," said Pat. He wore a white T-shirt, tight round the chest and shoulders, amplifying his muscles. Printed on the front, emblazoned in bright red, were the words *Warrior Spirit*. "And maybe a new carpet."

"The carpet's fine," responded Henderson. He had pulled himself a pint and was standing opposite them, heavy forearms planted on the bar.

"Except when it sticks to your shoes," Vincent said. "It's like walking on chewing gum."

Henderson shrugged. "It forms part of the appeal."

The big man – Eddie – shifted in his chair. Like Pat, he wore a T-shirt. Unlike Pat, it wasn't moulded round his physique. It was loose and baggy, which helped augment his massive size.

"Our friend hasn't left."

Docherty took another glug of lager, wiped away froth from his upper lip with the sleeve of his jacket.

"What?"

"The tramp from the woods. He was seen leaving Alison's house this morning."

"Alison's house?"

"Sniffing about like a fucking mangy rat," said Eddie. "Her son still warm in the grave. The fucking gall."

Docherty nodded slowly, digesting this information. A slow rage kindled in his gut.

"You should have taken care of him," he said.

"Next time," Pat said. "The guy won't know what hit him."

"Next time, I'll go with you. And we make it permanent."

"Sounds like someone's got you riled," Henderson said. He topped up Docherty's whisky glass.

"I want to kill that bastard so badly," muttered Docherty. "It's like a fucking itch I can't scratch."

Henderson gave a wheezy laugh. He reached under the bar, and produced a smooth piece of shiny wood, which he placed carefully on the bar top. It was about three feet long, thick and rounded at one end, tapering to a narrow column, bound in black leather.

"This little fucker," said Henderson, "is a Japanese Tetsubo war club. The real thing. I call it *Pain Maker*. You want 'permanent'? A couple of taps with this baby and it's goodnight Vienna."

Docherty picked it up, gauged its weight. "Nice. You could do damage with this one. Can I borrow it?"

"It's all yours," Henderson said. "But make sure you wipe it down afterwards. Don't want it back with pieces of the guy's brain stuck to the end."

"Hope it's not as sticky as your carpet," Jasper said, grinning. Another rumble of laughter. Docherty didn't join in. He was in no laughing mood. The news he'd been given had soured his disposition. He had blood on his mind.

"I say we pay him a visit," he said. He placed the club on the bar before him, stroked the smooth polished wood with the tips of his fingers. "Tomorrow. At night. We go tooled up and fucking bury the bastard."

"I want to make it slow," said Eddie, straightening in his chair, puffing out his chest. "Make him feel it."

"Slow sounds good to me," Docherty said. He sipped his

whisky, savouring the taste. He would also savour the violence. And when enough violence had been inflicted, he would pound the fucker's face with the Tetsubo war club like he was pounding a slab of meat.

His thoughts were suddenly interrupted. A noise echoed through the building, loud and sharp. The front entrance. Someone was knocking hard.

Henderson frowned. "Who the fuck is that?"

"Ignore it," Pat said. "They'll go away."

But whoever it was didn't follow Pat's prediction. The knocking continued. More than knocking. Hammering.

Henderson shook his head, his round face wrinkled in puzzlement. He looked at Docherty.

"The cops?"

Docherty shook his head emphatically. "No chance. Probably some drunk kids."

Henderson gave a deep sigh. "Christ," he said. "What does a man have to do nowadays to get a quiet drink? I'd better go."

"Maybe it's the carpet police," joked Jasper. "Found you at last."

"Fuck you."

Henderson went round the bar, lifted a section, opened the half-door, and made his way out of the room towards the front door.

The four men sat, pondering their drinks.

"We go tomorrow," Docherty said. "Under the cover of darkness. The mad fuck won't know what's hit him. Thinks he can come into my town and humiliate me. He needs a bit of 'correction'."

Eddie gave a deep, rumbling chuckle. "Correction. I like it. You have a way with words, Vincent."

"I still want to burn his shithole of a cabin down," Jasper said.

"You'll get your chance," Docherty replied. "We'll burn him with it."

A noise. The door of the bar opened. They all looked round, expecting the burly figure of Henderson.

Each face portrayed a similar expression – shock. Pure and undiluted. Docherty, glass raised to his mouth, stopped as if in freeze-frame.

It wasn't Henderson who entered the room.

It looked like the 'mad fuck' had come to visit.

## 41

S mith had no difficulty finding the Crafty Fox. It wasn't on
the main road but situated a little back, standing on its
own, adjacent to a dilapidated fairground overgrown with long
grass and vegetation. An unappealing building. A cube of
white stucco, flat roof, a single window at the front, the main
door accessed by a gravel path. A drinkers' pub, thought Smith.
Where men came to find cheap oblivion.

It was midnight. The place looked closed. The illumination
was poor, the only lighting from the street lamps on the main
road sixty yards away, for which Smith was grateful. He
hunkered down, keeping to the deep shadows and watched,
quiet as a whisper. He wore dark trousers, a hooded pullover,
ski mask, gloves. To the casual bystander, he was invisible.

At 12.30am a taxi pulled up. A man got out. Smith
recognised the hulking shape instantly. Vincent Docherty.
Some banter followed between Docherty and the driver.
Laughter. The taxi moved off. Docherty lumbered up the
gravel path to the front entrance. He knocked on the door
three times. A minute later, the door opened a fraction,
presumably for the occupier to check who was there. The door

opened wider, and Docherty disappeared inside. The door closed.

Smith waited ten minutes. Breathing deeply, composing himself. Preparing. Mindset was everything.

He got up, moved carefully, hugging the shadows, approached the entrance. There was no obvious sign of CCTV cameras. They could, of course, be concealed, but the place looked too much of a shithole to carry the expense. Smith waited another five minutes, again taking deep breaths, reining in the excitement he invariably experienced before confrontation.

He knocked at the door with the handle of his knife. Three sharp raps. He drew back a step. He knew they'd do nothing, hoping whoever it was would go away. He stepped forward, repeated the process, again withdrew into the shadows. He counted in his head. Thirty seconds. He heard the creak of movement from inside, heavy footsteps padding on the floor. The sound of a heavy key turning. The door opened by a sliver – the distance of three inches. The length of a lock chain. Smith glimpsed an eye peering through, checking to see who the hell was making the commotion. Smith waited, senses escalated to an increased competence.

A voice growled, "Who the fuck is there?"

The door closed. Smith remained still as stone. Five more seconds. The guy was debating. Then, the rattle of the chain lock sliding on its rail. The guy had to check to make sure nobody was there. The door opened. The guy was big. Round, fleshy face. Heavy chest, thick arms. Wearing a loose, collared golfing T-shirt, pale blue slacks. A dish towel slung over his shoulder. *The barman*, guessed Smith.

He squinted into the darkness. Smith moved, three long strides. The man jerked back, surprised, eyes flicking wide. Smith struck swift and hard, the heel of his hand connecting with the exposed throat. The man stumbled back, choking, unable to articulate, arms flailing. Smith was relentless. He kicked the man's groin. The man doubled over. Smith grabbed the back of his head, thrust down, yanked the man's face against his upraised knee, crushing bone, breaking teeth. The man slumped to the floor. Smith crouched, dealt a hammer blow to the side of the head rendering the man unconscious. The entire episode was performed quickly and silently. Clinically.

Smith left him lying in a gradually expanding pool of blood. He made his way through a corridor, to a pair of glass swing doors. He opened them, encountering a large lounge area. Red velvet drapes, a matching red carpet, somewhat worn. A bar on one side, tables and chairs on the other. The place was empty. Smith made his way to a door at the far end. The top half was glass. He looked through into another bar, smaller, more intimate. There, four men sitting on bar stools. Men he recognised. They were deep in conversation.

It had come to this. Smith felt exhilaration. This was what he was trained for. This was what he did best. This was all he knew. He removed the ski mask, tucked it in his pocket, opened the door, entered.

## 42

J acob was busy. It was late at night, but at this particular time, sleep was a rare commodity. Twenty-five guests had to be catered for. They were all arriving at different times from different parts of the world. Some stayed at rooms in Purkis's castle. Most stayed at hotels in Edinburgh and Glasgow. A few insisted on staying in London, which was a pain, requiring connecting flights. But Jacob was a master of organisation. The stakes were high. Dissatisfaction meant no return. No return meant a loss of revenue, which was an inconceivable notion in the world of Chadwick Purkis. A ticket to this particular show carried a three million price tag. Those who were invited expected something special. And Jacob made damn sure special was what they got.

The individuals concerned were all men. A real boys' club. From hedge fund managers to oil and gas oligarchs. From CEOs of multinational companies to media tycoons. Staggering wealth was the common theme. Jacob reckoned they each were billionaires. As such, their tastes differed from mere mortals. And Chadwick Purkis, the eternal entrepreneur, knew how to cater for such tastes. The product offered was unique. And extreme. It was Jacob's task to ensure the process was slick and trouble free.

Jacob had a theory. The more powerful one became, the more difficult it was to satisfy one's appetite. They each paid their three million entrance fee – loose change for such men – and got the fix they needed, compliments of Chadwick Purkis.

Jacob worked from a small, unobtrusive unit in a retail and commercial park on the outskirts of Perth. Purkis owned the whole thing – an area comprising thirty shops and offices, each one rented out. Just a fraction of Purkis's property empire.

The office was basic, no frills, on a floor above a travel agents. Some desks, chairs. The walls were bare, the illumination provided by strip lights on the ceiling. A kettle and a small fridge. Jacob only used the place for two days, in the run-up before the big event. He employed a couple of university undergrads who were clever on computers. They dealt with flights, restaurant bookings, hire cars, catering, oblivious to the reason behind the exercise. The guests who came arrived the day before the event, met at the castle on the day, stayed the night, then left the next morning. Three days every two months. For those three days, seventy-five million pounds, of which Jacob got a cut of two million. He could hardly complain. The funds were transferred to an offshore account in the British Virgin Islands, attracting minimum attention and minimal tax.

It was well past midnight. The two undergrads had left. Things were going to plan. The first guests would be arriving early morning, then others would follow during the course of the day, the last coming in late afternoon. Cornwall Pritchard had been driven to the usual hotel. The other contestants had all arrived, each taken from the airport to separate locations – hotels of similar luxury to Pritchard's. Booked for two nights. Given this was possibly – probably – their last two evenings alive, Purkis spared no expense. Plus, with the amount of cash rolling in, the expense was negligible.

Jacob sat, sipping coffee. Strong and black. It kept him alert. Though he had never required much sleep. A legacy from his days abroad, when sleep could get you dead. He thought back, as he often did at such quiet moments, to his youth. Abusive parents. Foster home. In and out of trouble. Working for a gang in Glasgow specialising in drug dealing and extortion. He'd killed his first man at twenty. The wrong man. A man with connections. Jacob had to flee, to hide, which he did. To Ireland and then to America. In particular the east coast, chasing the sun, eventually drifting down to Miami where, in certain circles, a raw cunning, a penchant for violence and a lack of remorse were valued commodities. He knew drugs, knew how the system worked. The process of import and supply, and ultimately distribution. He worked with a small outfit, organising cocaine shipments from such places as Colombia and Bolivia. He lasted twelve years and ended up spending most of his money evading the DEA, who were becoming more clever and inventive in their pursuit of crime. He decided it was time to leave. He returned to Scotland, started afresh. Did a little security work, got a job for Purkis's organisation. He came to Purkis's attention when he was asked to collect some rent arrears from tenants of a restaurant premises Purkis owned. It was tricky because the tenants were three brothers, none of whom were easily intimidated. Nightmare tenants in Purkis's book. Jacob performed with zeal. He broke both arms of one, fractured the jaw and skull of another, blinded a third in one eye. The brothers paid up. After that, they were never late again.

Jacob was the right fit. Purkis saw this, and elevated Jacob to personal assistant. Thereafter, Jacob's skills were exploited to the full, which he executed without compunction.

And to validate his actions, he had several million in an offshore bank account. Not bad for a boy from a foster home.

He took another sip. After the billionaire guests had all gone, each one back to his mansion in Malibu, or his villa at Lake Como, or wherever, he would partake in a quiet celebration. He would hire a woman for the night, get drunk. Then move on to the next task set by his employer, Chadwick Purkis.

Not a bad life, he thought.

Then he got the call.

Suddenly things got complicated.

# 43

---

S mith almost laughed at the expressions on their faces.

"Hello, gentlemen. Hope I haven't interrupted."

They didn't respond. Docherty had a pint glass in his hand, was in the process of lifting it to his mouth. He placed it slowly on the bar.

"Good to catch up again," Smith continued. "Did you miss me?" He noted the wooden club on the bar. "For me? A parting gift? You shouldn't have."

Still nothing.

Smith knew each of their names. Difficult to forget after their previous encounter.

He directed his attention to Jasper. "You. Fat man. If I recall, you tried to burn my house down."

He switched his gaze to Eddie. "You. Ape man. You were ready to crush my skull with a baseball bat."

Then to Pat. "You. Knucklehead. You're ugly and full of self-importance. Usually a sign of a small dick. Stay off the steroids. And shave the beard. It chafes the other guy's lips."

He turned to Docherty, gave him a burning gaze.

"And you." He reached into his jacket pocket, pulled out an

object which glittered in his hand. He tossed it onto the bar. "Did you lose this?"

Docherty stared at it, blinked. He said nothing.

"Do I get a finder's fee?" Smith said. "Maybe not. I found it at the side of the road. Is it 'V' for Vincent. Or 'V' for Murdering Bastard. It doesn't quite go. But you get the gist."

Docherty's face paled. Still he said nothing. Rather, he flicked a meaningful glance to the side, to his three friends.

The big man stood first – Eddie. He pushed the bar stool back, stretched to his full height, which was not inconsiderable. He was followed by Pat. Then Jasper, somewhat more hesitant.

"We've heard enough, fuckwit," said Pat. "You have one fucking nerve. Looks like we're gonna have us a little fun tonight."

"That's why I'm here," responded Smith. "For some entertainment." He lowered his voice, gave Pat a level stare. "The front door is locked. None of you will leave this place alive."

"Can you believe this guy?" Eddie snarled.

"Believe this," Smith said. In one fluid movement, he pulled the hunting knife from the scabbard on his belt, threw it spin style with his right hand. It flew across the short distance, a flash of steel, to imbed in Jasper's throat, almost to the hilt. Jasper remained motionless, transfixed, face a sudden combination of fear and confusion. He opened his mouth. Tried to speak. No words came forth. Instead, a volume of blood. He died on his feet. He fell forward onto the bar, face into his pint glass, then slumped to the ground. The sequence of events took all of four seconds.

The remaining men stepped back in unison, aghast.

*Welcome to real life.*

"Think his burning days are over," Smith said.

"What the fuck have you done!" It was Pat who spoke, his voice shrill.

"Introduced you to my world," Smith replied.

They were in shock. The situation had escalated to a level none of them had anticipated. Which suited Smith perfectly.

He strode forward. Pat stepped to meet him, hesitant, the hulking figure of Eddie at his shoulder. Eddie snatched up the club from the bar. Docherty had retreated to one side.

They came to him, Pat first, Eddie hovering, choosing a clear moment to strike. Pat seized Smith by the arm. Smith swivelled, broke his hold, brought a fearful blow to the throat, crushing the larynx. Pat staggered back. Smith followed through, relentless, slamming his fist into the man's temple, feeling the crush of bone. Eddie swooped in, swinging the club in a ponderous arc towards Smith's head. Eddie was big and powerful. But he was slow. Smith ducked, turned at a crouch, flung himself against Eddie's knees, who swayed, lurched back trying to maintain balance. In the process he dropped the club. Smith swept it up, struck him across the ribs. Eddie expelled a sudden gasp, winded. He made a grab, pulled Smith in towards him. Smith relaxed, allowed him to do so, augmenting Eddie's momentum, again rendering him off balance. Eddie toppled backwards. Smith fell with him, slamming his elbow into the square jaw. Eddie grunted in pain, shook Smith off. Smith rolled, leapt to his feet, agile as a cat, assumed a fighting stance. During the process, the club had slipped from his fingers.

Smith sensed movement to his side. Docherty held Smith's hunting knife, presumably plucked from the throat of his dead friend. He lashed out, intending a stab to Smith's abdomen. Smith stepped back, swung his arm down, brushing the blade to one side. It dropped to the floor. Smith leaned in, grabbed Docherty's arm in a lock, one hand on his wrist, the other just above the elbow, and thrust forward, snapping the ulna.

Docherty's arm broke with an audible crack. He shrieked, stumbled back.

Eddie had regained his feet. He sprang at Smith. Smith stooped, caught his shoulder in Eddie's belly, clutched the instantly raised thigh, tossed him through the air. Eddie hit the floor, on his back, breath knocked from his lungs. Smith planted his knee on the massive chest, used all his weight, brought his elbow down on the area between nose and upper lip, then again on the forehead. Eddie grunted in pain, body sagging as he drifted into unconsciousness. Smith rose to his feet, sweating and panting, and stamped his boot once, twice, three times, snapping Eddie's neck.

In less than thirty seconds he had killed three men. He turned his attention to Docherty, who had retrieved the club and backed into a corner, one arm hanging limp at his side. Smith had witnessed fear in all its forms and saw it now. Docherty, violent bully, was in a world he couldn't comprehend. Where death was not an abstract notion. Where death was real and imminent.

Smith's world.

"Jesus," Docherty said, his voice in short staccato bursts. "You've killed them all." The guy was in pain. *Good.*

Smith picked up his hunting knife. He made his way over to Docherty, halted two steps from him.

"Great to catch up again, Vincent."

"We can talk this through. Please. These guys. They went too far. But it was a stupid joke. This…" He waved the club about in a vague gesture. "…this is crazy. I… I don't even know your name."

Smith gave a wintry smile. "My name is irrelevant. And yes, I have to agree. The whole thing is crazy. Sometimes life gets like that. One second, you're having a quiet drink with your buddies. Next second, they're all dead. I'll bet, when you woke up this morning, this was not how you thought the day would end. And end it shall."

"I can get you money."

"Money? I'm the mangy nutjob who lives in a shithole in the woods. Do you think money's the answer?"

Docherty blinked sweat from his eyes. His arm hung at a bad angle. His breath came in short wheezy rattles.

"What do you want?"

"Two things. The first – enlightenment."

"I don't understand."

Smith's tone was almost conversational. "What happened, Vincent? You hit Paul. I get that. It was dark. You didn't see him. Maybe knocked him into the verge. And then what? You thought you'd make sure? A finishing touch? Indulge me, please."

Docherty licked his lips with the tip of his tongue. He shook his head a fraction. His voice lowered to a dry whisper. "I don't know what you're talking about."

"Of course you don't. Let me help."

Smith stepped close. Docherty raised the club. His bone was broken. He was in pain, his movement awkward. His effort in resisting Smith was feeble. Smith slapped Docherty's hand to one side. The club dropped to the floor. Smith performed a quick, vicious movement. Docherty gasped, looked numbly at his other dangling arm.

"I can keep going..." Smith said, "...until every bone is cracked, and you can only walk sideways like a crab."

Docherty's face crumpled like a squeezed pillow. He began to cry.

"Please. No more."

"What happened, Vincent?"

"It wasn't my fault. I wasn't driving. It happened so fast. There was nothing I could do. I swear."

Smith gave a grim smile. "Sure. You weren't to blame. Keep going."

Docherty swallowed, grimaced with the pain. Smith waited. He had all night.

"We had a job. The Royal Hotel? We set it on fire. On our way back, we hit Paul."

"We?"

Docherty hesitated. He was debating, thought Smith. Whether the pain to be inflicted for his silence outweighed the pain he might suffer at the hands of those who employed him.

"These people..." he said. "They're powerful. You can't cross them."

Smith rested his knife on Docherty's shoulder. "Let's start by cutting off your ears."

Docherty shrank back. "The driver is called Halliday. The guy in charge is Jacob. He gives the orders. It was them. They did it."

"Did what?"

"I liked the kid. He didn't deserve it. But there was nothing I could do."

"The kid had a name." Smith loomed in closer. "Say it!"

"Paul."

"That's better. Continue, please."

"Paul got hit. He was in a bad way. I pleaded with them. 'Take him to a hospital.' No way could we leave him there, like that. I pleaded with them, I swear. But you can't reason with these people. They made a decision."

"Of course they did," Smith said softly.

Docherty took a ragged breath. "Jacob ordered Halliday to kill him. He dropped a stone on his head. We moved him to some bushes. The whole thing was just one big fucking mistake."

"With just a sprinkling of premeditation."

Docherty sank to his knees. He began to sob. "I'm sorry. So fucking sorry."

"Stand up."

Docherty, restricted by two broken arms, struggled to his feet.

Smith gave him a measured stare. "Jacob. The man in charge. You can contact him?"

Docherty, avoiding Smith's eyes, responded with a nod of his head.

"Shall we?" said Smith.

"My mobile. Trouser pocket. I can't use my hands."

Smith patted the front of Docherty's trousers, found the phone, extracted it from his pocket. Docherty gave him the password. Smith scrolled down a list of contacts.

"J for Jacob?"

Another resigned nod of the head.

"Thank you. Excuse me while I chat. Won't be a minute."

Smith pressed the relevant symbol on the screen. The phone rang. A voice answered.

"Vincent?"

## 44

"Vincent?"

Silence.

"It's late," Jacob said, irritated. "What do you want?"

"Vincent's unavailable at the moment."

Jacob straightened in his chair, irritation suddenly evaporating.

"That's a shame. Who is this?"

"My name is really of no consequence. Another name is much more significant. Paul Davidson. You remember him, surely?"

Jacob said nothing.

"No? Let me remind you. He was the fourteen-year-old boy you murdered by the side of a road. Does that jog your memory?"

Jacob gave a mirthless laugh. "I think you've been drinking. What did you say your name was?"

"I didn't. Vincent has been most informative. I suppose the prospect of imminent death has that effect. I would love to meet. How you fixed?"

The gears in Jacob's mind clicked and turned, as he formulated a response.

"Of course I'd love to meet. Any friend of Vincent's is a friend of mine."

"I wouldn't describe him as a friend. More of an acquaintance. We're at the Crafty Fox. But it's rather busy and a tad messy. Let's meet tomorrow evening. My place. It's rather remote. I'll text you the details. Sound like a plan?"

"I look forward to it."

"Excellent. Any last words?"

Jacob frowned. "Last words?"

"For Vincent. Before I kill him."

Jacob took a long breath, said, "That's rather uncivilised of you."

The voice responded. "That's because I'm rather uncivilised. Tomorrow then?"

"I'll look forward to it."

"Me too, Jacob. Me too."

The line disconnected. Jacob gazed at the facing wall of the little office – a blank white rectangle, devoid of any ornamentation. Extraordinary, he thought, how in the space of two minutes, the circumstances of one's life could change so radically. But the ability to deal with such situations was precisely what he got paid for.

He tapped a contact on his mobile.

A voice answered. "Yes, Jacob."

"We have a problem, Mr Purkis."

## 45

Smith put Docherty's phone in his pocket.

"You don't mind, do you?"

Docherty's face reflected the pain he was suffering. His skin was tight and the colour of grey paste, his cheekbones harsh and sharp. Both arms hung at a queer angle.

"Did you mean that?"

"What?"

"That you intend to kill me?"

Smith drew up a seat. "Please. After all this exertion, you need some rest."

Docherty looked at Smith uncertainly. With difficulty he manoeuvred himself into the chair, lips drawn back with the effort.

Smith sat opposite. Clock was ticking. Jacob would, at this very moment, be marshalling a posse of goons to converge on the Crafty Fox. But not yet. Still time for a chat and a fond farewell.

"Do you remember where we first met?" he said.

"I'm sorry," muttered Docherty. "I can help. I'll turn myself in. Whatever you want."

Smith stretched over, tapped Docherty on the forehead.

"You have to stay focused and answer the question."

"In the garden," Docherty croaked.

"Correct. Do you remember what you were doing?"

Docherty didn't respond.

"I understand. Perhaps you're a little embarrassed. Let me remind you. You had just finished beating Alison, and if I recall, you were in the process of whipping Paul with the buckle end of your belt. Paul, being fourteen and a third of your size, could do little about it. Have I got that right?"

Docherty blinked, swallowed, bit his lower lip, but remained silent.

"Cat got your tongue?"

Smith waited.

"I'm sorry…"

Smith leaned forward, resting his elbows on his knees, studied Docherty's face as if he were studying a painting on a wall.

"Do you remember our conversation?"

Docherty's mouth twisted into a tight, pained smile. "I was only fooling about." Another rattling breath. "I didn't mean anything."

"Not quite how Paul and Alison saw it. But you need to concentrate, Vincent. Do you remember our conversation?"

Vincent's chin wobbled. He swallowed, but was unable to provide a coherent response.

"Your memory's a little hazy," Smith said. "I suppose it's an age thing. Thankfully, I remember. I said that if you ever hurt Alison or Paul again, I would first break your arm and then break your neck. You outdid yourself with Paul. And here we are. You and me. You did what you did. Now it's my turn."

"Please…"

"Hush. Relax. I'm not going to break your neck."

Smith saw the sudden shine of hope in Docherty's eyes.

"Thank you…"

"I wanted two things, remember? The first was enlightenment, which you've given me. Can you guess the second thing, Vincent?"

"I don't know."

Smith smiled. "Closure."

He stood, stepped deftly behind Docherty, grasped him under his chin, pulled his head back, and in one fluid movement slit his throat. Docherty coughed, spluttered, brought up a bubble of blood. Despite his broken bones, he raised his hands to staunch the flow. But the cut was deep, running like a smile from one side of the neck to the other. He slithered off the chair onto his knees, collapsed on his side, where he lay, twitching out the dregs of his life, until the twitching ceased, and he lay still.

Smith stared. He felt nothing. Empty. Which was always the way after a kill. Just as he had been trained. *Keep moving.*

He cleaned the blade on the cloth of the seat, slid it back in its leather sheath. He put the ski mask on, left the room, skirting around the litter of dead bodies. He made his way back out of the main lounge area, to the entrance hall. There, still slumped against the wall, the barman who had answered the door, chin resting on his collarbone, unconscious. Smith debated. To leave him alive would be sloppy. But the guy hadn't seen Smith's face. He hesitated. Easy to snap his neck. Decision made. It was the guy's lucky night.

He left the Crafty Fox, sliding into the shadows.

Next was the man called Jacob.

# 46

Chadwick Purkis, for the first time in years, felt the stirrings of unease in his chest. He'd received the call from Jacob. Trouble concerning Vincent Docherty at a place called the Crafty Fox. It seemed someone knew about the kid being killed and was on some vengeance trip. It was bad timing. He had his VIPs arriving later that day. Then, the day after, the gathering for the Glass Box. The last thing he needed was distraction.

But, he assured himself, a distraction was all it was. It hadn't escalated to a critical level. Not yet. Nor would it. Jacob would contain things. Jacob was good at that. Still, the killing of the boy had been careless.

It was late, but Purkis was wide awake. Dressed in a blue silk dressing gown and slippers, he opened the French doors of his conservatory, and made his way out into his fairy garden. There was a sharpness in the air. The whisper of autumn. He tightened his dressing gown. It seemed to him, regardless of the weather, a stillness existed. He had built his walls high. But no matter their height, nothing would ever expel the Scottish cold.

The place was suffused with soft illumination from box lanterns and silver globe lamps. He strolled past colours and scents, took a seat in a gabled arbour fashioned from polished oak, set on a lawn as flat and green as the baize of a pool table.

The situation could become complicated. Docherty had presumably provided the man with details of Jacob's involvement, possibly under duress. According to Jacob, the stranger had threatened to kill Vincent Docherty. Purkis pondered. Docherty was useful because of his police connection, but beyond that his usefulness was limited. As such, he was dispensable, and as a consequence Purkis was unconcerned whether he lived or died. It was safe to assume he was dead. What was more concerning was how the man discovered Docherty's involvement. Plus, now that the man knew about Jacob, he was closer to Purkis. Like an onion being peeled, each layer removed getting closer to the centre.

Leaves rustled. Purkis watched as a fox emerged from the shadows to wander languidly across the lawn, only yards from where Purkis sat, apparently unaware of his presence. It paused, bathed in the soft glow of the lighting, its fur shining vermillion red. Purkis raised his hand, pretending to shoot. The fox moved on, disappearing back into the shadows.

Purkis considered. The man hadn't gone to the police with his story. Which meant it was personal. Which meant the man had a connection with the boy. He wanted to meet Jacob. Probably not to extort money. Probably for vengeance. This seemed the logical explanation.

Purkis's instructions to Jacob were simple. Jacob would first go to the Crafty Fox and there, evaluate. Then wait for the man to contact him.

And then? A simple resolution, perhaps. Kill the problem.

It occurred to Purkis he'd never asked for the boy's name. The information might prove useful. Indeed, crucial.

If the man was on a personal crusade, the way to eradicate the problem might be to turn the table on its head – and get personal right back.

221

## 47

Jacob arrived at the pub called the Crafty Fox. It was 3am. He had left immediately after his call to Purkis. The journey from the office took just short of two hours. He met Halliday there. Contacting Halliday was never an issue. Halliday got well paid, his work involving activities he enjoyed and was particularly good at. Usually violence-related. As such, making arrangements in the early hours presented no problem to Halliday.

Jacob carried a Glock 19, tucked in a shoulder holster. Halliday, a Desert Eagle. The place looked closed and vacant. The front entrance was a solid wooden door. Jacob expected it to be locked. He turned the handle, pushed. The door opened. They were expected, apparently. Jacob crept in, wary, Halliday at his shoulder. There, lying sprawled on the floor, a man. Jacob crouched, examined him. Unconscious but alive. Instinctively, Jacob unbuttoned his jacket, unclipped the holster, pulled out the Glock. Halliday did the same. The pub felt empty. Nevertheless, it was wise to be cautious. Jacob suspected the man who had telephoned him had departed the scene long ago.

They both entered the lounge, then progressed to the smaller bar beyond. They stood, still as wood, surveying the scene. Four figures lay before them, the carpet saturated in a new vivid colour. Jacob, acquainted with death and all its forms, saw it now.

"Four of them," said Jacob quietly. "Looks like a tornado's hit them."

"Amateurs," grunted Mr Halliday.

"Perhaps. Still, four men. It shows our friend has skills."

"Let him try his luck with me."

"Luck? He possesses more than that, I think." Jacob stepped around the straggle of bodies, avoiding the blood. "One has a broken neck. This one looks like his skull's been caved in. And this one has a hole in his neck. A stab? Maybe a thrown knife? These were combat kills. Performed with accuracy and confidence." He made his way to the fourth body at the far end of the room. To Vincent Docherty. "But here we have an altogether different situation."

Halliday followed him, scrutinised the limp form, still and white in a puddle of blood.

"His throat's been cut," said Halliday, his voice toneless. He could have been describing a picture on a wall. "Clean and deep."

Jacob nodded. "Vincent was executed. Unlike his three pals. Which tells us something."

Halliday swivelled round, brow wrinkled in puzzlement.

"Our friend is on a mission," continued Jacob. "And he wants us to know it."

"A mission?"

"He's left carnage behind him. Which means he doesn't care about those he kills. About himself. And a man who isn't scared of death is the most dangerous enemy in the world."

Halliday passed the observation off with a shrug, clearly unconcerned.

"Let's see what our unconscious doorman knows," Jacob said.

They made their way back to the main door. The man lay groaning, finding some movement in his arms and legs. His mouth was a gash of blood.

Halliday grinned. "Looks like he's lost some teeth."

Jacob crouched, patted the man gently on the face. The man's eyes flickered, cracked open. He blinked, presumably trying to focus, gazed at Jacob with a look of dreamy confusion.

"What the hell happened?" Flecks of red spit sprayed with each syllable.

"Looks like you had an intruder," Jacob said.

The man shifted, nodded, realisation coming back.

"The bastard's broken my teeth."

"Looks like it. Did you know him?"

"He was wearing a mask. He just came at me. Fucking coward. Has he stolen any money?"

"Don't think so," said Jacob. "Did he say anything? This masked intruder?"

"Not a fucking word. I need to phone the police." His eyebrows puckered into a frown. "Are you the cops?"

"Not quite." Jacob stood, gave Halliday a look he had given many times. Halliday acknowledged with a nod, thrust his knee into the man's chest. The man emitted a rattling croak. Halliday leaned in, locked the man's head in the crook of his arm, adjusted his body and jerked, snapping the man's neck.

Halliday turned to Jacob.

"What now?"

"We get the hell out of here. And suggest to Mr Purkis that we'll need more men."

They left the building. They had each parked their cars at different locations, in dark, discreet places, away from the main road and more importantly, away from any CCTV cameras. Jacob decided they would leave the bodies where they lay. They would be found in due course. The dead man at the door had a key clutched in his hand. Jacob used it to lock up. He would throw it away later. The pub was a shithole. He doubted anyone would give a damn if it remained closed for a few days. Until the smell seeped through the cracks. Then the police would come. Then front-page news. Which was an irrelevance. There was nothing to connect him or Chadwick Purkis to the killings.

Except the stranger. This *vigilante*.

Jacob reached his car, parked in the shadows in a nameless side road a quarter mile from the building. He bleeped the alarm, got in, pondered.

The man wanted to meet tomorrow evening. His motive was clear. Revenge. He had admitted as much when he'd phoned Jacob. The boy. That was the link.

Jacob allowed himself a humourless smile. Life, he thought, consisted of nothing more than a series of moves. A combination of strategies. Rather like a chess game. A game which Jacob both enjoyed and excelled at.

The man had divulged more than perhaps he'd imagined, during their short conversation. The boy was the key. The boy was his Achilles heel.

Jacob drove into the night, back to Perth where he owned a penthouse flat overlooking the River Tay. He relayed the situation via Bluetooth back to his employer, Chadwick Purkis, who gave little reaction, listening with a heavy silence. Jacob, over the years, had gained a sensitivity to Purkis's moods. Silence was not good. Eventually Purkis responded.

"Call Leo. Tell him to get a team. Four men should do it."

"Short notice," replied Jacob.

"Treble his payment. 'Short notice' won't be an issue."

Jacob couldn't disagree. The line went dead. He made the call using a burner kept in the central console of the car for situations requiring caution and discretion. The line was picked up immediately.

"You don't sleep either. You busy?" said Jacob.

"Depends," replied the voice. It was clipped, educated.

"One hundred thousand a man. Four-man team."

"Who?"

"One target."

"When?"

"Tomorrow."

A pause, then, "One hundred and twenty-five. Plus thirty for expenses."

"Done. I'll text you the rendezvous point. Tomorrow, 10am."

Jacob hung up, slid his window down, snapped the phone, tossed it away.

Four men. His mind rolled back to the scene he confronted at the Crafty Fox. The man at the door. The four sprawled on the carpet in the back bar, and he wondered, with a twinge of dread, if four men were enough.

The boy was the key.

# 48

S mith got back to his cabin in just under two hours. He felt exhilarated. This was who he was. The last few years he had been a stranger, even to himself. Now, the stranger had been stripped away, allowing him to breathe. Allowing him to live. Restraint was lifted. In its place, a burning, elemental fury.

They would come for him as soon as he revealed to Jacob where he lived. *Jacob*. A biblical name. Perhaps such a man should be afforded a biblical death. Smith chided himself. Unwise to be overconfident. The situation could be easily reversed. Perhaps Smith might end up dead in a ditch. Smith had no illusions about the reality of war. Throughout his adult life, death had been a close companion. It hovered, a shadow on his shoulder, a whisper in his ear. Smith wasn't scared to die. He only hoped it waited long enough for him to exact a measure of revenge.

He dismissed such thoughts. They would come for him. Those who had orchestrated Paul's death were vulnerable. They had assumed they were free from repercussions. Which was not unreasonable. Paul had been killed on a deserted road in the middle of nowhere, no witnesses. Smith's sudden involvement would cause considerable consternation. Doubtless, they would wonder how he discovered them. But a more burning issue was containment. They would respond, and quickly. Capture Smith, extract information, then destroy him. Which, if the situation were reversed, is what he would do. He hoped, in their haste, they would prove careless. That their move was based on a knee-jerk reaction. They were aware of his purpose. They knew he sought retaliation for Paul's death. It was personal. They knew he wouldn't call the police, especially after the fun and games at the Crafty Fox. Therefore, rather than wait and evaluate, respond with crushing force.

He expected a posse of men. Probably trained. Nothing like the amateurs he had killed in the pub. They would come with heavy firepower if they had any sense. Which was manageable. In the dark, in the forest, a knife could be as lethal as an M16. They would have night vision or thermal scopes, but in the close confines of the trees such equipment was worse than useless.

*Jacob*. He'd spoken to the man only briefly. He seemed unfazed. No concern. No fear. Intelligent and insightful. Perhaps Smith was misjudging the situation. Perhaps this man Jacob was something more.

They would come. Smith was confident. Because they thought Smith was batshit crazy and mad for revenge.

Which he was.

# 49

Ten am the following morning.

The little boxes remained unopened. Alison had gone to her doctor because she didn't know what else to do. Anything to ease, even a little, the unbearable weight of sadness and guilt. It consumed her. It permeated her body, down to the marrow of her bones. The doctor had listened, and she believed he genuinely cared. She'd lost her son. The solution was simple and casual. Pills. Two boxes. More specifically Valium, plus 200mg of sertraline.

They remained unopened. She had removed them from the paper bag and placed them on the coffee table in her living room. Where they remained. She realised she didn't want to dull the pain. She wanted to feel every raw inch of it. She felt, somehow, if the pain were to lessen, that she would lose Paul. That her feelings were still a link to her dead son.

She sat watching daytime television. The images on the screen, the sounds they made held little interest for her. On the table beside the boxes was a full ashtray. She hadn't smoked since she was eighteen. Skiing and smoking didn't compute. Death and smoking computed perfectly. She'd started the day after Paul's death and didn't want to stop. She thought, grimly, that if she were lucky she might smoke herself to death.

On the armrest of her chair, a packet of Marlboro. She'd tried every brand, at last finding one that hit the spot, bit the lungs. She teased out a cigarette, lit up using a cheap plastic lighter, inhaled, exhaled. She hadn't eaten since the night before. Her appetite had vanished. A by-product of grief. The nicotine made her light-headed. She gazed about. The place needed to be cleaned. A fucking blitz. She couldn't have cared less. Cleaning was not on her list of priorities. On the window shelf, a line of condolence cards. She had bagfuls of them in a cupboard, most sent from strangers she'd never known. Funny, she thought, how life keeps people apart, yet death brings them together. Not funny. Sad. More than sad. Pathetic.

Her gaze drifted to the photo on the mantle above the fire, as it did every few seconds, as if it were a magnet for her eyes. The photo was of Paul, smiling his awkward smile, taken by the school at term end, his expression clear and candid. Before him, a life of promise. Not quite. More like violence and death. She bit back tears, took another deep drag, got up to fix a coffee. Coffee bean and nicotine. It rhymed. Recently, it had formed the basis of her nutrition.

She went to the kitchen. She clicked the kettle. She leaned against the worktop and studied the paintings on the opposite wall. Her paintings. Mountains and sky. Bleak colours – greys and blacks and dark blues. All darkness, without hope.

No one had ever paid any attention to them. Except Paul, who claimed he loved them. She allowed herself a small, wistful smile. He would say that, regardless.

And the stranger. The man called Smith. What had he said? She'd captured their soul. The soul of the mountains, if such a thing could exist. He had almost got it right. She'd captured her own soul. Sad and hopeless. For the millionth time, she pondered the idea of lying in a hot bath and quietly slitting her wrists.

Smith. Where was he now, she wondered? What manner of man was he? They had spoken. Reached an agreement. A pact, dark and dire. He would exact revenge on her behalf. The conversation seemed vague, dreamlike. Had she imagined it? She thought not.

She hoped not.

The kettle boiled. She reached for a coffee cup from a pile in the sink.

Suddenly, the doorbell rang. She frowned. She wasn't expecting visitors. She had no desire to talk to anyone. She waited, remaining still. It rang again. Then loud knocking.

"Fuck it."

She made her way towards the front entrance, glanced in the hall mirror, barely recognising the face that glanced back. She looked like shit. She didn't care. She got to the door, her hand hovering over the mortise lock. A fleeting image popped into her head. Vincent Docherty, drunk and enraged, causing mayhem.

She hesitated. The door was solid. She leaned forward. "Who is it?"

The voice that responded was clear and articulate. A voice she didn't recognise.

"I'm so sorry to trouble you, Mrs Davidson. I'll only take a few minutes of your time."

She responded, having little regard for pleasantries.

"What do you want?"

"It's about your son."

Her mind went into overdrive. "Paul?"

"It's important. I know this is difficult. I can't begin to imagine what you're going through, but it will only take five minutes. Please."

"Who are you?"

"William Bryce. I was one of Paul's teachers."

"A teacher?"

"Yes."

"You taught Paul?"

"Yes."

She opened the door. The man before her was lean, fit-looking, tanned. Dressed in a pale blue suit, white open-necked shirt.

He took a respectful step back.

"Sorry, Mrs Davidson, but it's important."

"Important?"

"Yes."

"Then I suppose you'd better come in."

# 50

On one level, things were progressing smoothly. Those arriving for the Glass Box were experiencing no delays. Flights were punctual, taxis were prompt, no hitches with hotel reservations. It was mid-morning. So far, so good. For those wishing to sample Purkis's castle in the country, he would arrange for staff to meet and greet them, and escort them to their rooms. They would be offered freedom of the facilities, which were numerous – pool, sauna, squash, gym, bar, drinks, snooker, a stroll through the fairy garden, if they so wished. More luxurious than any five-star hotel, thought Purkis.

He sat alone in his conservatory, the wall behind him glistening with his collection of weapons. Not quite alone. Outside, never far away, a security guard, his back to the glass, watchful. Purkis had many enemies. As indeed had most who had clawed their way to the top. And Purkis had clawed. And knifed. And shot. And much worse.

The conservatory was one of the few rooms out of bounds. Purkis coveted his privacy. He rarely left the confines of his home. His reclusive nature, he had come to realise, was a consequence of his success, and one he gladly accepted. Later, he would join his guests for dinner in the great dining room. Oaken beams criss-crossing the ceiling, oak panelling on the walls, oak flooring. A long, rough table able to sit twenty people. Like a Viking hall. Which they loved. He had hired a chef for the evening at a cost of £3,000. A small expense, given the context.

Those who stayed with him were all American. Coming here to this place, to Purkis's castle, was like coming to Camelot. A long-lost world. It added to the charm. The magic. Though the Glass Box offered little of both. Rather blood and gore. And they loved that too.

But his unease had blossomed into something more intense. The incident with Docherty festered in his mind. Plans had been implemented, but plans could go wrong. Jacob – the master of trouble containment – had organised a team. To clean things up. The obvious move. And one which this man – this enemy – would expect. Therefore, a little spice was required. Something to tip the scales. The trick was to introduce a new element into the equation. An element unexpected, and crushing. A *coup de grâce*. A killing blow that his enemy would not anticipate. Like the misericorde. The final thrust to make the bad things go away.

Like the room in a village in Afghanistan.

# 51

Smith walked into Aviemore and bought a cheap pay-as-you-go mobile. He had committed Jacob's number to memory and destroyed Docherty's phone. He took the shortest route – the back road, a mile from his cabin, the one Alison had used to reach him when she was searching for Paul. It cut the distance by two thirds. After buying the phone, he went to his next destination. The local library. It was small but functional. Three computer booths. It was empty, save a young woman behind the desk, headphones wrapped around her head. She gave a bored smile. Smith smiled back, paid for an hour on the computer. Smith had some research to do. A half hour later, he headed back. No sign of commotion. No massive police presence. Too early for the bodies of Vincent and company to be discovered. But eventually they would. And then? Lockdown. Four dead bodies. Shock and outrage. The media would descend, and suddenly Aviemore would be known for something other than its skiing and mountain climbing. Hell had come visiting. And it had only just started.

## 52

Alison didn't apologise for the mess of the place, and the man who had introduced himself as William Bryce didn't seem to care. She led him into the kitchen.

She gestured to a chair. The man sat.

"Coffee?"

"No, thank you."

She made herself one, sat opposite. She took a deep drag of her cigarette, flicked the ash into a saucer. She gave a mirthless smile.

"Difficult time," she said.

The man politely tilted his head. "Of course."

She studied his face. Angular cheekbones, sharp chin, inquisitive eyes. He sat, composed and at ease. The smoke didn't seem to bother him.

"You taught Paul?"

The man's lips curved into a small, sad smile.

"English. And Religious Education."

She nodded thoughtfully. "I didn't know they still taught that."

"RE? Yes. Which is why I'm here." He cocked his head, gazed at something past her shoulder.

"These are good," he said.

She blinked, perplexed at the shift. "What?"

"The paintings. Of the mountains."

She gave a dismissive twitch of her shoulders. "My hobby. Maybe I'll take it up again. Who knows. Everything's changed. Suddenly things don't seem as important as they used to be. You mentioned RE. The reason for your visit?"

"The purpose of RE isn't necessarily about religion." He pursed his lips, as if considering his words. "We encourage our students to chat. Open up. Sometimes it's easier to talk about things to a comparative stranger rather than someone close. Yes?"

Another deep drag. She stubbed the cigarette out on the saucer. She didn't know quite how to react.

"You're saying Paul opened up to you?"

"Not at school. During the summer break."

Alison was perplexed. And irked. Her voice took an edge. "Paul talked to you during summer break? I don't follow."

He raised his hands in placation. "Purely by chance. I was in Aviemore. I was having a coffee. He was passing. He saw me and came over. He came to me. We talked. Not for long."

"But long enough."

"I'm available at any time, should the need arise."

She fixed him a level stare. "And was there a need? You've come all this way to tell me something."

"I thought..." He hesitated. "I thought that what he said might be important to you during this time."

She put the coffee cup to her lips, sipped, placed it carefully back on the table, breathed, and said, "What did he say, Mr Bryson?"

"It's not what you think."

"And what do I think?"

"It was all good. We were talking. It was casual. He told me he was going to meet someone. His friend. A man. Someone he trusted. I got the feeling this 'friend' had made an impression on Paul. A positive impression."

Her anger subsided. Her confusion did not. "He must have meant John. Why would he mention this? I don't mean to be rude, but why the importance?"

He smiled again. His teeth, she noted, gleamed like pearls. "John? That was his name?"

She nodded, uncertain. "John Smith."

He kept his smile. "Easy name to remember. This man – John Smith – seemed to have a bearing. He seemed to matter to Paul. I think, maybe, it's important you know this. Is he local?"

"You got all this from a casual chat in Aviemore? I already knew about John. You're not telling me anything I don't know." She thought back, to Paul's daily sojourns to the forest, his pride that John had taken an interest. Her heart broke. Keeping her voice level took effort. "He was... good for Paul."

"Sounds like it. Sounds like quite a man. I'd like to meet him. To thank him."

"He doesn't need to be thanked. He doesn't want to be thanked."

"But still, if he's local what's the harm? Just to shake his hand."

She responded with a brittle laugh. "He's not the type of man to shake people's hands. He enjoys solitude."

He raised an eyebrow. "Solitude?"

"The old cabin by Loch an Eilein. Not most people's idea of a home. But then I suppose John isn't like most people."

"You knew him?"

"Not really."

"Thank you, Alison. You've been very helpful."

His demeanour seemed to shift. His face lost expression,

became… she grasped for the word – *businesslike*. He reached into the inside pocket of his jacket, took a mobile phone, tapped the screen.

She watched him, bewildered. "What are you doing?"

He ignored her. He spoke into his phone. "I have a possible location. I'll meet you in thirty."

He tucked the phone back into his pocket, fixed his full attention on Alison. She saw now the lines and edges of his face with a new perspective. Suddenly he was distant. His eyes seemed as blank as a lizard's. And suddenly, Alison was afraid. Afraid not for herself, but for John Smith.

She stood. "I don't know what's going on, Mr Bryce, but I'd like you to leave."

He responded, having no regard to her request. "We are cautious people, Alison. We like to know who we're dealing with. And with money at our disposal, and a lot of it, information isn't difficult to get."

"What?"

"Research. That's the key. I know both your parents are dead. You have no brothers or sisters. You have, I believe, an aunt who lives in Ohio. Your husband died some years ago. So, when someone claims to know Paul and wants a little… how can I say it… revenge, we know it's not an aggrieved family member. And we came to the reasonable conclusion that if this person knew Paul, he would also know you. Now we have to meet this person and tie up a loose end. Once again, thank you, Alison. We wouldn't have managed this without you."

"John," she breathed.

"Quite. As I explained, we're cautious people. We have to assume that whatever your friend John knows, you know. And John seems to know a lot. Loose ends, Alison."

She spoke, her voice tight. "Fuck you."

"Not so helpful." He stood up, now opposite Alison, the width of the kitchen table between them. He pulled his jacket to one side. Strapped under his arm was a leather holster and in the holster was a gun. In one deft motion, he pulled it free and pointed, almost casually, at Alison's midsection. Alison remained motionless, caught in the moment. She stared at the gun with dread fascination. A part of her thought she had to be dreaming. Another part was terrified.

The man smiled again, and Alison wondered how she could ever have been fooled. His smile was more horrifying than the gun in his hand.

"This," he said, conversationally, "is a Glock 19. It holds fifteen rounds. Plenty of opportunity to hit the target. It's semi-automatic. Do you know what that means? Let me tell you. It's self-loading which means that every time I fire a shot, it automatically loads the next cartridge into the chamber. All I need to do is keep squeezing the trigger and bam-bam. Out they pop. It takes a 9mm cartridge. 9mm is the width of the bullet. It might not seem much, but it does the trick. What I'm trying to say, is that I could fire five shots off before you took a step, and the paintings on the wall would shine with the spatter of your brain."

Alison gripped the back of the chair. She heard a sound – the beat of her heart. She opened her mouth, tried to speak, failed. Her mouth was dry, her throat tight. She tried again, found her voice, which came out as a dry croak.

"Why are you doing this?"

He gave the slightest shrug. "Because I must. Tell me, Alison, what did your friend John tell you?"

"Tell me?"

"I'll not ask again."

She licked her lips, took a breath, focused on the man. "Are you going to kill me? If that's your intention, then that's fine. I've got no trouble with that. In fact, I'd welcome it. But seeing as you've asked, John found a key ring beside the body of my dead son. The key ring belonged to Vincent Docherty.

Vincent must have lost it when he was moving his body. John intends to kill Vincent." She had a sudden thought. "Or maybe he's done that already. Maybe that's why you're here." She straightened, swallowed back her fear. "John's intention is to kill everybody who had a part in Paul's death. Which includes you, Mr Bryce, or whatever the fuck your name is. So just shoot your fucking Glock with your fucking 9mm bullets, and do what you need to do, or else get the fuck out of my house."

The man nodded thoughtfully. "Careless of Vincent. Just shows you. The simplest thing. But it's time to move on. My name is Jacob. And I'd like to introduce you to a friend of mine – Mr Halliday. He doesn't have my sweet nature."

# 53

When Leo Ruckert explained to his men that Chadwick Purkis had a job for them, their reaction was, to a man, enthusiastic. When he told them they would need to meet the following day at a derelict warehouse five miles outside Inverness, their enthusiasm waned. When he told them the payload was one hundred and twenty-five each for a day's work, their enthusiasm returned. More than enthusiasm. Exuberance.

Ruckert kept a small arsenal of weapons in a metal walk-in storage container on an industrial park on the outskirts of Paisley. To his mind, it was the perfect concealment, the container one amongst hundreds. After Jacob had provided the meeting point, he made arrangements. He contacted his colleagues, then at 6am, made the drive in a Ford transit van. It was early, but the gates to the park were always open. The place was deserted. He backed the van up. He unlocked the container door, shone his flashlight. On shelves, a variety of semi-automatic rifles – Rugers, Remingtons, ArmaLites, Colts. Also handguns, from Desert Eagles to Walthers. Plus Heckler and Koch sub-machine guns. Crates of cartridges. And a lot more. All of them illegal. Acquired over many months from contacts based in Germany and Russia, smuggled in usually via freight ships.

Ruckert chose his weapons, began to load up the van. In such situations he didn't believe in half measures. His view was simple and practical, and one he had tried and tested many times during his service with the special forces – when you're told to kill then kill the hell out the fella. Or woman. Ruckert didn't differentiate.

He packed the weapons and ammunition in plain wooden crates cushioned with bubble wrap, then covered the crates with a sheet. Also, Kevlar vests, night scopes, hunting knives, other accessories. He set off immediately north to Inverness. He would meet the others there. Three men. One from Manchester, the other two from Glasgow. Men he had fought alongside in the 22nd Regiment. Men who shared *esprit de corps* through the angst of battle.

Lethal men, adept at killing, lacking compunction. Like himself. Men who killed for money and who, if he were honest, enjoyed doing it.

## 54

"The power of technology," said Jacob.

They had brought up an aerial picture of Loch an Eilein on Google Maps, displayed in vivid colour on a laptop screen. With relative ease, they established where the man called John Smith was probably living. The probability was high. A single rooftop in a clearing in the woods, close to the loch with no other accommodation within several miles. *The old cabin,* as Alison had described it.

Jacob, after his visit with Alison, had driven straight to the meeting place – a warehouse outside Inverness. The building was a shell, derelict and abandoned. But it was isolated and safe. Little chance of prying eyes. A van and three cars were parked in a cracked forecourt. Four deckchairs and a foldaway table had been erected, around which Leo Ruckert and his men sat, scrutinising the laptop.

They were drinking coffee from flasks.

"The man's a loner," Ruckert said. He turned to Jacob. "A real rush job. He must have seriously pissed off your boss." Jacob regarded him. Ruckert wore mountain trek trousers, climbing boots, ski jacket, all neutral colours. Each man was similarly dressed. Ruckert was of medium height, thick in the neck and shoulders, wide at the hip: attributes indicating strength and agility.

Jacob responded with the slightest shrug. "It needs to be done quickly. It's time sensitive."

Ruckert gave a dry chuckle. "Things done in haste gives rise to carelessness."

"Mr Purkis has faith in you. Hence the big pay packet."

Ruckert flicked his attention back to the screen. "Normally there would be reconnaissance. Time constraints prevent this. Still, his location is favourable. The middle of a forest. No habitation close by. He'll have the advantage, presumably knowing the lay of the land. But he'll not be expecting us, so we'll have the advantage of surprise." He turned again to Jacob, raised an eyebrow. "I assume he'll not be expecting us?"

"Not if we move quickly. He said he'd phone me tonight. He wants to play by his rules. We need to change the game, seek him out earlier."

"Daylight makes it trickier, you understand," Ruckert responded. "Do we know what his firepower is?"

Jacob shook his head. "Not certain. Possibly nothing."

"*Possibly* doesn't crack it. We'll assume the worst and wear body armour. It'll slow us down but maybe save our lives. Is he skilled?"

Jacob thought back to the four dead men at the Crafty Fox. The way it looked, each had been dispatched with ease. 'Skilled' was perhaps an understatement.

"Yes," he said simply.

"And do we have a name?"

"John Smith."

"Fair enough." Ruckert gestured to one of his men, who opened a satchel, produced a Landranger survey paper map which he stretched out on the table. Ruckert studied it, comparing it to the Google Map on the screen. He pointed to a blue section. "There's the loch. The target's location is approximately there." He tapped his finger on an area shaded green. "The closest access for vehicles is a single-track road which stops about a mile from the location. But it's too exposed. Plus, it's the obvious route for an offensive." He considered, then ran his finger along the section of main road leading from Aviemore to the foot of the mountains. "We can leave the vehicles on the verge, and make our way through the forest straight from the road. I reckon it's about six miles, so it's a hike. Maybe a couple of hours, going cautiously. He'll not be expecting that."

"And what if he does?" said Jacob.

Ruckert looked at his men, gave a wolfish grin. "Then we cope."

"Mr Purkis wants this clean. Kill him. No fuss. Clean."

Ruckert gave a mirthless chuckle. "Clean? You've been watching too many movies, my friend. It's never clean. Shit happens. You want us to do this thing in daylight. Someone might be out walking their dog. Or going for a stroll in the woods. Or being all romantic and having a fucking shag in the bushes. What then?"

Jacob shrugged. "Then that's just bad luck. Collateral damage."

"Not so clean," Ruckert said.

"Just get it done. Call me when he's dead."

## 55

F our men. Each armed with a Remington 700 bolt-action rifle. A sniper's weapon. Able to kill at 300 yards. If slightly off target, capable of removing limbs. Concealed in a heavy rifle bag with shoulder straps. At first glance, easily mistaken for a slim rucksack.

Each man also had a Desert Eagle. Semi-automatic with a magazine of nine rounds. Powerful enough to remove a man's head from his shoulders. Strapped into leather holsters buckled to their belts beneath their ski jackets. Bulky but effective.

And each carried a fixed blade MTech hunter's knife, favoured by the US Marines. Consistent with his philosophy, Ruckert opted for too much rather than too little.

They went in one car, compliments of Chadwick Purkis. Later, it would be left somewhere remote, burnt and abandoned. They parked in a lay-by under the shade of packed pine trees. Ruckert had a map and compass. Two hours, he'd reckoned. Probably less. The day was bright with a slight breeze. In the forest, however, under the canopy of branches, the light would reduce, the breeze would disappear to stillness. Which was an advantage.

Cars passed. To a casual observer they were four guys going for a hike. Nothing more sinister. They slipped into the gloom of the trees, four shadows intent on destruction.

---

Some of his guests had arrived and were doubtless enjoying his hospitality. Purkis didn't know exactly where they were. His house was considerably larger than the average. Probably the jacuzzi, sipping champagne at £200 a bottle. At the present moment, he couldn't have cared less. There were places he knew they *wouldn't be*. His conservatory, where he was sitting. And the lower level. Where tomorrow the fun and games took place. Where the Glass Box was situated.

But such matters were not foremost in his mind. It was mid-afternoon. Since the update he'd received from Jacob earlier, he hadn't stirred from the room. His thoughts were preoccupied with the events taking place over a hundred miles away, somewhere in the Cairngorm mountains. His analysis of the situation had proved accurate. Jacob had come to the same conclusion. Find out about the boy, his background, his circumstances. The information was easy to acquire. His mother was a widow. No other relatives. She was the obvious target. And Jacob being Jacob had quickly established the relevant information. The name of their enemy – John Smith. And his location.

He stood by the open French doors, gazing out at the garden he'd spent over two million on, and wondered if he should build tennis courts. The notion had never occurred to him until this precise moment. And maybe a pavilion, constructed of blue marble and dark glass. With the money he would make from tomorrow's show he could build a hundred tennis courts, a hundred pavilions, and barely notice.

Then there was the hotel. Burnt to the ground. In due

course – a respectful period of time – he would erase its existence forever and replace it with luxury houses. More money. And money was God.

But his thoughts veered back to a forest in the Cairngorms. Where Leo Ruckert and his small team of assassins were hunting. Ruckert was dependable. A man skilled in resolving awkward situations. When diplomacy had failed. Though diplomacy had never played a major part in the rise of Purkis's success.

And if Ruckert failed? The thought had occurred to both him and Jacob, and both had arrived at the same conclusion. There was a contingency plan. A final card, so to speak.

Another place in his Camelot castle where his American friends were not allowed. A hidden place, windowless, with a locked door. Where his brand-new guest waited.

## 56

Ruckert and his men kept a distance of approximately fifteen feet apart from each other, single formation, a simple habit instilled from their patrol days. They moved quickly and carefully, not speaking. Ruckert stopped every twenty minutes, to check the map, check the compass. But he knew his bearings, having an instinctive ability for knowing where he was and where to go.

The forest was silent, save the chirp of birds and the murmur of a stream somewhere. They were well away from any trodden paths or trails, the route chosen obscure and uninviting. To Ruckert's mind, tactically, the least expected way in and a further advantage.

After an hour the trees thinned a little, the sunlight became stronger. They made their way through long grass and bracken. They kept going for a further half hour, increasing their pace. Ruckert stopped. A sound drifted towards them. The others stopped with him. He gestured with his hand. A signal they understood. In unison, they shrugged off their rifle bags, removed their rifles, folded the bags, tucked them into jacket pockets. They advanced forward. Ten minutes passed. The sound became more distinct. They slowed, stealthy as cats. Music. Specifically, 'Welcome to the Jungle'. Guns N' Roses. He glanced round. Their perplexed expressions mirrored his own. They crept forward for another five minutes. There! Ahead, maybe a hundred yards, a clearing. And a flat-roofed cabin, walls constructed of logs. No bigger than a large car.

*Jesus,* thought Ruckert. *Fucking Davy Crockett.* Another signal. His men fanned out, formed a loose semicircle. Their approach was masked by waist-high wild grass and sporadic clumps of bush and shrub.

Another two minutes. Visuals became clearer. On a window ledge, a portable CD player, facing outward, blasting noise. The door to the cabin was closed. Ruckert hunkered down, considered. Impossible to know if the guy was in. The music drowned out any noise of activity. Guns N' Roses dwindled to silence, then Led Zeppelin boomed across the forest – 'Rock and Roll'.

Ruckert assumed the guy was close by. *What was the music about?* To draw them in? To distract? Jacob wanted a quick kill. The tactical response, under the circumstances, would be to wait. To sit it out. Patience, until the target moved. Then kill. But there was a hundred-and-twenty-five-thousand-pound bounty to be collected per man. Jacob said the guy was skilled. Ruckert debated. How skilled could a man be against four trained and armed assailants?

The music drowned out all peripheral noise. Ruckert took a chance. He waved his hand, drew his men in towards him.

He lowered his voice to a whisper, though given the volume of the noise, it hardly mattered.

"I'm going to the front door," he said. "For a reaction." He nodded at the man closest to him. "Follow me, thirty paces behind. Keep your guard." He switched to the two others. "Spread out. Stay focused on the door. I'll knock, then stand to one side. If it opens, we shoot. Okay?"

They understood. Ruckert, with care, placed his rifle on the ground, opened his ski jacket, unclipped his pistol, tucked it under the belt of his trousers. He kept his jacket open, the pistol hidden.

He stood, made his way towards the cabin, his pace leisurely. A man out walking in the mountains for a little Scottish air. "Hello there!" Nothing. The door remained closed. The music played. If the guy was in, he probably wouldn't hear. Ruckert quickened his stride. He glanced behind. As instructed one of his men followed, wary of any peripheral activity. Ruckert got to a small, weathered porch, two steps up. On it, a single chair. He stopped. "Anyone in?" No response. He took a breath, took the two steps. The porch creaked under his weight. Another glance behind. Nothing untoward. There was only one window, which was smashed. On the windowsill, the CD player. He switched it off. Now, the only sound was his own breathing. He looked inside. The interior seemed neat. And empty. He went to the door, knocked, stepped to the side. He waited five seconds. Silence. Nothing to suggest human activity. He knocked on the door again, swept open the front of his jacket, pulled out the Desert Eagle, held it with a classic two-handed grip.

Still nothing. Slowly, holding the pistol with his right hand, he pressed his back flat against the wood beside the door, reached, and with his other hand tried the handle, pushed. The door opened.

He resumed his two-handed grip, waited. Counted to five, crouched, swivelled round, weapon pointing into the cabin.

The place was empty. He gave it a cursory examination. There was nothing to suggest any recent activity. No hot coffee, no plate of half-finished food. The place was clean and spartan.

*Lives like a fucking monk,* he thought. *But someone had switched the CD player on.*

He turned, got out onto the porch. Suddenly, in the daylight he felt exposed. He gestured to the man standing thirty paces away – *back to the forest*.

The man acknowledged with a nod. Too late. A sound – one Ruckert was well acquainted with – split the silence, sharp and clear. Like a whipcrack. Then a second. Ruckert stared as his fellow soldier's head exploded. A sudden violent eruption of brain and blood.

The shock lasted all of one second. Ruckert reacted. Instinct took over. He ducked, turned on his heel, dashed for the cabin entrance, thoughts tumbling in his head – the guy was armed. Either he always had a gun, or he took it from one of his men. Ruckert prayed it wasn't the latter. But his prayer ended abruptly. His legs folded. A quick searing pain. He fell on his stomach, unable to move. He tried to crawl but the effort was too great. With difficulty he craned his neck round. His right leg was gone.

Someone was approaching.

F our contestants. Two men against each other in the box.
The winners of each bout then fought. The winner of the
third bout got the money promised. In Cornwall Pritchard's
case it was £200,000, which was a sweet sum. Plus a trophy.
Not in the conventional sense. For Pritchard, trophy meant a
section of his opponent's anatomy.

He'd had lunch, comprising fresh linguini with roasted
fennel and a side dish of two baked potatoes. For dinner he
would have chicken salad and some fruit yoghurt. For supper,
some toast and peanut butter. Then early in the morning, before
the fights, a bowl of porridge and a helping of dried fruit.
Pritchard knew about nutrition. The trick was to keep the
glycogen store refuelled. But not too much – it was easy to
spike the blood glucose. If that happened the body would
experience lethargy and sluggishness, proving fatal.

Pritchard reclined on the bed in his hotel room, dressed in a
white courtesy robe. It was 4pm. He had been for a sauna and
felt good. He would order room service shortly. His room was
spacious, with a white marble en suite complete with hot tub.
All paid for by Jacob's employer. Cost was an irrelevance.

Rather like the last meal of the condemned man. The irony wasn't lost on Pritchard. But Pritchard hadn't lost a fight yet, and he had no intention of losing tomorrow.

On the bed beside him was an open laptop. Each contestant had been sent details of their opponents. Pritchard studied the screen. Two from America, one from Iceland. Who he faced in the first fight was a lottery. The guy from Iceland was big. As big as Pritchard. Long honey-gold hair, a trimmed beard, eyes blue as agate. His stats were reasonable. Some success in professional wrestling, black belt in aikido, a knowledge of sword play. He'd been a little overzealous in his last wrestling match, snapping his opponent's spine, rendering him paralysed from the waist down. He was lucky to have escaped prison, but his wrestling days were over. To Pritchard, he looked soft. Too fastidious about his appearance. Still, looks could fool.

Another was from Detroit. He looked the part. Scarred face, twisted nub of a nose, a boxer's brow. A foot shorter than Pritchard but wide and solid. Low centre of gravity. Someone difficult to knock down. A heavyweight boxer turned cage fighter, appearing in contests up and down the East Coast. He'd killed someone during a fight. Broke the guy's neck.

The third was from New York. Muscular to the point of ungainly, only an inch shorter than Pritchard. A face of chiselled bone, thin lips, head shaved to the skull. Expressionless. Eyes like obsidian beads. Neck of corded muscle. Champion boxer in the US Marines. Dishonourable discharge after alleged abuse of prisoners in Afghanistan. Expert in judo.

Three men who were desperate. Who needed the money because their livelihoods had dried up. Such were those who were tempted to the Glass Box. Which set him apart. Money, though important, was of little consequence to Pritchard. He went to satisfy a much more fundamental need.

He wondered what the others would make of his stats and

photos. Easy meat, probably. He was big, heavily muscled. Looked ungainly. Clumsy, almost. Beyond that there was little else. He had never boxed professionally, wasn't experienced in martial arts. His history was a blank sheet. But Pritchard had fought and won many times in the Glass Box. He was gifted in the process. *Gifted*. He liked that word. Dispensing death came easy to him. He was Titan. He was invincible. He was a fucking god.

# 58

---

They would come from the main road, through the heaviest forest. This had been Smith's assumption. His reasoning was simple. It was probably the most difficult route, with no discernable trails, the trees packed close together, uphill terrain, and therefore the least expected. Plus, it was what he would do if roles were reversed. The fact they came in the afternoon, however, came as a shock. He hadn't yet contacted the man called Jacob with his location, but they knew where he was, which suggested they had been given this information by a third party, raising a grim possibility. Suddenly the game had altered.

He had been lucky. He had made his way towards the main road, merely to convince himself that the route was tough enough to justify his theory. He'd spotted a man studying a map. Then others, waiting, maybe fifteen feet apart, classic formation. They didn't look right. This was not a group of hill walkers out for a leisurely afternoon trek. Their demeanour was rigid, focused. Committed. Plus, the satchels slung across their backs had all the hallmarks of rifle bags. Four men out for a little mayhem. There may have been others, spread wider, but

Smith didn't think so. A four-man team was a good number. Enough to move quickly, not enough to cause suspicion.

Sheer luck that Smith had seen them. But then, he mused, he had always been lucky when it came to killing the enemy. They had been about two miles from the cabin. Smith had darted back, the last half mile almost a sprint. He had little time to organise. The trick was to confuse. He had switched the CD player on, and suddenly the forest was alive with heavy rock. This would mask noise and distract their attention. An enemy bewildered was an enemy vulnerable.

He had raced back to the verge of the forest, a distance of about two hundred yards from the cabin. He wore a pale green tight-fitting pullover, green hard-wearing hiking trousers, blending well with the land. The forest was dense with Scots pine. He had chosen one thick with foliage and low branches. He had climbed a height of twenty feet, allowing a good vantage of the clearing to the cabin and the cabin itself. There, he had waited, perched in the branches, shrouded in twig and pine needles, virtually invisible.

And then they came.

———

Smith watched. Four men, stealthy, creeping from the line of trees into long grass and shrubs, silent as shadows, heading towards the cabin. No doubting their intentions. Each carried a rifle. Looked like Remington bolt-actions. Muscle weapons for long-range action. Looked like his new guests were in a killing mood.

One of them – the leader, Smith assumed – raised a hand. They were about thirty yards from Smith's position. They stopped in unison, forming a line. The leader waved his hand. They crept towards him. *Well trained*, thought Smith. *Probably ex-forces*. They hunkered down, formed a loose huddle. The leader was speaking to them, issuing instructions. Impossible to make out what was being said. The music drowned out everything. They nodded. An understanding was reached. The leader ditched the rifle, pulled out a pistol, hid it under his jacket. He made his way towards the cabin. The way he walked with a stiff gait, his torso bulked up, Smith guessed he was wearing a Kevlar. Wise, under the circumstances.

The music had created bewilderment, but not enough to deter them. They would know he was near. Either in the cabin or close to it. Caution would dictate they hold back, assimilate. But they hadn't. Which meant they were in a hurry, and the reward for Smith's life was big enough to take a risk. They were bringing the situation out. Bringing things to a head. After all, they had superior men and superior firepower. How could they fail? Such were the thoughts running through Smith's mind.

One of the men followed the first, keeping well behind, clutching his rifle. The remaining two fanned out, weapons ready. Smith made his move. He picked his way down through the branches. His assailants wouldn't hear a thing. He jumped to the ground, kept low. In his right hand, the hunting knife. The closest man was now about fifty yards away. He had assumed a cross-legged position, standard sniper's pose when the target was on higher ground, elbows resting on each knee to stabilise. He had a clear line of vision to the cabin, unrestricted.

Smith ran in a half crouch. Twenty yards. Ahead, the first man was stepping onto his front porch. Smith continued. Ten yards. Suddenly, the music stopped. The CD player had been turned off. Smith sprinted, aware of the noise he was creating. But he was too close to care. The sniper turned his head, his expression a mixture of shock and fear. Too late. Smith thrust the knife up through the man's chin, the blade piercing mouth, palate, nasal cavity, then withdrew and stabbed him in the neck. The entire action took two seconds. Exactly as Smith had been trained. A soundless kill. The man fell back onto the grass, blood soaking the soil.

Smith got the rifle. Three men remaining. Odds had improved. One at the cabin, the second trailing a little behind, the third knuckled down somewhere in the light bushes. Smith, with exquisite care, moved to his right in a direction roughly at right angles to the cabin. The music had been silenced. He was conscious of his every step, every twig he brushed against. Slowly, slowly. He heard, not far off, the rattle of his cabin door as the first guy rapped at it hard. Smith eased forward, undeterred. There! A figure assuming the same position as his deceased friend. Sitting, Indian style, elbows on knees, rifle pointed at Smith's front door, body rigid in concentration. Torso padded up with a Kevlar.

Smith stopped, knelt, raised his rifle. He heard his cabin door open. *Rude of them.* He aimed. The sniper was maybe forty feet away. Smith relaxed, breathed in, out. He squeezed the trigger, gentle as a whisper. The sound split the silence, stark and clear. The side of the guy's face vanished in a spume of bright colour. Smith stood up, rotated, aimed, fired again. The one following the leader had turned at the sound of the rifle shot, then crumpled, head shattered like an egg. The first guy, who was on his porch, tried to duck inside the cabin. Smith adjusted his aim, fired a third time. The guy collapsed, right leg disintegrated. Smith crouched down, waited thirty seconds. No other movement. He stood and advanced.

---

Smith got to the cabin. The guy was sprawled on the floor. His trouser leg was saturated. The bullet had entered the upper hamstring, detaching the limb. A testament to the power of the Remington.

The man groaned, tried to crawl, managed about two inches. Grasped in his hand, a Desert Eagle. Smith stepped forward, pressed his foot on the man's wrist, tugged the pistol from his fingers.

Smith picked it up. "Quite a weapon. I have a feeling you and your chums aren't Jehovah's Witnesses."

The man tried to speak, sputtered up a volume of phlegm.

"Cat caught your tongue?" said Smith. "I understand. The Remington 700 has the ability to render someone speechless."

Smith bent, grabbed the back of the man's ski jacket, hauled him round. The guy screamed. Smith allowed himself a cold smile.

"Sorry, old boy." He straightened. "You have a name?"

The man stared back, face pale and clenched with pain. He was losing blood fast. He had perhaps a minute left, perhaps less. Then unconsciousness, then death.

"I take it you're an acquaintance of Jacob? Yes?"

The man blew through his mouth, mustering the energy to speak. "Hospital."

Smith gave a short, harsh laugh. "That would be something. Not an option today. I think it's farewell for you."

The man swallowed, gave a dry cough. "Please."

Smith leaned in close. "Tell me, my friend, what would you do if you were me? I'm interested to hear your views on the matter. Nothing? My sentiments exactly."

Smith brought the rifle up, shot him in the forehead.

He took a deep breath. Four dead men. Old habits die hard. Strange, he thought, how some skills never left. He took out his mobile phone and tapped in the number belonging to the man called Jacob. It was picked up immediately.

"Hello again," Smith said.

A pause, then, "You met my friends."

"They weren't convivial. Our acquaintance was brief but

conclusive. Though one of them made a dreadful mess of my porch."

"That's a shame. Send me the bill. Or better, I can have someone come round."

"Maybe some other time. I was expecting your friends a little later."

"Call it a surprise visit."

"Thanks for that," Smith replied. "But still, I can't help wonder."

"I can imagine," said the man called Jacob. "You're not an easy man to find. Can't you guess?"

Smith took another deep breath, dreading what was to come next. He said nothing.

"She was chatty," continued Jacob. "Informative. And I love her artwork."

Smith spoke. "She likes the mountains." His voice dropped low. "Did you kill her?"

Silence. Smith waited.

"Alison is looking forward to seeing you. She says hi."

"That's nice. And?"

"Here's the situation, Mr Smith. Alison is currently enjoying our hospitality. Maybe enjoyment is the wrong word. But at least she's safe. For now. But her continued safety is fragile. You understand? What happens next is entirely up to you. It's rather simple. You and I meet. We chat. In return, Alison gets to go back to... her life. Like nothing happened. You get the drift?"

Smith kept his voice neutral. "Like nothing happened? You forget. You murdered her son. Or did it slip your mind?"

"The position remains. You come to me. In return, Alison doesn't linger in our company any longer than she has to."

"Like a trade?"

"That's one way of describing it."

"That's the only way to describe it. Here's the situation,

Jacob. You do what you have to do with Alison. That's fine. Because the way I see it, you're going to kill her anyway. But that doesn't remove your problem. Which is me. Who do you think I am? I'm nobody. I'm off the grid. I'm *elusive*. And I'll keep coming, Jacob. And I'll find you. Make no mistake. Because I'm good at finding people. You'll get up in the morning and wonder if you'll see nightfall. You'll go to sleep and wonder if you'll see daylight. I'm the cold whisper on your shoulder. Welcome to the rest of your life, Jacob."

Smith disconnected. He breathed, calmed. He sat on the chair on the porch and waited. He had dead men around him. Death followed him like a shadow, destroying everything it touched.

Paul had died. A fourteen-year-old innocent. Smith blamed himself. The kid wanted to impress him and in so doing, wound up dead. Now his mother. By merely getting involved, Smith, unwittingly, had orchestrated their doom.

The old fear rose up, a cold flutter in his chest. Fear not for himself, but for those he cared about. For Alison. Fear brought indecision, inertia. In his head he recited the litany, *The fear is in my mind...*

Then his mobile buzzed. And the situation turned from the desperate to the surreal.

## 59

Purkis got the call from Jacob. Not what he was expecting. The mercenaries were dead. The fact that Alison was effectively a prisoner seemed to hold no sway. Out there, somewhere, roamed a loose cannon intent on destruction. Four men dead. Each armed and experienced. *Who the hell was this John Smith?* The man was clearly skilled. And resourceful. Purkis listened in silence as Jacob explained the situation. On such occasions, silence was often the best way to communicate his disappointment. Which, in this case, was profound. Purkis asked for Smith's number. He hung up. Another tact was required.

A sudden thought occurred to him. Too outrageous to consider, and which he dismissed instantly. But still... John Smith was a common name. Probably the most common name in the Western hemisphere. He shook his head. The notion was ridiculous. Far-fetched. He shoved it from his mind and adjusted his thoughts to his new guest, and how she could still prove useful.

Purkis sent a text – *I'm in the conservatory*.

A minute later, there was a soft knock on the door. Mr Halliday entered.

"Where are our American friends?" Purkis asked.

"Splashing in the pool, Mr Purkis," replied Halliday.

"Let's visit our new guest." Halliday, a man not given to chatter, merely nodded. He followed Purkis out of the conservatory, a great hulking shadow. They made their way to another section of the castle – across a small courtyard of grey flagstones, to a red-bricked building with a single barred window and a heavy wooden door with top and bottom bolt latches.

Purkis stepped to one side. Halliday slid the latches, opened the door. They entered, Halliday first. The interior was comfortable – less austere than one would have assumed. A room of regular dimensions, soft beige carpet, a slate-grey Italian leather corner sofa, coffee table, television, bookshelf, coffee machine. Even a cute bijou fridge, stocked up with mineral water. A small end-suite bathroom and shower. *A gilded prison cell,* thought Purkis.

On the sofa sat a woman. Alison Davidson. On the coffee table was an opened bottle of water. She looked at the two men, face pale and sharp, lacking expression. *The eyes.* The eyes reveal all. Purkis saw nothing. Perhaps a quiet calmness. But no fear. He had to admire her composure.

Halliday moved to the side of the door. Purkis took centre stage.

"I trust Mr Halliday was a perfect gentleman?"

She seemed to consider the question. She responded in a toneless voice. "Is that his name? The first man I met pulled a gun on me and said if I didn't go with him he would kill me. He said his name was William Bryce, which he then changed to Jacob, so I think instantly he's a lying bastard. Then he introduced me to your friend Mr Halliday. He threatened to kill me, too, unless I did as I was told. He drove me here, again under the threat of death, to this place. Then he locked me in and told me, in a nice way, that if I caused any trouble he would snap my neck. Other than that, yes. A perfect gentleman."

Purkis gave a laugh, though it had a tinny undertone. "His manner can be a little gruff. He takes some getting used to. But you've arrived in one piece, and that's all that's important."

"Why am I here?"

"Direct. I like direct. Are you hungry?"

"No."

Purkis smiled. "Well then. You must understand, Alison, that we find ourselves in an awkward situation. To have this 'awkward situation' removed requires your assistance. Which is why you're here. To offer your assistance."

She stared at him. Her expression remained blank. "Offer? It doesn't feel like that. This awkward situation you mention. You mean John Smith. He's causing you trouble, yes? From which I assume you were involved."

Purkis raised an eyebrow, regarded her curiously. "Involved?"

"In the murder of my son."

Purkis pursed his lips, shook his head a fraction. "Your son? I'm sorry, but I believe you're misguided. I don't know anything about your son." He lowered his voice to a respectful tone. "Or his murder. But yes, you're correct. This man called John Smith seems to be the source of the trouble."

She snapped back an answer. "In which case go to the police like normal people, instead of making threats and kidnapping."

He made a placatory gesture. "It's not the way we work. We prefer to deal with matters internally. But we would still like your assistance. You know this man. I believe he may have a connection with you. You can talk to him. Persuade him to come in."

"Come in?"

"Meet us. Talk this through. Try to understand his motivations. Come to a civilised resolution."

"Civilised? Interesting word. Seems a bit out of context. How do you think I'll persuade him? I barely know him. I don't know what you want me to do."

Purkis cast a meaningful glance at Halliday, who stood silent to one side, a sinister presence.

"I think you do, Alison," Purkis said quietly. He paused, gave a sigh. "Perhaps you're right. Perhaps we should cut the bullshit. I'll make this as clear as I can. If your friend John Smith doesn't agree to hand himself over to us, then Mr Halliday will fulfil his threat and snap your neck like a twig. Mr Halliday lacks empathy and will complete the task with as much remorse as he might killing a fly. You begin to understand the position you're in?"

She blinked. Her eyes welled up. "Yes."

"Comply and then there's no problem. I'm going to phone Smith on my mobile. I'm going to put it on loudspeaker. I'll hand you the phone. When he answers you will tell him that unless he arranges to hand himself over to us, you will die. It's as simple as that. Clear?"

She took another long breath, biting back tears. Her bottom lip quivered. "Yes." She looked up. "Please don't kill me."

Now, thought Purkis, the eyes showed him what he wanted. Fear.

"Tell me your name," she said. "I'd like to know. Please."

It hardly mattered, thought Purkis. "Apologies. That was remiss. My name is Chadwick Purkis. Perhaps later, once all this nonsense is over, we can get to know each other."

She nodded, said nothing.

Purkis tapped in the number Jacob had given him. The number of John Smith. He tapped 'loudspeaker', handed it to Alison. She held it flat in the palm of her hand, close to her mouth. It rang three times, then was answered. Silence. She looked at Purkis. Purkis nodded, encouraging her to speak. Halliday stood close by, implacable. Terrifying.

"John?"

Silence.

"It's Alison."

Then, "Have they harmed you?"

"No."

"Where are you?"

"In some place in Perth. I was blindfolded for the last bit. They told me to phone you. I'm with two men. They've threatened to kill me." Her expression changed. She looked almost amused. Purkis was puzzled at her transformation. The puzzlement became enlightenment.

*Bravo,* thought Purkis. Her fear had been an act, performed well. But he let it play.

"One of the men is called Halliday," she said. She focused her attention on him. "He's big and stupid and looks like a fucking ape." She switched to Purkis and made sure she was looking him straight in the eye when she spoke, a small, serene smile never leaving her lips. "The other is an arrogant tosspot called Chadwick Purkis. They're scared of you, John. They know you're coming for them. And they're desperate. They murdered Paul. Kill them both."

# 60

Smith said nothing, mind churning. Coincidence? Possibly. He composed his thoughts, spoke in a carefully modulated voice.

"Gladly. Chadwick Purkis? That's an unusual name. This is on speaker? I once knew someone called Chadwick Purkis. The same Chadwick Purkis who was stabbed in the guts one summer afternoon for being in the wrong place at the wrong time?"

He picked up a rustle from the other end, indicating activity – the sound of the phone being moved.

He waited. A voice spoke.

"You're right. Wrong place, wrong time."

"Is this Chadwick Purkis?"

"Is this John Smith?"

Smith allowed himself a frosty smile. "The very one. How you been keeping? It's been a while."

"Good to hear the sound of your voice again, Johnny. Imagine that. After all those years. Now how do we sort this mess out?"

## 61

$S$ mith took five seconds to formulate a response. It was an effort to keep his voice in check.

"You've been busy," he said.

"Getting very rich, John. Life's good. Thanks to you. You gave me a second chance."

"And remember how you repaid me."

"To teach you a lesson. And what a lesson that was, Johnny. Did you ever think I could be so creative? It was sheer genius. But you had to be taught. Don't trust anyone. That's the golden rule."

"The golden rule. I'll remember that. Next time I'll be sure to finish what I started."

"But you didn't finish. That was your problem. You didn't see things through to their end."

Smith kept his voice low when he replied. "There's a village in Afghanistan which can testify to that."

"That was long ago."

"Five years and twenty-six days."

"You're counting. I get that. I really do. Come in, Johnny.

I'm not going to harm you. Just maybe we can come to an arrangement, which would suit both of us."

"You've just told me to trust no one."

A harsh laugh. "Let it go. That was long ago. I want peace. I don't want conflict."

"I'm sure you don't," said Smith. "And Alison?"

"She's fine. You come in, to me, we'll let her go."

"Just like that?"

"Just like that."

Smith looked up at the sky. It was late afternoon. Clouds were gathering like patches of gauze, blocking the sun, reducing the light to a sullen grey. Suddenly, the air felt cold. If there was a god, he thought, then he played a devilish game. Smith searched the clouds, the sky, but found no answers. He had no place to go. No tricks to play. He was dancing to the tune of a psychotic, and there was nothing he could do. He cursed his incompetence. He should have anticipated Alison being used as leverage. He should have got her away to somewhere safe, before he embarked on his voyage of retribution.

His fault. All his fault. A repeat performance of what had taken place five years ago.

He was venturing into the lair of a monster. Perhaps, he thought ruefully, this was the only way.

He took a deep breath. "How does this work?"

"That's it, Johnny, I knew you'd see sense. You're at the cabin? Stay there. Jacob will come and get you. He'll be with some men. You don't need to worry."

"But I do worry."

"Of course you do. It's your nature."

---

Smith had four dead bodies to deal with. He had a shovel he kept in a crawl space under the cabin. He buried three of them where they lay. Shallow graves. They would be found in time, perhaps, but he didn't care. He had other worries to preoccupy him. There was a fair chance he'd be dead before the day had finished.

He rolled each man into a hole, covered them up. He dragged the last one off his porch, the guy's head slapping on each step like a wet sponge. He buried him under a bush behind the cabin.

He got a half bottle of Glenmorangie whisky from his only cupboard. He'd brought it with him when he'd moved into his retreat in the mountains and hadn't touched it, planning to drink it when he had something worth drinking for. Well, he thought, if now was not the time, when was? With the exception of the cold beer he'd had at Alison's, he hadn't touched alcohol for five years. Now seemed a fitting time. He poured some into a tumbler, sat on the seat on his porch. He sipped. It tasted good. He thought back, to another world, to another time, to the nightmare he'd spent five years running from. The details were still fresh despite his efforts to forget. Fresh and clear. A fearful clarity. From the beginning – from his failure to complete his duty – to the end. To a room in an Afghan village.

A room beyond all comprehension.

# 62

Arrangements were made. Jacob, to his surprise, was instructed to fetch the man called John Smith. To add to his surprise, Purkis told him Smith was not to be harmed. That Smith would not present any trouble. Jacob, always cautious – and sceptical – armed himself regardless. Two cars, three men in each. Men forming part of Chadwick Purkis's private security team. Glorified bouncers in Jacob's opinion. But then Leo Ruckert and his men were hardly that and, if Smith were to be believed, were all dead. Safety in numbers, he thought.

To get to Smith's cabin, Jacob took a more civilised route. He knew the coordinates. He drove the single-lane track direct from Aviemore, parked at a location about a mile from the cabin, which was about the closest a car could get, then he and the others walked the rest.

They made their way along trails winding through thick forest. They arrived at a clearing. In it stood a log-built cabin house. Close by, a lochan the size of a swimming pool. Jacob had taken care to study the map. He knew they were close to Loch an Eilein, but far enough off the beaten track to avoid any casual hikers.

They approached. There on the porch sat a man. He seemed relaxed. He could have been contemplating the view.

Jacob drew his gun. "Mr Smith."

The man nodded, stood. "Jacob?"

"Yes."

"It's always nice to put a name to a face."

"I quite agree," Jacob replied. He appraised the man before him. Tall, maybe six two. Wearing outdoor garments of neutral colours – trekking trousers, close-fitting pullover, mountain boots. Unobtrusively muscular, harsh cheekbones, thick dark hair cropped short. A man, thought Jacob, who exuded lethal competence. He understood now how Ruckert ended up as he did.

"You've met my friends already," said Jacob. "Apologies for any inconvenience they may have caused."

"Not at all. They were very obliging. They died exactly when they were supposed to."

"Of course. Please come down from the porch."

Smith followed the instructions. One of the men approached, patted him down, searching for concealed weapons. He nodded to Jacob.

Jacob then stepped onto the porch, opened the cabin door, had a quick scan inside, went back out.

"There's blood on the floor," he remarked.

"I'll get that cleaned up later," Smith said.

Jacob smiled. "I'm sure you will. And the bodies?"

"I wouldn't worry too much about that."

Jacob made a polite assent, stepped off the porch to stand five feet away from Smith, still holding his pistol, men on either side.

"Mr Purkis has instructed us to ensure that you come to no harm."

"Glad to hear it," said Smith. "He wouldn't want me to

stub my toe. You'd better be careful, Jacob. You don't want to upset your boss."

"I'm a careful man, Mr Smith. Excessively so. Perhaps you would care to come with us. Maybe we can chit-chat later."

"I would like that," Smith said. "Very much."

They moved off, six men and John Smith, Jacob directly behind him, pistol at his back. Nothing was said. They moved at a brisk pace, the sound of their boots on the grass and dirt.

They arrived at the cars a half hour later. Two Range Rovers. Smith, politely, was gestured into the back of one of them, which he acceded to without complaint. Jacob sat on one side of him, a man on the other. A third sat in the front passenger seat. A fourth drove. The two remaining men got in the other car.

The cars lurched and bumped along the track, heading for Aviemore.

Smith turned to Jacob on his right. "This is cosy. Are we going far?"

"Not far," said Jacob. He still held the pistol, pointed in the vicinity of Smith's ribcage.

"I hope you've got the safety on," Smith said.

"As I said, I'm a careful man."

"Vincent Docherty and I had quite a conversation back at the Crafty Fox. He was… how can I put it… keen to unburden his soul."

"Now I know you have a sense of humour, Mr Smith – Vincent Docherty didn't have a soul."

"If he did," Smith said, "I helped it on its way. He mentioned your name. He gave me the strong impression you and another man called Halliday murdered a young boy called Paul. I would be interested to get your take on it."

"I can barely remember what I had for breakfast."

"I understand. You live a busy life. You should have done it back at the cabin."

Jacob was puzzled. "What's that?"

"Shoot me. It would have been the wise move."

Jacob fixed Smith a level stare. Smith's eyes were as cold as flint.

"Why?" said Jacob.

"Because I intend to kill you, Jacob."

"As I said, Mr Smith, you have a sense of humour. Where did you learn your skills?"

"Here and there."

Jacob nodded slowly. "I too have skills, of a similar vein."

"That's good. You'll need them."

Nothing more was said. The man in the passenger seat put the radio on. Jacob suspected Smith was right. A bullet in the back of the head at the cabin would have resolved the issue. But Purkis wanted Smith alive, for reasons unknown.

Jacob had a bad feeling in his guts. Smith seemed impervious to fear. This wasn't over, he thought. There was more to come, and Jacob didn't like it one bit.

## 63

A lison was taken from the room, Chadwick Purkis at her side, and Halliday following her closely. They were joined by another man, dressed in a sombre dark suit, hair cropped in a crew cut, face stern as stone. Extra security, she presumed.

She'd heard the conversation between Purkis and John Smith, was barely able to comprehend it. They knew each other? The world had turned mad. Or else she was insane. But still, despite the surreal quality of events, her mind was consumed by one burning thought which would never leave.

"He's still going to kill you," she said. "For the murder of my son. And if he doesn't, I will."

"Brave words," replied Purkis. "But the past is the past. You'll meet John presently and then we can all have a civilised conversation. Over dinner, I think."

"Fuck your dinner."

Chadwick gave a rasping chuckle, like the turn of rusty wheels. "You have spirit, I'll say that."

"Say what you want. I don't give a shit."

Chadwick glanced over his shoulder to Halliday. "She's a wild one." Halliday remained unresponsive.

"Fuck you," said Alison.

"They break wild horses. Don't make me break you, Alison. At least not before dinner." The smile never left Chadwick's face when he said this. Alison wondered if she had ever encountered anyone more terrifying.

She said nothing. She was in the realm of monsters, but this didn't scare her. What did scare her was them killing her before she avenged her son.

They entered the main building, walked along a high-ceilinged hallway to a set of wide, carpeted stairs, ascending in a gentle spiral. Something out of a Hollywood movie set, she thought. They went up to the first floor, to a bedroom considerably more lavish than the one she'd just left.

"You'll be more comfortable here, I think. Dinner at 9pm? Someone will be here to collect you. Enjoy. Make yourself comfortable."

They left her in the room, locking the door behind them. Despite the splendour, she was still a prisoner. The room was spacious. Four-poster bed, velvet drapes on stained-glass windows, heavy timber rafters criss-crossing the ceiling. *Medieval*, she thought. But the décor wasn't on her mind. She sat on the bed and wept.

---

She must have fallen into a light doze. She woke, checked her watch. She'd been sleeping for an hour. In one corner was a tufted chaise longue. Across it, placed with care, a pale green dress of silky fine chiffon, matching heels. Someone had been in the room. She looked at it and felt disgusted. She wanted to tear it to shreds. But she also wanted to survive. Because death was too easy. She went to the en suite, turned the shower on, and decided she would play the part – if only to extend her life long enough the see Chadwick and his accomplices die.

## 64

When Purkis left Alison in her new quarters, he gave instructions to Halliday, who was to inform the American guests he would not, regrettably, be able to join them for dinner in the evening. Matters would, however, proceed as normal, and he would meet them tomorrow for the fun and games in the Glass Box. The other man stationed himself outside Alison's room.

Purkis made arrangements. Specifically, dinner to be set for three in the conservatory. He then retreated to his library and sat at the window observing the fairy garden. Matters had taken a bizarre twist, one he could never have anticipated.

Jacob had phoned in. They would be arriving in an hour. Smith had given no trouble. Not so far, at any rate. Purkis pondered. If their places were exchanged, and he had been in Smith's position, he would have let the girl die. Such was the obvious move. But he didn't possess Smith's chivalrous attitude. And all this over a boy. A nobody. *An inconsequential.* Purkis smiled. He knew his adversary. Incapable of letting things go. Obstinate, some might say. To Purkis, just plain stupid. That, however, was the issue. John Smith was as tenacious as a terrier.

Purkis gave a long sigh. Rain pattered on the window. He was not prone to nostalgic bouts of introspection. Nevertheless, his thoughts were drawn back to his past. In particular, one fateful and momentous day in a public park, over thirty years ago. When everything changed for him. He remembered each detail. A hot and sticky summer's day. The sky a sheet of blue canvas. How thirsty he was. Then the surprise. The surprise turning quickly to fear. How events seemed to unfold beyond his control. The flash of the blade. The blood. A fresh and vivid colour. A colour that never quite leaves the memory, he thought. Indelible. Like a stain that won't wash away.

John Smith. Who would have thought? God played a quirky hand. But Purkis didn't believe in God. He believed in himself. And his capabilities. John Smith was a problem. An unexpected but interesting problem. And Purkis had an uncompromising attitude towards problems. Crush them. Like Tony French. Like the boy running on the road. Like a thousand others. Crush them. And move on.

Such was the world of Chadwick Purkis.

## 65

Purkis's home was five miles outside the city of Perth. It was invisible from the main thoroughfare, and accessed by a mile-long private road, winding through carefully managed woodland that eventually reached a fairy-tale castle set in a fairy-tale garden. Smith was impressed.

"Life's been good to your employer," he remarked. "His very own fortress."

"Mr Purkis has worked hard," replied Jacob.

"I'm sure he has. Blood, sweat and tears. Plenty of blood, for sure."

Jacob gave the tiniest shrug but made no response.

The cars passed the front of the building, continued round to a secluded parking area enclosed by high ivy-clad walls. Smith, escorted by Jacob and five men, was led through a side entrance, through a narrow hallway, and into an oak-panelled room devoid of furniture. In the centre, standing with hands clasped behind his back, was a man; heavyset, great hulking shoulders. Dressed in an elegant dark suit that was at odds with his flat, moonish face and round button-black eyes.

"This is Mr Halliday," said Jacob. "He'll escort you to your room."

Smith regarded the man called Mr Halliday. "I hope we get to know each other. Vincent Docherty mentioned your name. Not with any great fondness, I might add. Though he didn't warn me about your general ugliness. Perhaps, in future, you might consider wearing a bag? With holes, obviously, to allow you to see. People would thank you. They really would. Me especially."

Halliday's face didn't register, his expression bland.

"Please come with me, Mr Smith."

Smith followed him. Three of the men followed Smith. They emerged into a cathedral-style landing, the walls lined with bright tapestries fastened to silver rods. They went up a flight of stairs, along a further hallway, reaching a heavy oak door. Halliday unlocked it, gestured Smith with a tilt of his head. Smith smiled politely and entered.

"Dinner's at 9.10. Someone will come for you," Halliday said.

"Can't wait. And remember the bag. Otherwise you'll frighten the guests."

Halliday's gaze lingered on Smith. Whether he felt anger, or even irritation was impossible to say. His face could have been formed from stone. He left, the key turning in the lock.

The room was spacious and comfortable, complete with en suite. Smith went to the window, enclosed by bars, and looked out at the scenery before him. It seemed Chadwick Purkis had a keen interest in gardens. He wondered how many lives had been ruined to pay for the arbours and summer houses and pergolas. Too many to count.

Somewhere in the building, he hoped, Alison still lived and breathed. If so, there was a chance. He adjusted his thoughts. The reality was, there was little chance. He was in the lair of a monster. Difficult to see where his options lay. He thought back again to the pale, lifeless body of Paul, dumped by the roadside like a piece of garbage. He straightened. He would find options. He'd been trained all his life to do exactly that. And where there were options, there was hope.

---

Jacob joined Purkis in the library. He sat opposite, and for a brief second stared through the window at the gardens beyond.

"Your geraniums are dying."

"Everything dies, Jacob, or hadn't you noticed? Smith presented no difficulties?"

"Good as gold. Though a bit lippy. We have containment. Hard to imagine that such a man, after killing Ruckert and his men, should surrender so easily. Equally hard is understanding why you didn't want him killed when we had the chance."

"We have the boy's mother. He had no choice but to surrender."

"Still, he must have known that by coming here he was doomed. That we could never let the woman go. Unless he's stupid, or brave, or unbelievably noble."

Purkis chuckled. "Maybe all three. And something else."

Jacob said nothing.

"I know John Smith. We go… way back."

Jacob raised his eyebrows. *My*, thought Purkis. *A reaction. A rare event.*

Jacob nodded slowly. "An old acquaintance?"

"You could say that."

"You understand this man is on a crusade. He's crazy. He's the type that doesn't switch off."

"Unless we press the switch," said Purkis.

"In which case, if you don't mind me asking, why didn't you want him killed?"

Purkis brushed away non-existent specks from his lap.

"As I said, we go way back. An opportunity has arisen, a one in a million chance, and I can't waste it. It's important I see him again. To reminisce. To rekindle old memories. And to give him an answer."

Another raised eyebrow. "An answer? I don't understand."

"I don't expect you to."

Jacob was silent for a short spell, then spoke. "He's dangerous. You pay me to protect you. We should kill him now. I can send Mr Halliday and within the hour we'll have Smith's ashes scattered across your flower beds."

"Do you believe in God, Jacob?"

Jacob's face showed no reaction at the sudden switch in conversation. "Not instantly."

"Nor me. But Smith was sent here. Call it fate. Or destiny. Or karma. But if there is a God, I'm not passing up on this gift dropped in my lap."

"Gift?"

"Revenge, Jacob. The best gift of all."

## 66

At 9.10pm, as arranged, a key rattled and the door opened. Jacob stood, beckoned Smith. Smith obliged and followed him from the room. There, waiting in the hall, were six men. All smartly dressed. Dark suits, crisp white shirts, dark ties. They escorted Smith, surrounding him like a school of sharks, guiding him along the passageway, Jacob at the head. They made their way back down the stairs, through an arched doorway into another passage of plain stucco walls with doors on either side, then emerged into a much grander area – another hall, with a lofty ceiling from which hung candle chandeliers, the flames flickering like stars. In alcoves, Smith noted, stood armoured statues complete with broadswords.

They passed through, then entered another room. A large conservatory. There, a rectangular table with room for eight. Only three settings. Plates, cutlery, wine glasses. On one side, facing him, Alison. She looked up. Her eyes brightened. A glimmer of a smile. At one end sat another. A man, lean and sinewy. Tanned. Greying hair swept back from his forehead like a wave. Sharp cheekbones, chin tapering to a point. He turned his head when Smith and his entourage entered. His lips stretched into a smile.

"Welcome, John Smith."

"You're looking fit," Smith said.

"I run six miles every day," replied Purkis. "On the treadmill. Please, sit." He gestured Smith to the other end of the table. Smith gave a polite nod, made his way over. The men around him dispersed, stationing themselves in a prearranged format – two behind Purkis, two behind Smith, two at the door. Jacob stood a little off to the side, watching events from a wider perspective.

Smith sat. He smiled at Alison, switched his attention to Purkis. "Treadmill? You should try road running. Perhaps not. The traffic can be dangerous."

Purkis's smile broadened. "Deadly. How have you been, Johnny? You look well. Outdoor living is doing you good."

"Never been better." Smith switched his attention to Alison. "Have you been harmed?"

"They murdered my son. Other than that, I'm fine."

Purkis laughed out loud. A harsh, raw sound. "You must stop living in the past. We're here to enjoy the present. Fine food. Fine company." He put both elbows on the table, leaned forward. "I hope you like red wine."

A man appeared with a bottle, poured the contents into the three glasses, left the bottle on the table.

"Merlot's my favourite," continued Purkis. "I've been keeping this one back for a special occasion. A thousand pounds a bottle." He raised his glass, focused on Smith. "Here's to us, Johnny. Reunited."

Smith raised his glass, met Purkis's stare, allowed a half smile. "Here's to the death of twisted psychotics."

"I'll drink to that," said Alison.

Purkis reacted with more laughter. "I think you're ganging up on me."

"Is this really a thousand a bottle?" asked Alison.

"At least."

She poured the contents of her glass onto the floor. "Oops."

Purkis clapped his hands. "Isn't she wonderful!"

Smith said nothing. Purkis sipped, placed the glass on the table. Smith chose not to partake.

"Not drinking?" said Purkis. "It's exquisite."

"Maybe later."

"Quite right. Temperance. Discipline. That's the key to success. I thought we'd skip the starters and dive straight to the main. You both must be famished. Especially you, John, with all that exercise you've had in the woods today."

Smith gave the merest shrug of his shoulders. "You would send people to kill me. I suppose it works up an appetite."

The man who had brought the wine appeared with a trolley carrying three plates of food and an assortment of side dishes, which he distributed on the table.

"I hope you like T-bone. Done medium rare, the way it should be. I thought to myself, what should I feed my new guests? And then I thought, something I would like. Something simple, but satisfying. Something an ex-army man would like. Yes, John?"

Smith said nothing. Despite himself, he *was* famished. He ate. Alison pushed her plate to one side.

"Not hungry, Alison?" said Purkis.

"Not really. Eating beside you makes me feel nauseous."

"Your choice. But you really ought to. The body needs nourishment. Isn't that right, Johnny? When you're out in the badlands, deep in enemy territory, you learn to eat what you can. They train you to eat things that would make a billy goat puke. Did you know John was in the army?"

Alison said nothing. She looked pale and drawn. *This is killing her*, thought Smith.

Purkis continued, speaking through mouthfuls of food, clearly enjoying himself.

"I've being doing a little research on dear Johnny boy. Not difficult, if you pay the right money to the right folk. He's led an interesting career." Alison stared at Smith as Purkis spoke.

"There's no need for this," said Smith quietly.

"But there's every need. I want Alison to know about her new best friend. John left school and went to Sandhurst. Officer training. Then to the parachute regiment. I suppose young Johnny always wanted to jump out of planes. To me, a suicidal tendency. Lieutenant in Second Battalion. Promoted to captain. Then a little taste of counterterrorism. After that, he was accepted into the 22nd Special Air Service Regiment. Did you know that, Alison? Johnny was in the SAS. Scary. He showed uncommon valour in Sierra Leone, in the Occra Hills. The West Side Boys had kidnapped some hostages. John, with his band of merry men, parachuted in, rescued the hostages, and took out how many bad guys? A hundred? More? I suppose you lose count. Impressed, Alison?"

Alison said nothing, never once taking her eyes off Smith.

Purkis was enjoying himself. He ate with gusto, swallowing food down with gulps of wine. He topped up his glass, continued, "It gets better. Covert missions in Mogadishu and Bosnia. Then Iraq. Part of Task Force Kill. Deep behind the lines. Over thirty combat missions. And his job? To kill. Period. Because he was so damned good at it. But then, tragedy. Captured and held prisoner in Saddam's infamous *dungeons*. What happened, Johnny? A bit of torture? Mock executions. Water boarding. I heard Saddam introduced the rack to his prisons. Can you imagine? But guess what. Johnny boy escaped. Freed his men. Which earned him the Military Cross. Impressed yet, Alison?"

Alison remained silent.

"There's no point to this," Smith said.

"Indulge me," Purkis replied. "Please. So what did Johnny do? Retire? Resign? You could hardly blame him. No chance. Straight back in. This time, Afghanistan. Doing what he does. Excursions into hostile territory. Causing mischief and mayhem. Sprinkled with a good amount of killing. Because that's what John was skilled at. Killing. He and his team were known as *Hunters*. They hunted in little packs and destroyed everything in their way. And they really went to town. Nothing could hold John Smith back when it came to bloodshed."

Purkis put his knife and fork down, regarded Smith with a glittering gaze.

"And then we have the village of Zawa. You remember, Johnny? Where it all ended. Your final mission. When your neat little world caved in."

Silence. Smith took some wine. Suddenly, the palms of his hands felt clammy. A sound filled the silence – his heartbeat. Old memories. He spoke.

"A thousand a bottle? Think you've been scammed."

"What happened in Zawa?" Alison's voice sounded small and tight.

"Tell her what happened, Johnny. You have a captive audience."

Smith licked his lips, took a breath.

"You've given us a résumé of my life. Let me respond with what I know about your life. If that's all right?"

Purkis gave his beaming smile. "The stage is all yours."

"You're very kind." He turned his attention to Alison, who sat rigid, face set and focused on him.

"The man sitting beside us isn't Chadwick Purkis," he said. He paused, wondering how it had come to this.

"His real name is Billy Smith. Billy is my brother."

# 67

Alison remained still. Smith could not begin to conjecture the thoughts running through her mind.

He continued.

"When Billy was seventeen he was selling drugs to kids. I had a friend called Chadwick Purkis. By sheer chance, Chadwick and I stumbled across Billy dealing in a park. Billy stabbed Chadwick. Chadwick survived. Billy ran away. I never saw him again, until five years ago." He hesitated. "When everything changed…"

He took another drink. The wine glass trembled in his hand.

"What happened, John?" said Alison softly.

Smith held her stare. Memories, stark and clear, sprang up from the darkness.

*The mission was unusual. And possibly illegal. A grey area. One of those events the British army hoped would get consumed and forgotten through the general carnage of war.*

*Zawa. A village deep in the badlands of Afghanistan, in the Khogyani district. Approximately five-hundred occupants. Farmers. It had come to the attention of the Afghan authorities that the farmers of Zawa, and two neighbouring villages, were cultivating a large area of poppy fields for the production of heroin. In itself, nothing remarkable. Heroin was Afghanistan's biggest export. But Zawa was different. The drug cartel wasn't the Taliban. Rather, one individual heading a small band of mercenaries. A drug lord. And an outsider. A foreigner. Possibly a Brit or an American. And particularly vicious. This irked the Afghan government. On the outside, the manufacture of opium got the death penalty. On the inside, the government liked the vast profit it turned. In this particular instance they saw it as stolen revenue. But they also saw it as a problem to be dealt with by their Western allies. The British army agreed. The situation was a potential embarrassment.*

*The problem thus required solving.*

*Captain Smith commanded a tight unit of ten men. A hunter team. Covert. Highly effective. Their remit during the course of the war was to venture into enemy territory, cause disruption, return. Disruption was given a wide interpretation, involving generally the termination of warlords or Taliban or any other tribe of fundamentalists.*

*Killing a drug lord was a first. What made it unusual was that he was possibly a British subject. Also, the poppy fields had to be destroyed and the villagers persuaded to use the land for legitimate purposes. Between Smith and his men, they carried a hundred thousand American dollars. Compensation, explained Smith's commanding officer. The reality – bribe money to get the village elders to change their ways. Fat chance, thought Smith.*

*They had no photographs of their target. The implication therefore was to kill whoever they thought appropriate. He was, however, given a potential location. Five miles from Zawa in a compound nestled amongst low hills and scrub.*

*They set off from Jalalabad, a distance of approximately thirty miles. They travelled by night, hunkered down during the day, camouflaged and invisible. If they were caught by Taliban then death was immediate. Beheading, their heads displayed as trophies. Incentive was high to remain undetected.*

*Three nights. They arrived at their destination on the third night. A group of flat-roofed structures in a square area an acre in size, enclosed by six-foot-high walls and a metal gate the width of two cars. They'd studied aerial pictures of the place and knew the layout.*

*Two sentries standing outside. Smoking, chatting. Complacent. The massive chink in their armour – they thought they were invincible.*

*His men split into groups. Four at the front, three on either side. The sentries were easy kills. Two head shots from fifty yards, the sound of the rifle discharge no louder than two soft coughs.*

*They advanced as quietly as whispers. Over the wall. Converging. They were in a small courtyard. Another man wobbling on his feet, having a piss in a corner. Too much red wine, thought Smith. Shame. The man never got to finish, five bullets in the back, collapsing in his own urine. Another appeared from behind a corner, a bottle of beer in his hand. Maybe it was party night. The man's face for that fleeting second was almost comical, flashing from languid ease to dramatic shock. A bullet in the neck and two in the upper chest. He dropped, dead before he knew it.*

*Three buildings. Large structures. A dog began to bark. It hardly mattered. They took each building at the same time. Three men for the first, three for the second, Smith and the others the third. A slant of light beneath the door. They removed their night goggles. They shot the doors open. They entered.*

*Lights were on. Five men round a table, drinking, playing cards. Heads jerked up. Surprise. Fear. Death. They died where they sat, shredded and splintered, bodies saturated by a blast of bullets. A door at the far wall. Smith approached, shot the lock, kicked open the door, darted to one side.*

*A woman screamed. A man spoke: "You shoot, she dies. You understand this?"*

*Smith hesitated. A bright flicker of recognition. Impossible. But yet…*

*He motioned his men to hold back.*

*"Okay," he said. "No shooting." He took a breath, stepped toward the doorway. Before him, a bedroom. Spacious. A small, circular table. Candles. A setting for two. A bottle of wine, dinner plates. Beside the table, a man and woman. The man stood behind the woman, cradling her neck in the crook of his arm. In his hand a Smith and Wesson revolver, pressed on the woman's temple.*

*The man he recognised. The man was his brother.*

*They stared at each other. Time was measured by heartbeats.*

*"A small fucking world," said Billy. "Talk about coincidences. You couldn't make this up."*

*Smith said nothing.*

*"You really going to kill me, Johnny?"*

*Smith found his voice. "Put the gun down, Billy."*

*"What then?"*

*Smith stepped into the room. He glanced back at his men. The clock was ticking. They needed to get the hell out. They looked confused. No wonder. He gestured to them. Hold back. Stay vigilant. He closed the door behind him.*

*"Put the gun down," he said quietly. "I'm not going to shoot."*

*"Okay, Johnny."*

*Billy was smiling. To Smith it brought a thousand memories. Billy placed the pistol on the table, released the woman. She was maybe mid-twenties, an Afghan. Olive skin,* long glossy black hair. She scurried away to a corner of the room where she watched events unfold with wide-eyed terror.

"What now, Johnny?"

"I've been sent to kill you," said Smith.

"Sure you have," said Billy. "Look at you. Not changed a bit. And you joined the army. My little brother, all grown up with a rifle in his hands, killing people. Who would have believed that?"

"What happened, Billy?"

Billy raised his hands, as if the answer was obvious.

"I woke up! I saw the way of things. You should do the same." He stepped closer. His eyes shone. "I've made a fucking fortune. Let me go. We can share it. You'll live in luxury all your days."

"You stabbed Chadwick. Remember? You left him to die in the dirt."

Billy's eyes narrowed. "That was a lifetime ago." Another step closer. "Did he die?"

"Almost. He lived. What happened, Billy? Where did you go?"

"You going to kill me, Johnny?"

"Answer the fucking question!"

"That day. Best day of my life. It made me get the hell out. I had a stash of money. I went abroad. To France. I thought maybe I was in trouble. Maybe Chadwick was dead. I joined the Legion. They don't ask questions. I stayed with them for a few years, made contacts. We came over here to fight the war on terror." He laughed. "I didn't see terror. I saw a chance. So did a few of my friends. We set this up. It took time. But the fucking money rolled in."

"Your friends are all dead. We're going to destroy the poppy fields."

"Do what you have to do," Billy said. "It had to end sometime. And now? How does this end?"

"Goodbye, Billy." Smith aimed, fired three times at the ceiling. Rubble drizzled down. The two men stared at each other. "I'm leaving, Billy. I'm giving you this chance. Don't make me come back."

Billy didn't respond.

Smith left, closing the bedroom door behind him. He gave a sharp nod to his men. "Target eliminated. Let's get the fuck out of here."

---

They still had work to do. Smith contacted HQ at Lashkar Gah in Helmand province, five hundred miles away. Mission successful. Rendezvous in three hours. They made the five-mile trek to Zawa. The going was relatively easy, journeying across a flat landscape. They got there at dawn and approached the village warily. A cluster of traditional houses, flat-roofed, constructed of wooden poles, coated with mud and straw, each with a yard for bright flowers. They hid about two hundred yards away, waited.

Smith heard them before he saw them. The familiar and welcoming drone of rotor blades. There! Three Apache attack helicopters leaning in their direction. This was the 'legitimate' section of the mission. Discussions with the village elders. The formal destruction of the poppy fields by way of aerial defoliation. All witnessed and documented. Nothing about the elimination of their targets five miles distant. Nothing about the handover of one hundred thousand dollars hard cash.

The helicopters landed on the periphery of the village. A crowd had formed, women, kids, men all watching the events with bemusement. Smith waved his men forward. They got to the village.

A meeting was held in one of the houses. Smith, a colonel, and elders from three villages, plus an Afghan translator. Lots *of smiles and handshakes. Bergens were opened, cash distributed. The smiles got wider. The elders produced a map showing the fields. The colonel did all the talking, words converted into Farsi by the interpreter in a low monotone.*

*Another shake of the hands. Once the poppies were destroyed, the fields would be used to grow rice. Promises were made. Yet more smiles.*

*Smith and his men were transported back to Lashkar Gha. Mission completed. Job well done.*

*Only it wasn't.*

*A shitstorm brewed on the horizon, heralding an act of such profound malevolence the life of Captain John Smith would change forever.*

---

Smith answered Alison in a measured tone, keeping the shake from his voice.

"I met him five years ago. In some shithole in Afghanistan. I was there to kill him. He was running the biggest heroin factory in the region, if not the country. Supplying drugs to Europe and America. Essentially, a glorified drug dealer. Using villages, including Zawa, to grow his poppies on a massive scale."

Another sip of wine. "I killed his men. Unfortunately, I didn't kill Billy. I spared him. A flaw in my personality, I suppose. I try not to kill members of my family. The poppy fields were destroyed. After that–"

"You *spared* me," interrupted Purkis, his voice strident. "How fucking noble. You destroyed everything I had worked for. But I was like the phoenix. You set me free, Johnny. Just like Chadwick Purkis. I had over a hundred million syphoned off in offshore accounts. I came here, set up business." He raised his hands. "Built a property empire. Built all this."

"But that's not the full story," Alison said. "Tell me, John. What happened in Zawa?"

"Tell her, John," Purkis hissed. "Lance that fucking boil."

Smith took a deep breath. His heart thumped in his chest. "No."

"You're such a party pooper," Purkis said. "Which is just plain rude. Let me help. John very graciously chose not to kill me. He thought I would scurry away, like a scared cat. But I didn't. Not at all. Do you know what you did, John?"

Smith said nothing. He couldn't meet his brother's gaze, stared at the plate of food before him.

"You *underestimated* me. You broke the golden rule there, Johnny boy. Big style."

Still Smith couldn't find a response.

Alison snapped her head round to Purkis. "He doesn't want to talk about it."

"Yes he does," Purkis said in a low voice. "It's all he's ever wanted to talk about."

Smith raised his head, gave a gentle smile at Alison. Somehow, strangely, in this dreaded place, facing danger, he felt a burden lift.

"It was a room like no other," he said simply.

"A room?" said Alison.

And for the first time in just over five years, Smith spoke about the nightmare.

## 68

"The villagers agreed that the fields should be destroyed. I returned to base. I went back to the village eight weeks later. A routine visit to make sure the fields weren't being reused for poppy harvests." He paused. The events of that particular afternoon were as vivid in his mind as blood from a wound.

"The village was deserted. No one was there. No men, no women, no kids. No babies. Five hundred people, gone. Vanished."

"But not quite vanished," Purkis said. Smith didn't look at him. He continued.

"In the square in the centre was a new building. Maybe the size of a double garage. Maybe bigger. Like all the other houses the outside was coated with mud. It didn't look right, there in the village square." He licked his lips, took a deep breath, summoning up the courage to articulate into words the scene before him. "I couldn't understand it. The village was untouched. No visible signs of destruction."

He met Alison's gaze. Her face had softened. The lines didn't seem so harsh. *Keep going*, she was saying.

"I approached the building. It had a single door. It was... unusual. Its construction. It looked like oddly shaped planks of bleached wood. I opened it and went inside." Another deep breath.

"Tell her, Johnny. Tell her what you saw."

Smith saw it, every detail seared into his mind, to remain forever.

"The walls were made of human bones. As was the floor. And the ceiling. The work had been completed with skill and precision. There was a mixture of furniture; a dining table and six chairs, a sideboard, some low coffee tables, and shelves on the walls. And two candelabras suspended from the ceiling. The legs of the chairs were shins and femurs. The backs were complete spines and splayed ribs. The seats were a patchwork of finger bones held fast by human hair. The candelabras were the most intricate, each candle sitting in a hollowed-out skull, each skull cradled in hand bones. They were fastened to arms joined by wire and screws, each of the arms joined to the main pillar of the candelabra, which was the skeleton of a small child hanging by the ankles. The building had been built from the bones of the villagers. Walls, ceiling, floor, furniture. It was an obscenity."

The room was silent. Then Purkis clapped his hands. "Ta-da! It was a work of fucking art! Do you know how long that took us? I had to get guys with a strong stomach. But you pay a mercenary enough, he'll do anything. Ten men, a million each. I was very clever, Johnny. I poisoned the fucking water. How simple was that! It wiped out most of them in one day. The rest were shot. Then you know what we did?"

Smith turned to him, stony-faced. "Let it go."

"We piled the bodies in a pit, doused them in oil and burnt them. Do you know what the smell of burning bodies is like, Alison? No? Bacon. It gives you a real appetite. When the flesh was burnt, we scraped the bones clean and left them to bake in the sun. Ten men, a three-day job. A fucking wonder of modern architecture. But when you're committed to a task, anything's possible."

Purkis pushed his plate to one side. All that remained was the bone of his steak. "But I left you a message. Tell Alison what I said. It was screwed onto the wall. Tell her what I said. This is the best bit."

Smith said nothing.

"Don't be so mawkish, John. It's not your style."

The message his brother had left was one Smith would never forget. He answered in a whisper.

*"All your fault, Johnny Boy."*

Purkis sat back, sighed. "And there we are. You understand now what happens when you go trusting someone. You let me live. You *felt sorry for me,* yes? You wanted to give me another chance. As if I should be grateful. You thought, seriously, I would accept fucking clemency? From you? You insulted me with your arrogance. You disrespected me. You needed to understand, little brother. Actions have consequences. It was *you* who killed those villagers. It was *you* who destroyed Zawa. So fucking own it!"

Smith sensed the men around the table stiffen, poised for trouble. But at that moment he lacked the fight. He felt drained. Exhausted. Like he had been hollowed out. Plus, if he attempted any form of attack, he would probably survive all of three seconds.

"You killed all those people because your pride was dented," he said. "I guess that says it all."

"Beware the wrath of the dragon," said Purkis.

"Jesus," muttered Alison. "You're full of bullshit."

Purkis laughed, raised his glass, acknowledged the comment with a polite tilt of his head, downed the last of his wine. He immediately topped it up.

"Why use Chadwick's name?" asked Smith.

"Why do you think?"

Smith gave a weary shrug. "Because you're psychotic?"

Purkis ignored the remark. "If it wasn't for Chadwick Purkis, I would never have run away. I would have stayed selling drugs to kids on street corners for a pittance. Chadwick... how can I describe it... empowered me. Emboldened me." He laughed – a harsh, metallic sound. "In a sense he gave me freedom. He allowed me to see the bigger picture. I used his name. His legacy. Billy Smith vanished. Chadwick Purkis was reborn."

"Would you like to know what happened to Chadwick?" asked Smith quietly.

"Not particularly."

"Sure you do. When he got out of hospital, they moved away. Not far, but far enough. We stayed in touch for a year. But as a result of his injury, Chadwick was in constant pain and couldn't walk far, and he fell into a deep depression. One evening, on his seventeenth birthday, Chadwick Purkis went to his bedroom and hanged himself. As you say, actions have consequences."

"Such a sad story," said Purkis, lips drooping at the corners like a sad clown. He cocked his head at Alison. "A sad story, don't you think?"

Alison deigned not to reply.

"Wherever you go you leave sad stories," said Smith. "But let's move on to more pressing matters."

"Let's," said Purkis. "I'm so enjoying this family reunion."

"You've done your research on me," continued Smith. "I'm impressed. But I did a little too. Vincent Docherty was quite the conversationalist at the end. You remember Vincent? He mentioned the Royal Hotel. How he had been given a job, which was, essentially, to burn it to the ground. Which he did, with Jacob and Halliday. I went to the library in Aviemore. There's not much there, but it does have a computer. I checked the land register. The owner of the hotel is a company. Guess what it's called?"

"I can't imagine."

"Zawa Holdings. I checked Companies House. It transpires the owner of Zawa Holdings is Chadwick Purkis. Any relation? I thought so. Here's my take. Vincent, Jacob and Halliday were instructed to burn the hotel down. The reason why is irrelevant. Presumably about money. On their way back they hit Paul." Smith leaned forward. "Suddenly, they had one huge problem. Way above their pay grade. They'd hit a child, and the child was still alive. What should they do? They phone their paymaster and ask for instructions. Which are given. And which are followed. Am I warm?"

Purkis gave another long sigh. "Does it matter?"

Alison responded. "It matters to me, you sick fuck."

"That's not polite talk at the dinner table, Alison. If Paul were here, what would he say?"

"Fuck you."

Purkis blew through his lips, looked at Smith. "You really should train your women better."

Smith ignored the remark. They were now at the core of the situation.

"What now?" he said. "I'm here, which is what you wanted. What now?"

Purkis took a long breath, tapped his chin with the tip of his index finger.

"You owe me, Johnny. You were sent to kill me."

"But I didn't."

"You took away my livelihood. You killed my men. You dishonoured me."

"Trade," said Smith. "Let Alison leave, unharmed. You've got me. It's me you want."

Purkis gave a small, sad smile, turned to Alison, gestured with a sympathetic shake of his head.

"This really isn't a trade situation, Johnny. You have no leverage. I have you both. Why should I let anyone go? The situation is clear. You're trouble. Both of you. And trouble has to be removed. Excised. Like a malignant cancer before it spreads. And in the process I intend to enjoy myself. I'm going to introduce you to something very special. A most unique construction. Rather like my little chamber of bones. Interested?"

"Not really."

"You should be. It's called the Glass Box."

## 69

Smith was escorted back to his room. Alison was taken back to a different part of the castle. Where, he had no idea. The future seemed bleak. But now he understood. His brother was insane. He had come at his brother's request, in the hope there was a chance. A chance for Alison. He saw now there was little hope.

He sat on the bed, despondent. He had no coherent plan. *Keep moving.* He had been trained to endure. To cope. To maintain a sense of purpose, despite often impossible odds. He thought back to Paul, running up and down the mountainside, exhausted, spent, but still staggering on, refusing to fold. The boy hadn't given up. Not once. Nor then would Smith. In honour of a young boy's memory.

Despondency evaporated. In its place a quiet rage.

His brother had mentioned the Glass Box but hadn't expanded further. Presumably he had something exotic planned for Smith's demise, in keeping with his brother's state of mind. Which gave Smith a chance. He could have been summarily executed while he ate his T-bone steak. He had been given more time. More time meant more opportunity. Perhaps there was hope.

When things were bad the SAS taught their warriors to react in a most specific way. Get mean. Mad-dog crazy mean. Kill, kill, kill. Take as many of the fuckers with you.

Or die trying.

---

Alison was taken back to her room, the door locked behind her. She kicked at it for good measure, hurled some obscenities to which there was no response, which made her all the more furious. A reaction, anything at all, would have been more palatable than silence. She craved a cigarette. She paced up and down the room, mind in overdrive.

The conversation between Smith and his brother had been, what... she struggled for a word. A number of descriptions came to mind. Surreal, unbelievable, horrific. But none of it mattered. Something terrible was being planned. Probably for both of them. She thought back to Purkis's résumé of Smith's army life. Colourful. She adjusted her thoughts – *fearful*. She would never have guessed. He'd never hinted. Why would he? The events in Afghanistan were beyond imagination.

She allowed herself a cold smile. Smith had been trained all his adult life to do one thing, which he appeared to have a talent for. Killing. Perhaps things weren't so bad. At this moment, she couldn't think of a better person than John Smith to be at her side.

---

Jacob met Halliday just before midnight. Jacob, able to function with limited sleep, was nevertheless bone weary. Long day. They sat together in the kitchen, hunched over bowls of thick soup. The room was empty. The staff, including the chef Purkis had hired for the evening, had left, with the exception being a night porter, who would see the American guests to their rooms after they'd drunk themselves into semi-oblivion. Jacob had checked on security. Twenty men from an outside agency had been brought in for three days at a cost of three thousand a man. Per day. All because of the man upstairs. John Smith.

Jacob tore off a wedge of bread, dunked it in his soup. "They were okay with things?"

"They're half pissed. I don't think they noticed Mr Purkis wasn't there. If they did, they didn't care."

"Where are they now?"

"Snooker room. Drinking brandy. Excited about tomorrow."

"So they should be. Mr Purkis has, I believe, added a new dimension to the games."

Halliday nodded slowly, owl-like with his round face and dark eyes. "John Smith?"

"He's an interesting character. He killed our soldiers in the woods. He killed Vincent and his chums in the Crafty Fox. With apparent ease, I might add. Eight men in two days. That's quite a tally. One could describe him as ruthless. And competent. But yet he comes here to this place on his own volition, knowing there was a high chance he would die. For the life of a woman? Through brotherly love?"

Halliday frowned. "Brotherly love? I don't follow."

Jacob chewed on the bread, swallowed. "John Smith is Purkis's brother."

Halliday remained impassive. If the information came as any form of a revelation to Halliday, it was not reflected on his face.

"What does that tell us about this man?" continued Jacob. "That he should come here at such huge personal risk."

"If he was expecting a brother's love from Chadwick Purkis, then he's stupid," Halliday said. "If he came to save the woman's life, then he's weak."

Jacob gave a small smile. "I think there's more, my friend. He came for revenge. And a man who ventures into the wolves' den to balance an injustice is a man who doesn't care."

Halliday grunted, slurped his soup, said, "He'll care all right when he steps into the Glass Box."

*I'm not so sure*, thought Jacob. *A man who doesn't care is a man who doesn't fear. Which makes for a formidable enemy.*

He had a bad feeling. His gut told him this wasn't over. Not by a long, long way.

---

Cornwall Pritchard, as was the norm before a contest, was unable to sleep. In the beginning, in the early days he had tried to fight his insomnia, tossing and turning in bed, his mind demanding sleep. But it remained elusive and the effort was counterproductive. The more he tried, the worse it got. Now, he accepted it. Embraced it. He kept the light on, listened to the radio, scrolled for random things on his mobile. At 1am he left his room and went for a walk. The hotel Jacob had chosen was set in the country. Pritchard, with the aid of a torch, padded along paths and tracks, his great body lumbering with every stride, always keeping the lights of the hotel within range, the sounds of the woods for company.

He had pictured scenarios in his mind a thousand times, over and over. The men he would face, the manner in which he would orchestrate their deaths. Slow kills. Plenty of blood. They liked that. Pritchard was an expert in the art of the slow kill. Once, for the entertainment of those who watched, hors d'oeuvre involved tearing out his opponent's tongue, down to the root. He'd used his fingers. Main course was eyes, nose, limbs. How the crowd had roared.

Pritchard did not require sleep. Adrenaline fired through his blood. He was invincible.

---

The dishes were removed. The table was cleaned and returned to another room. Furniture was placed back to its rightful place. The conservatory was restored to its original form.

Purkis stood at the wall adorned with his display of swords. Carefully, he took down the misericorde, balanced its weight in his hand, ran his finger along the blade. The same blade which pierced the heart of Tony French an eternity ago.

Perhaps, at the end, he would administer it again. When his brother was broken and bloodied. When his brother pleaded and begged to be released from the pain. A final, mortal stroke.

His brother had sought to destroy him in Afghanistan. Instead, his brother had shown mercy. *Mercy!* The word disgusted Purkis. It offended his dignity.

He placed the dagger back on its mantle. He thought not. Such an end was too quick.

The misericorde was way too good for his little brother.

## 70

At 9 the following morning, breakfast was brought up to Smith's room. Some porridge, a plate of fruit, yoghurt. The man who brought it was accompanied by three others, who stood at the doorway watching, as he placed the tray of food on a drawing table beside the window.

"Going for the healthy option," Smith remarked. The man ignored him, left the room, the rest following, the lock clicking. Smith ate. He had little appetite but required energy. The day ahead would be undoubtedly eventful.

At 11.30am there was a soft knock, the key turned, the door opened. Jacob entered. Behind him the same entourage of men, poised for any hint of violence. Draped over his arm, garments in a polythene wrapper. He placed them on the bed.

"Mr Purkis would like you to change into this, please. I'll return at 2pm."

Smith's lips twitched into the semblance of a smile. "You know that's not his real name."

Jacob stared at Smith, the hard angles of his face softened in sympathy. "It hardly matters, Mr Smith."

"I'm sure it doesn't." Smith gestured at the clothing on the bed. "What's this?"

Jacob's smile broadened. There was little humour in it. "Part of the performance. Each of the contestants plays a character."

"This sounds like fun. And what character does Mr Purkis wish me to play?"

Jacob raised his shoulders and hands, indicating ignorance. "I have no earthly idea. But I can say this." He lowered his voice, inched a little closer. "It won't be pleasant for you."

"Really?" Smith jerked his head back, then forward, slamming the top of his forehead into the bridge of Jacob's nose. Jacob grunted, staggered away. The men at the door, shocked for a second, bundled in.

"Leave it!" snarled Jacob. He went to the en suite, got a towel which he held to his face to staunch the blood. He glared at Smith, nose burst, nostrils streaming.

"I think it's broken," said Smith. "At least I hope so."

Jacob gave a ghastly smile. "Two o'clock. Be ready. If you're not, the woman gets taken to a shed and then shot. Your choice."

He gave a curt nod to the men in the room. He followed them out, turned. "Today is the day you get to die, Mr Smith. Think on that."

"Today is the day you got your nose broken. Think on that, fuckwit."

# 71

At 2pm precisely, Halliday and four others arrived at Smith's room. Smith had complied with Jacob's instructions and changed into the new clothes. Black combat fatigues. Dread stirred in the pit of his stomach. His brother had a wild imagination, capable of creating nightmarish scenarios. Smith had no doubt he was a main player in one such scenario. But he was still alive. Where there was life, there was hope.

He was taken down a different set of stairs, to a short narrow hall devoid of lavish ornamentation. The place was a rat run, he thought. A maze. Like the workings of his brother's mind.

Then down steep, rough-hewn stone stairs to a corridor, almost cylindrical, as if hollowed through the earth by a monstrous worm, lit by strip lights on the ceiling, casting a cold amber glow.

"This is nice," he said. The hulking figure of Halliday lumbered at his side, silent. Two men in front, two men behind. Undoubtedly carrying firearms. Escape was a distant dream.

"How's Jacob?" he asked.

Halliday turned his head a fraction. "Upset."

"That's all? I was hoping for some pain and suffering."

"That's what you're going to get."

"And you, my friend. Don't doubt it."

The corridor snaked on. Smith reckoned they had travelled the length of the castle. They came to a stretch where suddenly the lighting changed. Now, torches fastened to the stone by metal brackets burned with real flames.

"Theatrical," remarked Smith.

Halliday grunted. "Mr Purkis likes his fun."

"I really wish you'd stop calling him that."

They stopped at a door to one side.

"For you," Halliday said. "Where you wait before the performance."

"Looking forward to it," Smith said. "If it's Shakespeare, tell my brother I was never a fan. And another thing. Tell him, next time we meet, I'll kill him."

"I'll be sure to pass it on."

The door was thick wood. Halliday slid open a heavy bolt lock, gestured Smith in. Smith entered. The door closed behind him, the bolt rattling.

The interior was surprisingly comfortable. Regular dimensions, thick carpet. Couch, chair. A small en suite. Bottles of mineral water and energy drinks in a small cooler. Music played in the background. Classical. On a coffee table, bowls of fruit and nuts and protein bars.

Smith sat. There was nothing further he could do, other than wait. He took deep breaths...

*The fear is in my mind.*

*The fear is not real.*

*The fear will not kill me...*

He took another deep, calming breath. He had seen death in

all its forms. It had, throughout his life, been a close companion. It had never scared him. But now it did. Not for himself. For Paul. For Alison.

He didn't want to die.

Not yet.

# 72

All the guests had arrived at Purkis's castle. Full attendance. There were rarely any absences. It was 3pm. The rain had stayed away, the sun was out, which pleased Chadwick Purkis. His *fairy* garden – like most gardens – looked best in the sunshine. Not that sunlight was relevant to the activities in the Glass Box, given they took place underground in the basement, where there were no windows.

Each guest had paid the required entrance fee. £3,000,000. Twenty-five guests. £75,000,000. Jacob, the consummate organiser, confirmed the transfers, all to an offshore account in the British Virgin Islands. His bonus was a cool £2,000,000. He hoped the Glass Box would last forever.

They were congregated in a reception room, dressed immaculately in dinner suits. Decorum had to be maintained. On a long, gleaming dining table, bottles of champagne. They sipped from fluted crystal glasses. These men met every two months. In the intervening period, they never contacted each other. Such was the rule. They had a lot to catch up on. The atmosphere was relaxed, convivial. Quiet, civilised conversation. Ripples of laughter. As the day progressed and drink was consumed, the laughter would get louder, more raucous, the conversations graduating to shouts and cheers and whoops of unbridled excitement. Inhibitions disappeared. Formality removed. Bloodlust was up. The Glass Box was their release. The fulfilment of a need. Which was why they always came back. And Purkis exploited it to the full.

The ritual never changed. The sound of a soft gong, then Purkis led them down stone steps to the basement, the lighting supplied by real flames on real torches. They got to the wide wooden doors, and opposite, red velvet drapes. Here, Purkis addressed his guests.

"Good to see you all. Once again, the Glass Box is ready for our pleasure. What will it be, I wonder? What weapons will our gladiators be given?"

A hush. The talking had stopped. Purkis nodded at a man standing quietly at his side. The man stepped forward, pulled a cord, opening the drapes.

There, the metal circle on a spindle attached to the wall, apportioned into six sections, above which, a simple red mark painted on the stone.

The man grasped an edge, spun. The circle, greased on its spindle, flashed round. A full fifteen seconds passed, the circle slowed, stopped. Purkis allowed himself a smile. He couldn't have wished for better.

He turned to the group.

"Broadsword!"

The group cheered. Purkis opened the double wooden doors, and they filed through to the Glass Box.

# 73

---

Cornwall Pritchard had been driven to the castle. He had been escorted to a room similar to Smith's but without a lock on the door. There, waiting for him, was Jacob. His nose was puffed up, cotton wool saturated with blood inserted in each nostril. His eyes were blackening. Pritchard made no comment.

"You feeling good, Cornwall?" said Jacob, his voice nasal.

"Never better."

"Good to hear. There might be 'an addition'. A very special one."

Pritchard cocked his head. "An addition?"

Jacob smiled, wincing at the pain the motion caused. "On the assumption you win – and I have no doubt you will – Mr Purkis has asked that you engage in an extra fight."

Pritchard frowned. "Who will I be fighting?"

"His brother."

"I don't know anything about him."

"Does it matter?"

"Perhaps. And?"

"Two million for the fight. As I said, it's special."

Pritchard straightened, rolled his massive shoulders. "Deal."

Jacob gave a polite nod. "Make it interesting. Exotic."

"You mean – make him suffer."

"Yes."

"You mean – more than usual?"

"Yes."

## 74

---

6 pm.
　　The bolt slid open. Smith readied himself. At the door was Jacob, behind him the hulking figure of Halliday and several men. Jacob had a pistol in his hand. Looked like a Glock.

"Time," said Jacob.

"But I've only just got here."

"No bullshit. Let's go."

"If you insist. Love the nose."

He exited from the room. Nothing was said. They walked further down the corridor, a solemn procession, Smith in black fatigues, those around him in dark suits. Smith's senses were sharpened to a pre-battle level of competence. Nerves tingled. He maintained steady breathing. His heart thumped at an accelerated speed. Sights and sounds were accentuated.

They arrived at a set of wide double doors. From within came the sound of men's voices, loud and harsh. Halliday opened the door. They stepped inside.

The room was huge. The smell of sweat assailed the nostrils. Scattered about, in apparently random fashion, couches, armchairs, divans, low tables. Tapestries and thick drapes covered the walls. The carpet felt thick underfoot. The ceiling was flat and smooth, illumination from downlighters creating a soft reddish hue. On one side, a bar. Men were sitting or standing, drinking, laughing, talking loudly, at ease with themselves.

The noise stopped when Smith entered the room. He looked about. He was the sole focus of their attention. There, sitting on a couch, was Alison. They locked eyes. She gave a brief, tremulous smile. She looked pale and scared. Smith smiled back. He imagined his smile was equally as tremulous. On either side of her sat men, one being Purkis.

The furniture was placed around a structure in the centre of the room. The Glass Box. Glass walls about twelve feet high. A single door. An area about twice the size of a boxing ring. Maybe bigger. No ceiling. Smith's attention, however, was drawn to the interior. The scene was such his steps faltered, his breath caught. So shocking, so divorced from reality it seemed unfeasible.

The glass walls were patterned in sprays and streaks. On the glass floor, strewn about, body parts and puddles of blood. Difficult to assess how many people had been dismembered, the limbs scattered like broken sticks. Smith counted three torsos. Sitting on a chair amongst the carnage, apparently unconcerned, was a man wearing loose white breeches stained at the hips and thighs. He was naked from the waist up, massively muscled, skin the colour of gleaming ivory, blood-soaked. As Smith watched, he was casually wiping the blood off his chest and arms with a towel. The man looked up. His hair was long and tied back behind his head in a ponytail. Cheeks flat and angular like two sharp wedges. Square chin. Neck thick as a tree trunk. Sloe-eyed. Resting on his lap was a sword.

The procession of men stopped at the couch where Purkis and Alison sat.

"They're monsters, John!" Alison's face shone with terror in the muted glow.

Purkis stood, square with Smith. "She's way too melodramatic," he said. "You weren't particularly polite to Jacob." Jacob, standing next to Smith, looked on, the swelling now rendering his features unrecognisable. Whether he displayed any anger was impossible to say. Probably. Hopefully, thought Smith.

"We'd better push on," continued Purkis. "Yonder, in the Glass Box, sits Titan. You can see how he earned such a title. Every two months four men are invited to the Glass Box, the prize being a life-changing amount of money. There are three fights. 'Contests' as I like to call them. Two are set against each other. Then the next two. The winner of each battle it out. Simple, yes? You've missed the event, I'm afraid. But I'm sure Alison enjoyed it, despite her remonstrations. Titan won. He's difficult, if not impossible, to beat. He has won many times. He has justifiably garnered the respect of those sitting around you. Titan doesn't do it for the money. He does it for the sheer enjoyment. Which makes for a wonderful spectacle. Titan has agreed to a further contest. And the guests around you are thrilled because they get to see something extra for free."

"Where do I sit?" said Smith. "It should be fun."

"If it were only that simple, Johnny. And you dressed up for me. All in black." Suddenly he leaned in, held Smith close. "I don't want this, little brother," he whispered. "But you brought this on yourself. You should have killed me. But you didn't. Your mercy was a violation. It's all about respect. You've got to pay, Johnny."

He stepped back. He raised his voice.

"The last contest, gentlemen. Our brave contender pits his agility and wit against the strength and muscle of Titan. And the name of our hero, all dressed in black? He is *The Demon Prince*." He regarded Smith with a steady stare. "A night-time killer! A ghoul in the shadows! An assassin!"

The men around them, silent up until this moment, whooped and howled.

Purkis made a gesture. Halliday padded off, and returned with a sword sheathed in a silver scabbard resting on a silk cushion. He gave it to Purkis, who held it out to Smith.

"For you," he said. "The chosen weapon is broadsword. This is a two-handed claymore. Fifty-five inches long. Double edged. The blade has been sharpened for the occasion."

"You're very kind," replied Smith. "What stops me from decapitating you at this very moment."

Purkis's face opened in mock surprise. "You would do such a thing? But then poor Alison. She'd be dead before you moved an inch. Then you'd follow straight after."

"What if I don't care about Alison, big brother?"

"But you do care, Johnny. Which is your weakness."

"What happens afterwards?"

"My, I admire your optimism. You and your lady get to live a little longer, I suppose. Let's cross that bridge when it comes."

"Let's."

Smith picked up the sword. It was heavy and clumsy. He had never used such a weapon before. It felt strange in his hands. The SAS didn't include broadsword training in its repertoire.

The men around him stepped back. The Glass Box beckoned.

## 75

Smith made his way towards the door, his brother following a little behind, flanked by men on either side. Smith turned briefly. Alison sat, rigid, back straight as a lance, regarding him with a fixed stare. Beside her, Jacob, who gave Smith a polite nod as if to say *one wrong move, and I'll shoot her.*

Smith waved politely back as if to say *I'm going to kill you.*

He entered the Glass Box.

The man referred to as Titan stood up. He was big. He was maybe six five. Maybe taller. His flesh looked as hard as horn. He held his sword in his right hand – the same design as Smith's – which he swung playfully, as if light as a twig.

With his left hand, he tossed the chair contemptuously to one side. He regarded Smith, grinned.

"Welcome, little prince."

"We don't need to do this."

Titan cast him a quizzical look. "But I want to do it."

Smith said nothing. He held the sword out in his two hands, the weight a pressure on his wrists. He sidled warily round the great hulk, careful not to trip on scattered limbs or slip on spilled blood. Titan watched him, the grin never leaving his face.

Smith hoped the man's size would prove to be his disadvantage. If he could avoid the sword strokes and dart in and out of range, then he might have a chance. If he misjudged, oblivion. Titan stood, feet planted, waving his sword almost idly. Smith moved closer, gauging Titan's reach. Titan moved, quick as a snake. The sword flicked out. Smith jerked to the side, the blade whistling close to his body. Around him great cheers rose up. Smith focused, ignoring all distractions. He tried to slide around the towering body. Titan turned, swung the sword high, struck down. Smith brought his sword up to deflect the blade. The swords met. The force was staggering, jolting his arms and shoulders.

Smith retreated. Titan swung again. Smith was out of reach. The blade flashed through empty air. Titan was momentarily unbalanced. Smith jabbed forward, nicked Titan's elbow. Titan tried a clever backhanded slash. Smith dodged, jabbed again, piercing Titan's elbow a second time. Titan glared, the grin gone. He sidestepped, this time his sword flashing in a horizontal sweep, the purpose to cleave through Smith's ribcage. Smith twisted his body, agile as an acrobat, parried the blow. The force again was jarring. Smith was knocked to his knees. Titan, perhaps sensing victory, released a great cry, raised his sword, brought it down. Smith dodged away frantically. The sword fell, lodging into the carcass of a previous contestant. Titan tried to wrench it free. Smith saw his chance, swung towards the thick neck. Titan bellowed, abandoned his sword, ducked, lashed out with a vicious kick. Smith took the full force in his stomach, was propelled backwards, sword slipping from his grasp.

He stood, winded, panting and sweating. Now both men

had lost their weapons. The voices of those watching had risen to a clamour.

Titan advanced. Smith aimed an apparent random blow towards the head. Instantly, Titan's hand seized his wrist. Smith disengaged with a jerk, swung a left-handed blow, landing on Titan's neck. It felt like a wedge of concrete. Titan moved with disconcerting speed, caught Smith in an armlock, the intention to snap the ulna. Smith allowed his knees to sag, leapt back in a kind of mad half somersault, pulling his arm free.

The movement unbalanced Titan. He staggered back. Smith sprang forward, struck at the right eye, moved back. Too late. Titan seized his wrist, pulled him in. Smith drove forward, slamming his shoulder into Titan's rock-hard stomach. Titan thrust a knee up, battering Smith in the chest, crushing his lungs. Smith gasped, swept his fist up, a hard uppercut connecting with Titan's chin. Titan reacted, a dazzling fast blow buffeting the side of Smith's face. Both men reeled back. Smith's head felt dizzy. The impact had disorientated him. He was struggling for breath. He was losing his agility. Titan's right eye was closing, his elbow was cut, blood flowing.

Both men stood, regarding each other. Titan rolled his shoulders, flexed his arms and again advanced, this time with caution. Smith circled him. He was close to his fallen sword. As if sensing Smith's intention, Titan roared and jumped forward. Summoning his last resources, Smith lurched to engage, thrust his elbow into Titan's throat. Titan gave a rattling wheeze, gathered Smith in his great arms, squeezed. Smith headbutted Titan's nose, mouth and chin. Titan reacted with snapping teeth. Smith kicked at his knees. One folded backwards. Titan bellowed like a bull, loosening his hold. Smith headbutted again, breaking Titan's nose. Both toppled, Titan landing heavily on his back. Smith scuttled away on hands and knees, slipping and slithering.

He gripped his sword hilt, stood up. Titan was dazed. Blood oozed out the back of his head where it had struck the glass floor. Titan struggled to rise. Smith swept the sword down on Titan's neck – again and again until the head rolled loose.

Smith stepped away and leaned on the sword handle. He met his brother's gaze. His brother responded with a salute and an approving twitch of his head. Those watching were silent. Presumably not the conclusion they had anticipated.

Purkis made a motion. Men approached the box, their intentions not benign. One had drawn a handgun.

*The end*, thought Smith. He took a long breath, raised his weapon. *A sword against bullets. It doesn't quite cut it.*

And then all hell broke loose.

## 76

Alison watched, unable to avert her eyes. Her dread slowly turned to hope. Smith was using his speed and agility, almost as a weapon. The monstrous bulk of the man called Titan was unable to handle him properly. His arrogance changed to caution, his caution changed to fear, causing recklessness. She saw this played out before her eyes. She dared to believe.

The seconds ticked on. Smith dodged and darted. Blades flickered. The air quivered with the sound of steel. The big man was tiring. The men around her were in a frenzy. Jacob, sitting next to her, was silent and solemn. This, she imagined, was not going according to plan. He sipped from a bottle of mineral water. She caught a glimpse of his pistol, in a shoulder holster under his jacket.

Titan fell heavily. The glass reverberated at the force. He struggled to rise. Smith seized the opportunity, found his sword, swung down. Alison looked away.

The battle was over. Smith had won. Never had she witnessed such a macabre and terrifying spectacle. The place was silent. The man next to her – Jacob – sat stiff as a board.

"Looks like Titan lost his head," she said.

He cast her a scathing glance. "It's not over yet."

"Glad to hear it." She darted her hand out, grabbed the pistol. She'd never held a gun in her life. Jacob twisted round, startled. She leapt up.

"John!"

All eyes turned. She tossed the pistol up and over the glass walls.

Then, crushing pain, and she drifted into darkness.

# 77

The pistol landed two yards from Smith, skittering across the greasy floor. He strode over, scooped it up. It was Jacob's Glock, holding ten cartridges. The walls suddenly reverberated. The approaching men were firing, punching craters in the glass. But the glass held. Toughened, assumed Smith. Designed to prevent punctures from weapons of all sorts.

The silence from the spectators switched to frantic noise. Panic and consternation. Bullets were unexpected. Bullets were indiscriminate, meaning anyone could get hurt. Suddenly, those watching were inadvertently taking an active role in the contest. Smith allowed himself a grim, mirthless smile. Doubtless they would want a refund.

Men in dinner suits began to flee to the exit, creating pandemonium. Smith pulled open the door of the Glass Box, crouched, fired three pops so fast they morphed into one. Exactly as he had been trained. Three men dropped, three chest shots, white shirts suddenly sparkling with blood. He ducked back in. The glass vibrated, absorbing the impact. Two of the guests collapsed, hit by stray bullets, heightening the panic. He saw his brother shrieking orders, voice drowned in the chaos. Smith grabbed the opportunity. He sprang forward, out through the open door, rolled, crouched, fired in one smooth action. Another fell, the top section of his skull a froth of blood and hair. Smith kept going, ran to one of the fallen guards. Another guest crumpled, a bullet in the stomach. Smith picked up a pistol and like a gunslinger in an old Western, a weapon in each hand, started firing, not caring who he hit. More went down. The place was emptying fast. Not only guests were leaving. Purkis's guards were equally inclined. Their pay packet didn't merit being killed.

There. The unmistakable figure of Halliday, lurching towards the door. Smith raced towards him. Halliday was slow and clumsy. He slipped on spilled wine. He got up, glanced round, his round owl face suddenly animated. He took another step, slipped again, fell on his stomach. Smith pounced on him, jabbed his knee into his spine, cupped his hand under Halliday's chin.

"For Paul," he hissed. He wrenched the chin up, snapped Halliday's spine. Halliday's body spasmed, went still.

He got up, swivelled, expecting more gunfire. Silence, save his own ragged breathing. He made his way to where Alison had been sitting, picking through the dead. There, slumped on the couch was Jacob. He'd taken a shot to the shoulder. He groaned, stirred, his eyes flickered, drifting in and out of consciousness. Beside him lay Alison, one arm drooped onto the floor. He knelt, lifted her head gently. She shifted. Her lips twitched. She was alive. She gave a fleeting smile.

"The bastard hit me on the head. Did I miss much?"

"Nothing worth speaking about."

She raised herself up onto her elbows, gazed about. "Jesus, John. You don't believe in half measures."

"I try to finish a job."

"And is it finished?"

"Not quite."

She found her feet, wobbling slightly, regarded the semi-conscious figure of Jacob.

"You remember you asked me for permission," she said to Smith.

"Yes."

"Would you give me permission?"

"You don't need to ask."

He handed her one of the pistols. She took it, balanced the weight in her hand, pointed it a foot from Jacob's face. Jacob's eyes fluttered open. He focused. He swallowed and found his voice, a dry croak.

"I don't want to die."

"Nor did my son."

Her hand trembled. She blinked away sweat and tears, heaved a deep sigh. She lowered her arm.

"I can't do this."

Smith nodded. It took a lot to kill. Something – perhaps the only thing – he had ever been good at. Hence the self-loathing.

He prised the gun gently from her fingers.

"Let's try something else," he said.

"What?"

Smith pointed to the Glass Box.

"Look."

# 78

## THE FINAL OUTRAGE

Sitting on the chair once occupied by the man called Titan, was Chadwick Purkis. Otherwise known as Billy Smith. He seemed oblivious to the bodies littered around him, gazing beyond the glass to some indeterminate distance, that perhaps only he saw in his mind. Dressed in his dinner suit, both hands resting politely on his lap, he could have been waiting for the opera to begin. His bow tie was missing, presumably lost in the confusion. There was a small red stain on his shirt. Possibly wine. Possibly not.

Smith grabbed the lapels of Jacob's jacket, hoisted him up and half dragged, half carried him to the Glass Box, Jacob moaning in pain and protesting at every step. Once inside, Smith dropped him to the floor, where he remained on his knees, head bowed, clutching his shoulder, swaying back and forth.

Smith ignored him, appraised his brother, who blinked and looked around as if just noticing his surroundings.

His attention levelled on Smith. "I'm not running, Johnny. Not from you. Not again."

"Fair enough, Billy."

Smith picked up the sword he had used to kill Titan, still glossy with blood, and tossed it on the floor beside Jacob. He picked up Titan's sword, and rested it on his brother's lap.

He stood back. "Seeing as we're in the Glass Box, and seeing as it's broadsword night, why don't we have some entertainment. That's what you like, isn't it, Billy? A little fun? Your turn to be part of the spectacle." He turned to Jacob, still kneeling on the floor. "What do you say, Jacob? A bit of sport? You and your boss?"

"I need a doctor," muttered Jacob.

Smith pursed his lips, deliberated, came to a decision.

"I have something better," he said. "Complete relief." He shot Jacob in the head.

The noise was loud and sharp within the close confines of the box. His brother roused himself, took a deep breath and gave Smith a strange, dreamy look. "You've destroyed everything. That's what you do, Johnny. Like Zawa. You destroyed that village and everyone in it."

"That was you, Billy. Just you. Don't twist it."

"I love you, Johnny. I've done bad things. You've got to do this."

Smith pointed the pistol. Like Alison, his hand trembled. His throat felt dry. He was weary to the core. He took a steady breath, aimed. His brother looked at him. His mouth quivered into a hint of a smile. He seemed almost serene. Smith blinked sweat from his eyes. Or was it tears?

"I can't do this," he whispered. He lowered the weapon.

"A second chance, Johnny?" said his brother. "No thanks." The expression changed. From calm acceptance to unbridled fury, lips drawn in a snarl, eyes gleaming. He grasped the sword on his lap, and sprang at Smith like a wild beast. Smith stepped back, raised the pistol once again. Still, he hesitated. "I can't do it!"

"But I can." A voice behind him. Alison. A gunshot. The

impact caused his brother's face to implode – eyes, nose and lips vanished in a tangle of blood and vein. He collapsed to the ground, to join the many who had fallen in the Glass Box.

She stepped forward to stand at Smith's side. "It's over," she said. "What do we do now?"

Smith gazed at the body of his brother. He felt nothing. No grief. No guilt. No remorse. Halliday was dead. Jacob was dead. And now Billy. He and Alison had exacted revenge for Paul. But there was no sense of gratification. He felt hollow and cold. Not a man, but merely a husk, sucked dry of emotion. Revenge had that effect. It added nothing. Rather, it ate at the soul until there was little left. He turned to Alison and gave a small, weary smile.

"What do we do now? We keep moving. Because that's all there is. That's all we can do. There's nothing else. And something you should know."

"Yes?"

"It's never over."

# AFTERMATH

Alison Davidson visited Paul's grave every day. Despite the snow, the cold, the rain, she was there, by her son's side. Sometimes, in the rustle of leaves, or the sway of branches, or the stir of the breeze, she thought to catch the whisper of his voice. And she would whisper back and tell him how much she missed him. The seasons passed. Time slipped by. He was never far from her thoughts. His smile, his laughter. His love. On a summer's day she would walk through the forest to the mountains, taking the trails and paths she imagined Paul would have travelled with the man called John Smith. She never returned to the cabin, which she'd heard was abandoned and in disrepair.

She was sitting in one of the many coffee shops in Aviemore. On a whim she had ordered hot chocolate with a cream and marshmallow topping. Paul's choice. She was reading a book. Movement caught her eye. A man stood at the table. She looked up. She smiled.

"You came back."

He returned her smile.

"I never left."

THE END

# A NOTE FROM THE PUBLISHER

**Thank you for reading this book**. If you enjoyed it please do consider leaving a review on Amazon to help others find it too.

**We hate typos.** All of our books have been rigorously edited and proofread, but sometimes mistakes do slip through. If you have spotted a typo, please do let us know and we can get it amended within hours.

**info@bloodhoundbooks.com**

Printed in Great Britain
by Amazon

12080998R10202